USA TODAY BESTSELLING AUTHOR

MJ FIELDS

Copyright

Copyright © 2024 by MJ Fields
All rights reserved.
Visit my website at
www.mjfieldsbooks.com

No part of this book may be reproduced or transmitted in any form or by any means, electronic or mechanical,
including photocopying, recording, or by any information storage and retrieval system without the written permission of the author, except for the use of brief quotations in a book review.
This book is a work of fiction. Names, characters, places, and incidents either are products of the author's imagination
or are used fictitiously. Any resemblance to actual persons, living or dead, events, or locales is entirely coincidental.

Rounding The Bases

The Series
EACH BOOK 'FIRMLY' STANDS ALONE

If you love binging a series, this order 'hits it home'!

Taking First
Stealing Second
Force at Third
Catching Feels

Catching Feels

From USA Today Bestselling author, MJ Fields, comes a brand-new enemy to lovers, brother's best friend, standalone baseball romance

Jillian

My whole life, **I've been a planner**. Every aspiration I've ever had was on a spreadsheet, chart, or graph that flowed from one step to the next, all leading to my goal. I, Jillian Hart, younger sister of **two professional athletes**, would be the **first in my family to hold a Doctorate**.

After graduating with honors in **both of my majors**, I was sure I'd soar to the top of all the acceptance lists of my dream colleges. When I received my first acceptance letter to Montana University, **my safety school**, I knew it wouldn't be the last. I was wrong. I'd been waitlisted at the two universities **I wanted** the most.

Feeling a **quarter-life crisis** closing in, I felt the need to have a focus. So, I decided I was going to conduct a little **research project of my own**.

My thesis is built around the need to understand why so many

girls I grew up with —*who chased a boy instead of dreams*— are **happier than me**.
My hypothesis: ***it's sex, not love.***
Set on proving I'm right, I now have a new goal to achieve, and **my crisis will be averted.**
Step one: *lose my* **V-card** *in the name of research.*

<u>Nour</u>

My batting average was one of the **top in our league in the minors**; since moving to the majors, it's drastically declined. No matter how many times I've tried to **approach it logically**, all things point to the fact I'm **not getting any action off the field**. Don't get me wrong; I could have **so much I'd drown in it**, but I've read the cautionary tales of men in my position and do not plan on adding my name to a **chapter in that book**.
The answer: **FlingShot**, a hookup app.

It's all fun and games until someone ends up catching feels.

The Players

Pitcher- #34 Blake Bennett
1st Base - #22 John Paul- Pope
2nd Base - #13 Roman Hart
Short Stop - #4 Amias Steel
3rd Base - #72 Leland Locke
Catcher - #10 Nour Uyar
Right Field - #99 Rudy Galleon
Center Field - #18 AJ Pereira
DH - #2 Chuck Turner
AJ Tereira

Playlist

Talk Dirty To Me — Jason Derulo
CandyShop — 50 Cent
Signs — Tesla
Love Song — Tesla
Walk This Way — Run DMC, Aerosmith
Baby One More Time — Britney Spears
Raindrops Keep Fallin' On My Head — B.J.Thomas
Kiss The Rain — Billie Myers
Piano Man — Billy Joel

Prologue

FlingShot

NOUR

AFTER MOM MADE Tommy White spit his gum out in her hand and freaked him the fuck out by telling him that chewing gum turned into the flesh of the dead after dark, I stopped inviting friends over to stay the night. She didn't do this to be problematic; she actually believed it. My parents would cross the street if they saw a black cat and repeat statements exactly forty times because it was supposed to make whatever they were saying happen. They would pinch their right earlobe and knock on wood twice with their left while saying *mashallah*—even though they were Christians when they immigrated here from Turkey—to ensure evil wouldn't be alerted of their good fortune.

Once I started playing high school baseball, I began thinking my parents might not be as crazy as I had thought they were. In college, it was much the same. The oddities, including my own, were amped up when I played in the minors.

My first RBI was hit while I was wearing the only jockstrap I could find, one left in place of all the others that my team had stolen as part of their hazing. It was hot pink and bedazzled with a heart that read, "*SWEATY BALLS.*" I wore it for an entire season.

There's more, so much more. It's almost embarrassing, and it gets worse every damn day. But it is what it is, and that's not what has me all in my fucking head right now.

It's been weeks since the fire at "Slugger Row," which is a row of townhomes all rented by fellow Jersey Jags players. Although no one was hurt and really no personal items were damaged by the fire, well, the smoke stench isn't coming out of anything we own, but that's really it. It was an electrical fire, so most of the damage was inside the walls, and now the electrical system and walls have to be fully replaced and repaired.

Our second baseman and owner of the property, Roman Hart, is dating the neighbor, CeCe, who owns a Victorian house that's as big as any bed and breakfast my family stayed at when Mom and Dad dragged us on our annual leaf-peeping trips up the coast. Luckily, she's letting us crash here. I'm sure it has way too much to do with her feeling responsible due to the fact the man responsible for dicking with the electrical system that started the fire is CeCe's piece of shit father. He's now behind bars, where he belongs, and everyone knows she's not responsible.

We could easily find a new apartment, but our place is so close to Revolutionary Field and the local hangout, O'Donnell's Pub, that we're all willing to wait. It also has a hell of a lot to do with the fact we've all grown close, something I never expected would happen, but I'm glad it has. I've missed being part of a close family.

We're all alive and have a roof over our heads. CeCe, her

family, and girlfriends are amazing and love to cook as much as I do. Add their pup to the mix, and it's a win.

A win is a good thing in my profession—no, it's a great thing—and for the Jags, who have never been at the top in the fifty-two years since becoming an MLB team. Not ever. But now we're winning games and slowly pulling up in the ranks, which is also great. And it's not just the team doing well; my batting average is the best it has ever been since we moved into CeCe's.

But there is one major problem: I haven't had sex since we moved into Slugger Row, and with how packed this place is, even ten minutes in the bathroom is a luxury I don't often get. What does this mean? I barely have enough alone time to get myself off, and it's crucial I release before a game.

That's right; me, the guy who hated superstitions the whole twenty years I lived with my parents, has game day rituals that include a big, early morning breakfast that always consists of a loaded omelet and two pieces of toast, one with butter and the other with strawberry jam. Next, I shower and do some self-care—jerk off—before chilling and watching two episodes of *Real Housewives*, which is my form of relationship control. I nap, then head to a yoga class at Revolutionary Field when we're in town. If I can't find a class when we're on the road, I find a place by a body of water or in a park and do an hour before heading to the stadium, where even more game day rituals—superstitions—take place.

It's time to take things, other than my dick, into my own hands, to go where this man has never gone before.

Looking down at my phone, I flex my fingers before hitting the app store. Then I search dating apps and look for one that's more the opposite.

"Bingo."

. . .

Welcome to Flingshot
Whether looking for a fling or a spontaneous connection, Flingshot is your go-to app for instant sparks and unforgettable moments.
Shoot your shot!

AFTER CAREFUL THOUGHT, I tap out a ridiculous bio.

Profile name: SportsManSam
I've surfed the biggest waves … in my bathtub, scored a touchdown in a hockey game, and hit a home run in chess. My secret talent? Outrunning cheetahs on the track. They're fast, but I have better sneakers. When I'm not busy winning Olympic gold in musical chairs, I enjoy coaching unicorns in the art of pole dancing. Hit me up for a lesson.

I UPLOADED a few mirror selfies that hid my face: one in a suit, one in a towel showcasing my abs, and one on a surfboard that one of my friends back home took. Then I hit "*submit*."

AJ walks into our shared room. "Bathroom's yours, man. Come down when you're done. CeCe's making popcorn, and we're going to watch—"

"I'm not into murder documentaries when I'm rooming with a guy who sounds like he's running a chainsaw in the—"

He cuts me off with a laugh. "Rome's family's here; she's not going to watch that shit and freak them out. We're watching highlights." He knocks on the wooden doorjamb before walking away. "Let's go."

Standing, I look down and briefly contemplate changing out of my favorite comfy sweats but decide against it. I'm living here until the townhouse is finished; I'm not going to a fucking party. Sweats will work, but it's probably a good idea to wear a shirt, too.

Walking out of my room, I head for the bathroom just as Bennett walks into it.

Of course.

JILLIAN

Is it normal to peruse dating apps when you're peeing? I'm not sure, but the likelihood of me meeting my next "maybe" while on the toilet is high. Imagine telling that story to your grandchildren. Not that I think the next maybe will be husband material. Hell, I'm not even sure I even want to get married. Finding a man to fool around with *is* the objective.

Middle and high school were a bust. No one was interested in the girl whose brothers—plural—popped up in on every situation where a guy dared take a second glance at me. Hell, even after they graduated and went on to college, the whispers of the threats they'd made still followed me around our town and our school. I was sure my undergrad years would be promising, but they blew up my phone with warnings about what they would do to any jock or frat boy who added me to the list of girls they nailed and how they'd end up in jail.

Could they have been blowing smoke? Yes. Could they have been serious? Also, yes. But worse than that was I didn't want to be a number on some immature asshole's list of ass he tapped. A man who has a list like that clearly has issues, and I know all about men with issues.

My brothers are the men they are because our mother raised good men. Hell, they even give *her* Father's Day cards. They won't admit our father ever taught them a thing, but he did teach me a thing or two. He taught me what I didn't want in a man. My list of red flags could span a mile, if not more, all thanks to him.

Add to all that the classes I took outside of my exercise science degree requirements, ones of a more personal interest that ended up giving me a second major in Women's and Gender Studies, and I am now confident in what I, Jillian Hart, want in a man.

Yes, I know it's more PC to say "partner," but I'm not looking for that yet, maybe not ever. What I want right now is a man to … experiment with. That sounds cold, but it is what it is. Limited experience doesn't negate my desire to feel, to touch, to taste, and to be touched and tasted.

Yes, undergrad would have been an epic exploration of all of that if not ruined by the pandemic. Then, after that shitshow, Rome and Hudson were drafted, and Grandma Hart got sick and passed away. That loss? Devastating.

Mom and I traveled as much as we could to watch and cheer Rome and Hudson on as they played. Their seasons, for the most part, are opposite of one another, and Hudson's is shorter, so he traveled with us when he could. It was awesome. There was no years' worth of planning and saving; Hudson simply whipped out his card.

Mom still insisted on using coupons, discount codes, and scouring the best price on the web, if available, and always reminded him to think twice before a purchase. He owns a kick-ass house on Skaneateles Lake near the Knights training facility and playing field, Legacy Stadium, in Blue Valley,

New York.

"It's bought and paid for; that's my savings account," he always tells her.

Now that prices of real estate have gone through the roof, she agrees it was a wise investment.

Roman went straight from the minors to the majors and bought rental properties, yet he still drives his old pickup.

We used to live in Grandma's house and had planned to until I graduate in a couple of weeks. Yes, used to. However, a few weeks ago, when we returned to Virginia, we found my father had moved into Grandma Hart's house—his mother—and had changed the locks. It didn't matter that it had been at her request that we moved in because her only child—my father—had taken her savings and had been cashing her social security checks, meaning she had been on the verge of losing her home. It didn't matter that Mom paid the taxes and utilities, and we all took care of Grandma when she was sick for more than eight years. It didn't matter that Rome, Hudson, and I painted the house and maintained the property because we loved her, and it was home. It didn't matter that we loved her and knew he never visited her, even when she was dying, because he was her son and Rome's ex-girlfriend was the sheriff's daughter.

My plan to go to grad school is now on hold. I've been accepted to Montana University's program, but I really don't want to be that far away. I'm still waiting to see if I get pulled off the waitlist for Binghamton University in Central New York or Rutgers here in Jersey.

Being as busy as they are, I have yet to bring this up with Mom or my brothers. Why? I know Mom will pack us up and move West, but that's not fair to her or my brothers, who are only a four-hour drive from each other.

Hudson bought a freaking RV, and Mom loves driving the

damn thing. He has a whole setup for it on his property, which is amazing.

He recently lied and told Mom that he sold a half-acre to a teammate whose family lives in the South so they had a little place here. The truth is he and Rome are having a house built where everything is on the main level, and the upstairs is a loft where we can all stay one day. The front, all windows facing the lake, and "we" are giving her the deed to it on Mother's Day. The reality is, I'll never make the money they do, even with a Doctorate, and it sucks I can't ante in a third, but wallowing in that feels gross.

I will not begrudge their success, and I don't, not even a little. I'll celebrate their success, born of hard work, and bask in the love they have for the woman who deserves all the Father's Day cards she gets because she played both roles.

Mom and I rolled into town this afternoon, and she made me drive the huge RV. Okay, it's not *that* huge. It's not like a rock band bus, but it's bigger than Grandma Hart's seven-year-old Prius. She was so proud of that car; it was the first vehicle she'd bought brand new. She gave it to me when she could no longer drive, and I have sworn I'll drive it until the wheels fall off.

I focus back on the app and swipe through the profile pics until I see abs—perfect abs—the kind that all others should be measured by.

I click to read the bio.

Profile name: SportsManSam
I've surfed the biggest waves ... in my bathtub, scored a touchdown in a hockey game, and hit a home run in chess.
My secret talent? Outrunning cheetahs on the track.
They're fast, but I have better sneakers. When I'm not

busy winning Olympic gold in musical chairs, I enjoy coaching unicorns in the art of pole dancing. Hit me up for a lesson.

OH. My. God. That's freaking priceless! I laugh to myself and decide, *Screw it*. Then I slide my finger back on the slingshot and release to—

"Jillian," Mom calls to me through the door. "I'm going to the RV to get some sleep."

I set my phone down, wipe quickly, flush, wash my hands, and hurry out, catching her before she leaves. "You're not going to watch the highlights?"

"I watched it all in real time. It's been a long day." Then Mom yawns as she gives me a hug, which does as yawns do and makes me yawn, too.

"Oh no, you can't leave, too." Cora's worried whisper comes from behind me.

Stepping back, I give Mom a peck on the cheek. "See you in less than an hour."

"Take your time. That purple mattress your brothers bought me was way too expensive, but I have to admit, it is a dream."

"My brothers are professional athletes; they can afford it," I remind Mom.

"Can afford what?" Roman asks from behind me.

"She's swooning over the purple mattress again."

"It's a double." Roman kisses her cheek. "You swoon over a king, not a double."

"I'd get lost in a king." She kisses his cheek back. "I'm more than happy with a good book in a double. Goodnight, my Harts."

"I'll walk you out," Roman says, following behind her.

"Reels starting in ten … nine … eight … seven … six …" AJ Tereira, six-foot-two, hot as hell Brooklyn raised center fielder and one of the three displaced Slugger Row players still crashing at CeCe's, calls to us.

Blaze Bennett Jr, the Jags' starting pitcher, is also hot as hell, but that stick up his ass and the fact he acts uncomfortable around us takes him from ten to nine-point-five; and Nour Uyar, the six-foot-three, two-hundred-twenty-three-pound catcher who is so hard to read, are the other two.

"Rome's walking his mom out. Chill." Nour Uyar's deep voice pours over me like warm water on a cold day.

Sweet Jesus, I think as he passes me, leaving the smell of man, soap, and a hint of something extremely sexual to waft in the air.

If all three of these players' books were on a shelf, I'd find Nour's dark exterior the most alluring, and it would be the one I'd pull down from the shelf and read first. On the surface, he seems so laid back, yet I've witnessed his quiet restraint and find it extremely sexy.

A few weeks ago, there was a fight at O'Donnell's, and when others jumped in, he stood back but not too far. His dark brown eyes were honed in entirely on the situation, as if he were assessing the situation and would step in if needed.

There have been games where Bennett's pitches have been called poorly on the field, and from sixty feet and six inches, you can tell Nour remains calm and soothes Bennett's anger or anxiety.

His body is so sexy. He's built like a Greek statue. Okay, well, the body type. But the dick size? Those statues always seem to have below-average-size cocks. I know Nour is packing—I've seen the outline of his dick in sweats, sans the cup.

I'm not all that experienced because, hello, two brothers made me any decent guy's little sister, but I've done my research, and his dick isn't resting on his balls; it's hanging long, thick, and proud. It passed Go and collected two hundred dollars, *if you know what I'm saying.* You can even see the outline of his head, and even though giving a BJ isn't something I'd like to do for fun, my mouth has watered more than once when I've been able to sneak a peek. I imagine he has the kind of dick you'd want to high-five for being awesome but fear you'd hurt it.

His ass? Perfection. Not that I'd be into eating ass, but I'd love to bite his to see if it's as hard as it looks. Catchers have the best asses, anyway, due to the fact they squat for half the game. And then there are those nipples, and I am generally not turned on by a man's nipples, but Nour's are so perfectly placed and proportionate on his pecs that I'd love to bite them, too.

"You wanna help me out?" Cora laughs, drawing my attention back to the here and now while she juggles plastic movie-theater-looking popcorn containers. She nearly drops them when she looks at me. "Are you okay?"

"I'm fine." I force a laugh.

"Yeah," she sighs as I take a couple of the containers from her hand. "You and me both." Then she whispers, "I need to get laid."

We both start laughing but stop when we hear the clearing of a voice.

Thinking it's Roman returning, I look back and see Nour freaking Uyar holding up my phone. "This either of yours?"

1

JILLIAN

May

JILLIAN

I wake to the sound of my phone vibrating on the nightstand and slap at the surface before finally finding it. Rolling to my side, I rub my eyes with one hand and squint as the bright light from the phone screen renders me temporarily blind.

When I'm finally able to see, I realize it's a notification from Flingshot.

"What the hell?" I mumble, wondering how I managed to turn the notifications back on since I always make sure to check, only when the app is in use. But then I see it's from *SportsManSam* and am a little less annoyed because at least he's funny and has a hot body.

<u>***SportsManSam:***</u>
What's up?

I blink a few times, contemplating closing the app and trying to fall back to sleep but fuck that, he's already disappointed me in bed, and he deserves to hear about it. Well, read it, anyway.

> ***GoodtimesOnly:***
> *Are you seriously coming at me with 'What's up?' After that bio, I was sure you'd give good banter.*

> ***SportsManSam:***
> *My bad. Lost the race against the cheetah today. My shoes were untied. I'll do better.*

I sit up, trying to decide if that's good enough to continue, but then I remember his abs.

> ***GoodtimesOnly:***
> *You already disappointed me in bed once; let's make sure that doesn't happen again.*

> ***SportsManSam:***
> *So, we're already in bed together?*

> ***GoodtimesOnly:***
> *Isn't that the point of this app?*

> ***SportsManSam:***
> *That's what I thought. Glad to see we're on the same page.*

> ***GoodtimesOnly:***
> *I may be reading between the lines*

here, but it seems like you've had some bad experiences. Same. My bio says looking for fun and interested in men. Apparently, that reads differently to couples wanting to add a third to spice things up.

<u>SportsManSam</u>: You won't get that here. I haven't been part of a couple in years, and if I ever traveled the marriage route, sharing isn't an option.

<u>GoodtimesOnly</u>:
laughing emoji *teacher emoji* Reading between the lines again, but lemme help you out, SMS. You can't even mention the M word on here. Once we know it's in your head, we women could possibly believe our vijay-jay will rub enough of its magic on you to procure a ring.

<u>SportsManSam</u>:
notepad and pencil emoji Added to the list. Keep them coming. So far, on my own, I have learned: 1 - that I'm a *shit emoji* because if "she" identifies as a woman, I should be DTF. 2 - Few want to meet; they just want a pen pal. 3 - Me stating I travel for work means I'm married or in a relationship.
4 - People don't post their own pictures.

<u>GoodtimesOnly</u>:
Ouch. 1 - Try adding CIS man looking for CIS woman. 2 - That's unfortunate. If I lose interest, I block.

3 - Travel for work could also make people question if you have a girl in every city.
4 - Make them send you a picture.

I hold my phone, make sure a boob hasn't escaped my tank top, bow my head to hide my face, snap a picture, and send the message. Then I send another.

<u>GoodtimesOnly</u>:
I have curves and love them. If you're not a fan, that's your loss. You don't get face until I know you're real, and SMS, I'm beautiful.

<u>SportsManSam</u>:
Real men love curves.

A picture comes through of himself with a black ball cap covering his face while leaning against the headboard of a bed, a white sheet draped across his lower half.

<u>SportsManSam</u>:
Excuse the semi if you must, but you did cause it.

<u>GoodtimesOnly</u>:
I don't mind it at all, but tell me, how did I cause it?

<u>SportsManSam</u>:
Cami's thin enough that I'm pretty damn certain I spied with my little eyes a pretty little piercing.

I pull the phone closer to my face for a better look. *Well, there you have it.*

> ***GoodtimesOnly:***
> ****winky face emoji****

He doesn't respond. Fuck.

> ***GoodtimesOnly:***
> ***You still there?***

> ***SportsManSam:***
> ***Of course. We should meet.***

> ***GoodtimesOnly:***
> ***I'm down. Let's figure out a date and time.***

> ***SportsManSam:***
> ***As mentioned, I work out of town a lot. I don't have time for a relationship, but it's important to me that you feel respected. I'd like to know what will make you feel as such.***

Respected? I mean, that's a given, but I'd also like to feel fucked.

> ***GoodtimesOnly:***
> ****thinking face emoji* I'd like to get off. I'd like you to get off. I don't want an awkward goodbye or hello.***

> ***SportsManSam:***
> ***Your place or mine?***

Definitely can't be my house. I don't have one, and I'm not going to his.

> ***GoodtimesOnly:***

Why not meet at a hotel?

SportsManSam:
I'm down for whatever as long as you're comfortable with that. Your bio says New York. You close to NYC?

I should be freaking out right now, but honestly, I just want to know if it lives up to the hype. And yeah, it's kind of shitty that I lied to my mom and told her that I had a boyfriend senior year in high school just so she'd stop asking me if there was anyone "special." Hell, I even agreed to go on the pill so she thought I'd had sex.

GoodtimesOnly:
Yep.

SportsManSam:
You sure about this, GTO? Yep, is one of those words we men sometimes lump in with that other word that freaks a guy out—"fine."

I roll my eyes at the fact that that's even a thing. If it's not fine, say so.

GoodtimesOnly:
I'm not like other girls. *laughing face emoji* Yep means yep. Fine means fine unless it's coupled with an eye roll or a foot stop. I'm drama free, SMS. The profile name says it all: Good Times Only. I'm living my best drama-free life.

SportsManSam:
A gif of a man striking gold comes through

> ***SportsManSam:***
> ***Let's agree now then, that if it's not fun, it's a one-off.***

> ***GoodtimesOnly:***
> ***Let's not pretend it's something more. It is a one-off.***

> ***SportsManSam:***
> ***Guessing you like variety?***

Ew, no. Okay, maybe? I don't fucking know.

> ***GoodtimesOnly:***
> ***They say it's the spice of life.***

Aaaand … nothing.

> ***GoodtimesOnly:***
> ***Did I lose you?***

> ***SportsManSam:***
> ***Hell no. I'm just trying to figure out how I'm going to sneak a portable pole into a hotel. You're the real deal, a fucking unicorn, you get a free lesson.***

Grinning, I start to respond, but he beats me to it.

> ***SportsManSam:***
> ***I want you to sleep on this. Send me a message tomorrow after you've slept on it to let me know either way. Sleep well, GTO.***

> ***GoodtimesOnly:***
> ***Sleep well.***

Knowing damn well I'm not going to be able to sleep, I decide to slide out of bed to grab my little bullet to curb the ache between my legs caused by staring at SMS's pics and the wicked thought of what lies ahead.

Sliding off the bed, I am startled when I hear, "Are you okay, Jillian?"

Fuck! I scream in my head, thankful I manage to keep it contained and eventually am able to answer. "Sorry, Mom, must have been dreaming."

"Do you want me to call down and have some warm milk brought to the room?" She begins to sit up.

"No, no, no. Go back to sleep. I'm fine."

The door to our room in the suite opens, and Hudson peeks in. "You ladies good?" Before I can answer, he huffs and looks up. "Jill, one of the girls escaped. Fix that, yeah?"

I look down, and sure enough … *fuck!*

I fix my damn shirt on my way to the bathroom. Eyes spring up to meet his, and he arches a brow. *Busted.*

I throw daggers from my eyes, hoping they penetrate deep enough that he doesn't say a word to Mom about the piercing.

"You sure you don't want some warm milk?" Mom calls after me.

"I'm good. Promise. Go back to sleep, Mom." *Please!*

STANDING in front of yet another hotel mirror, I have to dig deep to remember where I am. California. Today's the last game in the series against the Angels, and then we hop on a plane to Syracuse and head to Hudson's house for Mom's Mother's Day surprise, and then …

Fuck, fuck, fuck, do not cry, do not—

A light tap on the door, and then it opens just a crack. "It's—"

"I know who it is. It's Hudson. You crack the door and wait to hear me say, *I'm decent*. Mom would knock and walk in, and Rome would wait until I opened it."

"All right." He flings the door open, eyes closed. "Coming in because you sound like you're crying and … fuck." He walks into the damn wall. "Well, that's gonna leave a mark."

"You're such a jackass." I laugh and cry at the same time. "I'm freaking decent."

He walks over and wraps me in his big, stupid arms. "Stop crying over pierced nips, Jills."

I sock him in the stomach. "I'm not. But you really should get your ass back to the gym."

"Fuck, J." He takes a dramatic step back and acts as if I've wounded him.

"Oh, please, no one could bruise that massive ego of yours." I move to lean against the counter as I bat away tears. "For your information, I'm not upset you saw my—"

"And you shouldn't be. You're a girl; you have boobs. Boobs that have gotten me into many a fight since they started sprouting when you were fifteen."

I sock him again, but he keeps on going.

"You pissed you skipped walking at your graduation? I told you—"

"That was *my* decision. No regrets." No one I wanted to see, anyway. I saw through all those bitches in my classes who acted like they wanted to be my friend. It was the same shit growing up.

He brushes a hand over his face then lifts his shirt. "Same."

"What the hell?" I gasp, seeing gold barbells through his man nips.

"Are you judging me?" he asks, dead serious.

I nod as I ask, "Why gold?" As soon as the question leaves my lips, I realize the answer. "Your team's black and gold."

He nods. "Got black, too, and even though we're oversharing tonight, tits are different than the parts south of the border, so if you have—"

"You pierced your dick?"

"Fuck no," he states, looking at me like I'm insane. Then he grins. "Tags did it."

"One of the Jags' owners? He and Bella have that reality show and—"

"Yep," he says proudly. Then he narrows his eyes. "Don't tell Rome."

"*Pfft*, he has more ink than you—he can't judge." I step back and push myself up on the counter.

"I'll have more. Planning on a back piece and the other sleeve next off-season."

"What are you planning?"

He shakes his head. "We'll discuss that later. How about we talk about what had you in tears?"

I shake my head. "It's stupid."

"You being upset isn't stupid, Jillian."

"Our lives have changed so fast that sometimes it's hard to keep up." It's not a lie, but not the whole truth.

"It's a whirlwind, for sure. I'd love to say it'll get better, but if the Jags keep kicking ass, Roman's season will overlap ours even more. Mom's going to be flying in a million different directions. But you, you're going to be in school with no interruptions. No Covid, no Dad squatting at the house, no—"

"I got waitlisted at Binghamton and Rutgers."

"Appeal that shit. You're Jillian fucking Hart."

I shake my head and close my eyes. "I got into Montana University's program."

His pause in response warms my heart.

"What do you want?"

Tears prick my eyes again, and I see him swallow hard. Hudson doesn't get emotional; he and Roman weren't made to fall.

"Hard to grow being in the shade for so long." He walks over and hugs me. "Never got the chance to figure it out."

"Not your fault."

"Maybe not." He steps back. "Gonna suck not knowing my little sister's cheering me on every game, but it's your time, and when you figure it out, I'm gonna be in the stands, cheering you on."

"I know." I sniff.

"If it's Montana, then—"

"That's the only option right now."

"Fuck it is. Take a gap year. Travel," he suggests, then laughs. "Who'd have thought the Harts would be in a position to use the term gap year?"

I can't help but smile. "I knew you'd make it."

"I knew Rome would."

"So did I," I defend myself. "Just shocked that it took a little longer."

"A year longer. His gap year. Now take yours."

"How is that going to help me?" I roll my eyes. "If anything, it would slow my growth."

"CeCe's little sister, Cora, got waitlisted. She's going to take a couple of online classes and work at Wags."

I knew this. The poor girl had her life turned upside down

her freshman year and ended up with some shitty grades, so she's retaking those classes.

"I don't want to be a vet."

"Not sure she does anymore, either." He scratches his head. "You don't have to work. You—"

"I worked from the time I was thirteen until Covid at the snack shack," I cut him off real quick. "I enjoyed working. I loved people. I want to be that me again."

NOUR

Family Matters

Nour

WALKING OUT ON THE FIELD, I mentally go over my game day checklist.

1 - Loaded omelet.

2 - Two pieces of toast; one with butter, one with strawberry jam.

3 - Showered and jerked off.

To the image of GTO's curvy as fuck body and pierced nips. Not just in my head, either; I propped the phone up in the shower. Also did that last night. *Let's see what happens there.*

5 - Watched *Real Housewives of Beverly Hills.*

6 - Napped liked champ.

7 - Yoga.

Amias and Locke joined me, which was interesting since Locke hated yoga just a couple months ago. *Another deviation, but it's gotta be worth something that Locke wanted to do yoga.*

8 - Played a game of chess.

It was against two of the gen three, Archer and Cooper, Jase and Carly Steel's grandsons.

9 - I'm wearing a new jock since I've yet to hit for shit this season. It's tie-dyed.

Tereira thinks it's a rainbow and gave me a fist-bump for being an LGBTQ ally. I mean, I'll be an ally to anyone who needs one, so yeah, it's cool.

10- I'm wearing the gold chain I bought in Turkey the first and only time I visited.

11 - The bracelets the kids from the center gave me when I got pulled up to the majors are on my wrist.

Stepping out of the tunnel and onto the field, I look up at the sun, seeking its warmth and repeat my mantra in my head, *It's a good day to win.*

And then ... the crowd notices us and immediately starts booing.

Chuck Turner, who is our designated hitter, *once catcher*, cups his ear and smiles. "That's Angels fans accepting they're getting an ass kicking today, Jags!"

Smirking, I look up, scan the crowd, and spot her immediately. Even knowing she's going to be here, it's shocking. It's one thing for me to turn away from our family, but Amira taking the stand that she has, by simply being here, is making a statement to the family, and it doesn't sit right with me.

She's beautiful, educated, and successful. She'll have a wonderful life, but it could have been much easier had she not said fuck the patriarchy in the way she did when moving to Trenton.

"Who's the hot as fuck brunette with the Wags?" AJ asks loudly, knowing damn well it's my sister.

"Jesus, Mary, and Joesph," Rudy Galleon says then bites his fist.

"That's Dr. Uyar." Amias Steel, our short stop, says, smacking him in the stomach with his glove.

Rudy narrows his eyes at AJ as he takes the glove and accuses, "You knew?"

"Damn right, I did." He laughs his ass off as he takes off toward centerfield.

I watch all of this from the corner of my eye.

"Nour, I was—"

I cut him off with, "Nope."

Roman Hart, second base, chuckles. "Galleon, he says no more than ten words to anyone, other than Bennett, until he catches the first warmup pitch." It's eight, but he's clearly caught on to my superstition. "After that, I'm sure he'll give you the ass chewing you deserve for disrespecting his sister."

"How the fuck did I disrespect her? Said she was hot," Galleon defends himself. "Didn't say I wanted to add her to the rotation."

"She's a decade under your preferred demographic," Cody Vanders, our left fieldsman, states as he passes by.

Following him out, Galleon gives him shit right back, "Vanders, you really wanna open that door and grant me access to talk about your—"

"Don't go there, G," Vander warns.

He and Locke "*played as a team*" before Locke got the only girl he ever wanted to call his and his alone. To each their own.

I watch as Bennett walks away from whatever pearls of wisdom he and his pitching coach—a.k.a. his father, Blaze Bennett Sr.—has just instilled in him, and just like always, he looks pissed.

I glance at our manager, Josè Evans, and wonder when he's gonna clue into the fact Jr. despises his old man. He's an amazing pitcher, and the minute he's not under his old man's thumb, he'll be one of the best, if not *the* best, in the entire league.

"Kid's gonna be okay," Pope says, nodding toward the stands.

I look up and see a few of the owners—Justice, Truth, Brisa, Tris, Bella, Kiki, Max, and Patrick—all staring toward Bennett. Behind them, the team's property owners—their parents—are doing the same.

Patrick Steel sees me looking at them and nods to me. I lift my chin, hoping he sees what I do.

I then shift my line of vision to Amira. She's laughing at something being said, and so is everyone sitting in that area. Jillian Hart isn't, though. She lifts a shoulder, rolls her big doe eyes, and then bats lashes that are no doubt false. I'm pretty sure her tits are, too. No woman, no human, is that naturally sexy. I'm honestly shocked her brothers allow that. Not that I'd say that to her or them, but it's a safe assumption that they paid for it so, clearly, they support her choice to put Ds on a five-foot-three, maybe four, frame. Safer yet to assume it was Hudson—Rome's the more conservative of the two.

"You good, man?"

Remembering the first time the two women walked into the bar, both incredibly stunning, and how any man with a pulse, even those who prefer men, took a second look, and then AJ asked in a way that showed obvious interest, "What have we here?"

Roman glared at him, and Hudson laid it right out there.

"What we have is the mother and sister of two protective, give-no-fucks men, especially when it comes to them. Jail? Sure, I'll do time. Stitches? Line 'em up. Take on the whole bar? Been there, done that."

So, I turned to avoid eye contact with Rome since I had

been one hundred percent just checking out his sister's rack and simply nodded.

"Bennett's heading out to the hill."

"Thanks."

I glance up at my sister again, and she points a finger toward her open mouth then acts as if she's spitting something into her hands.

I blow a big-ass bubble and wink at her before pulling down my facemask and heading out to home plate, making damn sure to step over all the foul lines on my way.

Even if I couldn't see his face, from the first pitch, I can feel it against my palm that Bennett's pissed. I don't know his and his old man's story, but I can relate. I can't imagine having to work with mine which, ironically, is what led me to playing in the minors and now here.

After warming up, we head in.

Coach T yells, "Listen up; the batting order's different tonight. They're starting their rookie, so we're going with Steel, Pope, Galleon, Turner, Uyar, Locke, Vander, Hart, and Tereira."

"The fuck?" Bennett mumbles.

"You're tight," comes from behind us.

"Fuck I am," he replies without looking back at his old man.

"Let's get you loosened up," Bennett Senior says, ignoring the fact that his son clearly wants nothing to do with him.

Sucks not being able to tell his old man to fuck off because he's a coach, but that doesn't mean I don't let him know I think he's a dick.

"Nothing here changes a thing you and I do out there."

His jaw tightens, and he gives a firm nod before heading toward "Coach Bennett."

After taking my gear off, I stand outside the dugout with the guys, watching the pitcher warm up, when the song "Talk Dirty to Me" by Jason Derula starts.

Laughing to myself, I glance at Amias, who's looking up at his family, shaking his head.

AJ Tereira nudges me and nods to Bennett, who's looking at us, no doubt remembering the night we were all drinking and the four Steel brothers were busting on Patrick and showing us his TikToks. This song came up on his feed with people all over the damn world doing a dance. All of us learned that damn dance, and yeah, we posted it. That video went viral.

"Fuck it." I wave him over, knowing it will lift his spirits.

"Hell yes!" Tereira cheers.

AJ, Rudy G, myself, and Blaze fall in line. We all slap hands and wait for the chorus to begin.

"Been around the world, don't speak the language ..."

Once we've sufficiently shaken our asses, made fools of ourselves, and have Bennett smiling, I look around. The owners and WAGs who are in the stands are all on their feet, cheering like we just won the fucking series, and the Angels fans are no longer booing the Jersey Jags but fully engaged and whistling, clapping and having a good damn time. And I feel damn good. Then I remember Amira is up there, too. I force myself to look up, half-expecting her to be hiding under her seat, but she's not. She's beaming from ear-to-car.

When she notices me looking at her, she does the whole spit your gum out routine again.

I turn and look at the sun. It's coming down, but it's still in the sky. Then I glance back and shake my head, which causes her to smile in a way that I remember my older sister smiling at me before everything went to shit.

"Ladies and gentlemen, welcome to Anaheim Stadium!

It's a perfect day for baseball as the Angels take on the Jersey Jaguars. We are moments away from the first pitch, so grab your snacks, find your seats, and get ready for an exciting game. Let's ... play ball!"

Steel steps up to the plate, swings at the first pitch, and connects, sending a rocket into the outfield for a double. The crowd roars as he stands proudly on second base.

Next up is Pope. He connects with a solid hit just over the shortstop's head and races to first base while Steel holds his ground on second.

Rudy G is now up. With two strikes and two balls, he swings and delivers a powerful hit to right field. But he's thrown out one step from first base.

We're all on our feet, cheering on Steel and Pope, who seize the opportunity to advance to third and second respectively.

Turner heads to bat, and Coach T looks at me. "Keep it on the ground, and you're all good."

I nod as I watch Turner approaches the plate. The second pitch, he smashes a single. The crowd is on their feet, but Steel and Pope stay put.

No pressure, I think as I head to home, holding the barrel of my favorite bat, flipping it, catching the knob, and tapping it on the ground four times—once for each base I want to make it to. After three swings, I step into the box, grind my left toe into the dirt, and then nod to the pitcher.

Eyes locked on his, I then watch as the ball leaves his hand and grip the bat tighter, seeing as I watch the fastball heading straight for my sweet spot, just above my knees. I exhale the tension from my body as I step forward and swing.

The moment leather and wood connect, I feel an energy course through me that is stronger than anything I've ever felt. I don't even need to watch the ball to know it's soaring between center and right, and I'm not sure where it will drop, but I am sure at least two of my teammates will make it home.

I watch our first base coach motioning me on as I approach. Then I hit first and head to second, making it seconds before the second baseman has it in his hand.

"Fuck!" he roars, hurling the ball to the rookie pitcher, who misses it.

Our third base coach waves me on as it flies past the first baseline.

Their first base man grabs the ball and throws it to the catcher as Turner slides into home.

"Safe!" the ump yells.

"One hell of a hit, Uyar!" Our third base coach smiles as he claps his hands. "One hell of a fucking hit."

"You wanna come home or hang on third for a while?" Locke yells to me as he heads to bat.

"Bring me home," I answer.

"You got it."

Truth be told, it shouldn't matter either way, but my focus right now is leaning heavily toward going through the list of every fucking thing I did today to make damn sure it's repeated next game.

When I got pulled up, my ultimate goal was completed. I just wanted my shot. But now I want more than anything to play for this team for as long as I possibly can.

INSIDE THE VISITOR LOCKER ROOM, we're celebrating our second win, when the men of the Steel family walk in.

"You made us proud tonight, Jaguars," Jase Steel says.

Xavier adds, "Had fuck not to do with the two out of three

wins you delivered here in Anaheim, and everything to do with the fact you played like brothers, and you had fun from beginning to end."

He's not wrong. Tonight was the first away game we've really engaged with the crowd. Those months of lockdown and learning TikTok dances to pass time, paid off.

"Had a little to do with the win," Cyrus adds.

"To celebrate, we're giving you all two straight days with no games," Max Steel jokes, because it's not a gift; it's scheduled.

Justice Steel shakes his head. "Shower up, and then let's get home, kiss our mothers, then it's back to business in Trenton against the Tigers."

WALKING out of the visitor locker room, I hit the Flingshot app, send a message to GTO, and see she's sent me one.

<u>GoodTimesOnly</u>:
Slept on it. Looking forward to meeting up, sooner than later. *hourglass emoji*

I tap out a reply.

<u>SportsManSam</u>:
You going to be around in about an hour? If so, hit me up. Let's nail *hammer emoji* this down.

When I round the corner in the corridor, I see Amira standing with Roman Hart's crew—CeCe, her sister, Cora, Hudson, Linda, and Jillian Hart—and shove my phone in my pocket.

"MVP of the game right here," Hudson yells to me. "Killed it out there tonight, Uyar."

"It was a good night." I try not to smile too damn big, and it's not easy.

"Six RBIs in one game," Roman says from behind me. "Twelve's the record."

Hitching my duffle over my shoulder, I ask, "Wanna place a bet on which of us breaks it first?"

We fist-bump, and then Amira steps forward. "You played like a pro."

"That's because I am one."

"You certainly are." She smiles. "I'm so proud of you, Nour."

"Just doing my job." I wink.

"I was able to change my flight home. I hope you don't mind, Dr. Shaw. Cora—"

"Please, call me CeCe." CeCe laughs.

"I'll try." Amira smiles at her then looks back at me. "They're all flying to New York for Mother's Day. I thought you and I could possibly do something after catching up on our sleep?"

3

JILLIAN

BV or Bust

JILLIAN

LIFTING MY SLEEP MASK, I glance over at Cora, who has not been able to keep still for the past twenty minutes. "You okay?"

"Yeah, I'm okay. You?"

"I'm okay."

I catch her smirking as she looks down and fixes her lap blanket, and I immediately know what it's about.

"You're never going to let that go, are you?"

"Yes," she states then follows it up with, "Eventually."

"Better make it happen, because the sooner you do, the less time I'll spend plotting my revenge."

"Revenge?"

"Oh please, you started it with your little micro-O when *Blaze Bennett* walked out of the tunnel."

She squirms again, and I position my seat back to try to figure out what the hell her problem is.

"I have to pee, okay?" she whimpers.

"Then go."

"It's been occupied for like fifteen minutes. I've waited so long I'm afraid if I go all the way to the other one, I won't make it."

"Knock on the damn door. Tell whoever the asshole is—"

"Holes—plural. Two people."

"Oh, fuck them and their mile-high fantasy." I start to stand, but little Cora Parker grabs my knee to stop me. She's strong, too. Her hand's like has a damn vice grip.

"Those assholes include my sister and your brother."

I snort out a laugh. "I should wake up Mom. She always has to pee. She'd go—"

"You're not hearing me. I'm going to piss my pants if I have to wait for anyone else," she sneers.

I grin. "That revenge I was talking about …"

"Not funny," she replies as if she's in pain.

"Don't worry about it. I don't have to do shit. Karma showed up and took care of it."

"I really don't like you right now."

"You do, too." I stand.

"What are you doing?"

I nod a few rows ahead where a man is standing and stretching. "I'm going to hold your place in line so he doesn't get there first."

I step over her and do just that.

POOR CECE LOOKS COMPLETELY SCANDALIZED when she comes out of the bathroom and sees me standing here.

"No need to freak out; Hudson and Mom are asleep." I glance at Cora, who stands slowly and does the slowest pee-

pee walk I've ever seen up the aisle toward us. "Your sister's going to piss her pants, so we need to move."

"Oh my God," she murmurs as she moves out of Cora's way. "I'm so sorry."

"Move it, Romeo," Cora grumbles at Rome as he walks out.

I glance back at the two of them once Cora is in the bathroom, hopefully not pissing herself. I point back and forth between the two of them. "There's nothing either of you can say to make this go away. Just move along."

"I'm so sorry," CeCe whispers again.

Rome leans in, narrows his eyes, and whispers to me, "I'm not."

When Cora is done, I decide I may as well go, too. I still have another brother on this plane, and as chummy as he's gotten with the brunette flight attendant, I may be the one almost pissing my pants in a couple hours.

When I return, Cora gets up to let me back in my seat by the window. "I owe you big."

"Not for that, you don't. But for not warning me that Nour's sister is the new vet at Wags and allowing me to say he looks like baseball Jesus, you owe me big."

She bites back a laugh. "If I'd have thought you didn't know who she was, and that was going to come out of your mouth, I would have done whatever I could to stop it."

I sigh. "I'll never be able to face either one of them again."

"I wouldn't worry about it. She's cool, and even if she wasn't, they're not close like you and your brothers. I'm not sure many people are."

"Thought the same thing, but the Steel family, they're tight, and so are the owners of Hudson's team." I yawn.

When she doesn't reply, I nudge her. "I hope you still don't feel weird about going with us."

She shrugs. "I feel bad about Dad being alone. But he's picking me up at JFK, and we're going to hit a couple plays."

"Your mom was a Broadway enthusiast, right?"

She nods.

"Never been to a show. We're all sports in this—"

"You should come with us." She smiles. "CeCe and Roman could stay another day and—"

"You and your dad have plans." The idea of going somewhere with anyone other than my brothers or Mom is tempting, but … I don't want—"

"Seriously, he'd probably love to get to know some of the people I spend time with. But if you don't want to, then—"

"I'd actually love to."

"Perfect." She smiles big. "I'll message CeCe now."

We message back and forth with Rome and CeCe, and it's a go. Rome changes his ticket from his name to mine, and even books me a room at the hotel where Cora and her dad are staying.

It doesn't take long before she falls asleep, and I decide to check the app to see if he's responded.

I feel my face spilt into a grin when I see he has.

SportsManSam:
You going to be around in about an hour? If so, hit me up. Let's nail *hammer emoji* this down.

GoodTimesOnly:
Sorry, spotty service. Any chance you'd be up to meeting in NYC Monday late evening? I have "a thing" with my girls, so I probably won't have a moment alone until late, but I do have a room that's all mine. Think about it. Let me know tomorrow? Sleep well, SMS.

X

SportsManSam:
No need to think about it. Can't wait to meet up with you. Send me deets when you get them.

It may be in poor judgment to play this game, but I'm resigned to go through with this. But I won't be sending him details until an hour before I have them. So, instead of replying right away, I scroll up and look at his pictures again. Those abs of his … yeah, I am totally doing this.

I'M NOT one to use words like "picturesque," but Skaneateles, New York, is deserving of such a word.

"It's beautiful here," Cora says, looking out the window as we pass by the stone buildings.

"You'll have to come up at Christmastime. They have Dickens weekends." Hudson chuckles. "Kind of cool."

A few minutes later, as we're turning down West Lake Road, I watch Hudson's eyes shine with restrained excitement and pride.

I lean forward and squeeze his shoulder. "Feel like home?"

"More and more every day," he admits.

A few minutes later, he's turning into the driveway.

"My goodness, that went quickly," Mom says as the new home on his property comes into view. "I love that they decided to match the exterior to your house."

"Looks like it belongs, yeah?" Rome asks.

Mom smiles. "Certainly does."

Hudson pulls in behind the contractors' vehicles in the driveway. "Let's check it out." He then throws the vehicle in park and gets out.

Rome climbs out of the passenger side and opens CeCe's door, while Hudson opens Mom's. Cora and I file out of the third row behind them.

Stepping out on the porch, Ryan Brooks, the general contractor and a seriously handsome man in his fifties, says with a smile, "Look, it's the Harts."

His stunning daughter, Riley, who is tall, all legs, with thick, long black hair, steps out, and her brother, Jackson, the strong, silent, and also hot as hell type, nods.

"Look, it's the Brooks family, working on Mother's Day." Hudson shakes his head. "Say it ain't so."

Ryan's wife, Jade, steps out of the house, her long, black hair in a thick braid hanging over her shoulder. "We're heading to brunch at the brewery to meet the rest of the family. I insisted they show me their latest project." She looks at her husband and kids. "It's incredible."

Riley takes her hand. "Let's leave them to it."

Roman shakes their hands. "Thank you."

I watch as Mom tips her head to the side, clearly curious at his choice of words.

"We're open until seven tonight; you should all stop by and celebrate," Riley says, walking down the porch stairs. She smiles at Mom. "Happy Mother's Day."

"Thank you," Mom says then looks at Jade. "Happy Mother's Day to you, too."

"Let's check it out." I take Mom's hand.

"Will the owners mind?" Mom asks, voice shaking slightly as we head up the stairs. Rome. Hudson, CeCe, and Cora follow behind us.

She knows.

"Not sure." Hudson steps around us and opens one of the wooden double doors. Rome opens the other.

As is the plan, I step into what one would call a quaint yet luxurious country lake cottage, but people like us, the Harts before my brothers became pro athletes, would drop the word quaint and admit it would be more than we ever dared dream of to live in a place like this.

If she had any questions before, they are being answered now.

To the left, the spacious living area is furnished with all the plush, overstuffed sofas draped in soft earth-toned throws that she added to one of many Pinterest boards that Mom and I have going. She and I were dreaming of the home we'd have once I finished school. A large stone fireplace's flickering flames cast a warm glow across the room. Above, wooden beams cross the ceiling, adding a touch of rustic charm.

In the center of the room will sit a coffee table, if Mom wants one. The bare walls, a blank slate where I imagine she'll hang pictures from the shops lining Main Street or ones she'll take. The only exception is the large wooden plaque with the words, "*Where Harts gather and love grows.*"

She shakes her head and wipes away a tear with the hand not still holding tight to mine.

I lead her to the kitchen that has sleek granite countertops and custom-built cabinets, with maple finish that matches the beams. A farmhouse sink beneath a window offers a picturesque view of the lake, unobstructed by Hudson's massive home. The scent of freshly brewed coffee wafts from a gleaming espresso machine nestled next to a row of polished copper cookware. Beside it are flowers with a card peeking out that says, "*Welcome Home, Linda.*"

More tears fall, this time hers and mine.

Beyond the kitchen, the dining area features a wooden table, surrounded by cushioned chairs, each one draped with a woven throw. Soft sunlight filters through lace curtains, casting patterns onto the hardwood floors below.

"I can't find words." She sniffs. "I—"

"Find them after we're done exploring your new home, yeah?" Rome suggests as he moves past us and heads toward the master bedroom.

Inside the master is a wrought iron bed, covered in white linens. The drapes are open, exposing the French doors leading to the side porch, offering another spectacular view of the lake. There's the writing desk she's dreamed of having in the corner and a vintage armoire that looks like the one I found on Pinterest and sent to them in our sibling group text we used while planning.

I look at Hudson, and he gives me a wink.

Another set of French doors leads to her en suite bathroom, with a soaker tub and separate shower. Inside the bathroom is also a walk-in closet.

Hudson nods back toward the kitchen. "Follow me."

We pass the kitchen to the stairs, and he points up to the balcony of the second story. "There's another master suite upstairs with a balcony, a smaller bedroom, and a second living area." He opens the door under the stairs. "Half-bath here for guests."

He looks at Roman, who stands by the bottom of the stairs, pulling the small ball of wood, called a newel cap, off the bottom post—newel post—and pulls out the deed. "This is yours."

When she begins to sob, there's not a dry eye in the house. *Where Harts gather and love grows*.

THE PARKING LOT IS PACKED, but Hudson manages to find a place to park his massive Escalade.

"It' a barn." Roman chuckles.

"It's a gambrel-roofed barn," Hudson states as he opens his door and slides out. "Stick around here, and you'll learn shit you never thought you needed to know."

I look at Cora. "It's a red barn."

"With silos," she adds as she moves to exit the third row.

"Silos?" I ask.

"Animal person, farm people, we're like not the same but kind of."

"Makes perfect sense, kind of." I laugh as I follow her out.

The sign over the entry doors reads "*Brooks Barn and Brew*."

Mom's, still misty-eyed and still looks to be in a bit of shock.

I love today. Truly love it.

Inside the entry, an easel is set, telling us, "*Seat yourself. We're busy*," which makes me giggle, but it's speaking truth —the place is packed.

We all follow Hudson toward the bar, three sides of which are seating. On the back wall is a one of the massive TVs, between two doorways, which I assume lead to the kitchen.

Smiling, Riley Brooks comes out of the back and spots us. "Hey, look, it's the Harts."

"Sure is." Hudson winks.

A sandy-brown-haired, nice-looking guy comes up behind her and wraps an arm around her waist. "It's the off season; what are you doing back from"—he pauses—"where in Bumfuck, Virginia?"

Hudson lifts his chin. "I own a house here, and so does my beautiful mother." He pulls her under his arm. "This is home no matter the seasons."

"Should have been here earlier. Not looking good for even a Knight to find a place to—"

Riley elbows him and laughs. "The loft has plenty of space. Grab a table. I'll send a server up."

Hudson winks at her. "Family-style works. Load us up. To the round table we go, fam."

Before we walk away, I hear Riley's boyfriend say, "This was supposed to be a day off for you. I thought we'd get some time together."

"Guy's a fucking tool," Hudson mutters under his breath as we make our way to the stairs.

The loft is freaking awesome. One side overlooks the bar below, and just like the main level, it has a wall of windows overlooking the lake.

"How many lakes are there around here?" Cora asks.

"It's called the Finger Lakes region," Hudson replies. "There's eleven close by. Mom's lake is the best."

Upstairs, there's one family and, of course, Hudson knows them.

"Hey, look, it's the Rosses."

"Hey, look, it's the Harts." A blonde woman smiles. "Come sit with us."

Hudson looks at CeCe. "Alex and his son, Liam, are veterinarians."

"Dad's a part-time vet now." Liam, the son, chuckles.

"Not part-time yet," Alex corrects his son. "Not until the fall."

"Too young to retire." Roman shakes his hand. "I'm—"

"We know who you are. You're Roman Hart." She holds out her hand. "I'm Phoebe, and this is Remington. The other Rosses."

Hudson sucks in a breath. "No disrespect met, Mrs. Ross. Roman's girlfriend's a vet, too, and her sister's going to be."

"Once I get off the waitlist at Rutgers." Cora shrugs.

"You apply to Cornell?" Alex asks.

"As in, the Ivy League college?" She shakes her head. "No way. My grades tanked last semester."

"Extenuating circumstances." CeCe shakes her head. "You'll get there again."

"Get those grades up next semester and apply. You never know," Alex says, sitting back down at the table.

"I'm retaking the classes, but I'm not Cornell material." Cora shrugs.

"Alex and Liam both graduated from Cornell." Phoebe winks at Cora. "And Alex starts teaching there in the fall."

While everyone is talking, I excuse myself and head down to use the bathroom—a.k.a. check my phone to see if SMS has messaged me again—when one of the servers drops a whole tray of drinks at my feet.

"Oh shit, I am so sorry." She bends down and starts picking up cups, shockingly, none of them broke. "Oh my God, look at your shoes."

I bend down and help her. "No big deal."

"You better fire that one," someone yells over the crowd.

"Can't fire free help!" she calls back then looks at me. "Totally why I shouldn't be allowed behind the bar. I'm—"

"London Links." I laugh.

"Guilty." She smiles and looks up at me. "Fuck, leave it to me to trash Hudson Hart's sister …"

"Jillian." I shake my head. "Put me behind the bar or counter any day. Out here, I'd have dumped them, too."

"Better not say that too loud. Riley will snatch you up." We both stand; her with the tray, me with hands full of cups.

I look at the tray. "Yeah, these won't fit. I'll follow you."

And that's just what I do.

Behind the bar, London announces, "Hart's not for hire, so don't get any ideas."

"Not even for events during the off season?" Riley jokes.

"Off season? Which one—baseball or football?" I laugh.

Riley cocks her head to the side. "We're fully staffed during football season, but the holiday parties, we can always use a hand."

"Told you." London shakes her head as Riley follows us back to the massive kitchen area.

"I might be available?"

"Is that a question or—"

"No, seriously, maybe, but I'm no good on the floor."

"I'll take a maybe." Riley starts emptying my hands. "Good money in events, and it's only like five or six hours. I'll take you any Friday, Saturday, or Sunday from December first to New Year's Day. You'll make an easy five hundred a shift. Obviously, you're busy when the Knights play, so that's a non-issue."

"You're being serious?"

London sighs. "She is."

"Cool."

UPSTAIRS, I decide to make an announcement. "I got accepted to Montana and waitlisted at Rutgers and Binghamton."

My whole family and the Rosses look at me.

"I don't want to go to Montana."

Hudson smiles. "Good."

I continue, "Riley Brooks just offered me a job here during events that aren't on game days. I think it'll be fun, and I also think I'm going to take a couple online classes toward a Master's in Women and Gender Studies."

They all just look at me.

"I am going to just see where it all leads."

Hudson grins. "Gap year, baby."

I can't help but smile, and then I look at Mom. "Are you okay with this?"

"I'm over the moon."

4

NOUR

Sexting

Nour

SportsManSam:
*No need to think about it. Can't wait to meet up with you.
Send me deets when you get them.*

It was nearly twenty hours since I sent that message before her reply.

GoodTimesOnly:
*Time Square area, around ten at night okay with you?
We're going to see a show.*

SportsManSam:
Ten's good. You think we should exchange names?

GoodTimesOnly:
A one-night stand doesn't require names. It requires body

parts, *eggplant emoji* *peach emoji* sex you'll remember for months, and orgasms, *wave emoji* preferably multiples.

SportsManSam:
Give me a second; I need to pinch myself to make sure you're not a dream GTO

GoodTimesOnly:
Dream? No, I'm a *unicorn emoji*

SportsManSam:
You can dance on my pole all night.

GoodTimesOnly:
This pole comes up a lot, SMS.

SportsManSam:
We all have our fantasies. Tell me yours.

GoodTimesOnly:
Is this the part you ask for a picture of my tits so you can jerk off while I tell you how wet I get at the thought of one night with a stranger?

SportsManSam:
If you want to send a picture of your gorgeous tits, I'm not going to tell you no.

There's no way in hell I'm going to admit that I've been rubbing one out to the same picture every morning and each night since she gifted me the one she did. The one I zoomed in on and found out she was pierced. Then I may have to admit it's now part of a routine I need to keep up until my next game to see if it's her unicorn tits that improved my game to defend against the allegation she would no doubt have that I'm "just like all the guys." One of several things would inevitably happen, but two are most disconcerting. One, she'd tell me that she hates baseball and I'll never get it up again while "pregaming" in the shower; or two, a one-night stand would be off the table because she'd see the value in fucking a pro player.

It feels like forever has passed, and I'm starting to worry that I went a little overboard.

<u>**SportsManSam**</u>**:**
I don't need a picture, GTO.

As soon as I send the message, I get a blurry mirror selfie of a hot as hell, curvy brunette with a hand full of her own tit, fingers pinching a silver barbell, and I curl up into a seated position.

<u>**GoodTimesOnly**</u>**:**
Well, I guess that was a bad idea.

<u>**SportsManSam**</u>**:**
No, no, no, that wasn't bad at all. It was good, GTO, so good.

<u>**GoodTimesOnly**</u>**:**
So...

<u>**SportsManSam**</u>**:**
Such a good girl.

A few more minutes pass, and I again think I've fucked up with the good girl thing, but whatever, it's too late.

GoodTimesOnly:
***kissy face emoji* I'll shoot you the details when I get my room number.**

SportsManSam:
Sleep well, gorgeous. Excited to be in you tomorrow.

SportsManSam:
Proof of excitement or it's not true.

Not honoring her request would be a major dick move, but having a picture of my cock out there to be passed around is unsettling. So, I hold the phone in the correct position, grab my hard cock through my boxers, snap a picture, and then … I hit *send*.

GoodTimesOnly:
Very nice. *drooly face emoji* See you tomorrow, SMS.

"Please tell me you didn't just send a dick pic while I am literally four feet away from you," AJ grumbles.

Fuck.

"I needed to see if these boxers make my dick look big."

He rolls over and props his head up on his hand. "Endorsement?"

What?

"Not sure yet." I only sort of lie, because it may happen one day.

"After our last game, I knew they'd be all over you. Happy for you, man." He lies back down and rolls over.

"What time are you and Amira heading to the city tomorrow?"

Okay, this is an actual lie.

"Not sure yet, but probably afternoon."

"Cool." He yawns. "Going to work out tomorrow?"

"Yeah. Around six."

"Catch a ride with you?" he asks.

"Of course."

He yawns again. "Night."

"Night."

NOT THAT I have ever questioned the fact that men think about sex more than we should, but it's more evident today than ever in the gym, where that is the topic of conversation.

It started with Locke walking in with a shit-ass grin on his face, and Vanders shaking his head and saying, "I give it a year before you walk in here looking like the Locke we all know."

"That's because you don't know Gwendolyn Locke." Leland points to his face. "Ask Pope when he gets here. He'll confirm."

As if on que, John Paul walks into the gym. "Ask me what?"

"Vanders said this look"—Locke circles his face with his hand—"will fade in a year."

"This look?" he asks.

"Vanders"—Turner shakes his head—"you and I both should know better than to act like experts when it comes to relationships."

Turner's not wrong; he's been married more times than I can keep track of, even if I gave a shit enough to keep track, and Vanders' marriage has been open for pretty much its entirety. Apparently, since becoming Jags, Locke and he strictly stuck to threesomes. Vanders because his wife doesn't like sex, and Locke because one-on-one was messy. He only ever loved one girl, and that girl is now back in his life, his bed, and shares his last name.

I get where Locke is coming from; I only thought I was falling in love once, and that was enough for me to never allow myself to blindly fall into anything like that again.

"We're not the same," Vanders states as he adds more weight to his bar.

"Same boat, different ocean," Turner admits.

"Nah, man, not even close. You've cruised in the Atlantic; I set anchor in the Artic."

I watch as a look passes between Steel and Pope, one that says, *Defuse the situation*.

Pope chuckles. "I don't know about all that, but I will confirm that Locke's not wrong. He's had that same stupid look on his face from the day Gwendolyn York moved to Walton, Texas, until the breakup. It's back, and it's not going anywhere. The whole team needs to learn to deal with it, just like the Walton Warriors did back in the day."

"No disrespect to your wife, Pope—she's a smoke show, too—but having known Gwen before they got married, I'm having no doubt they'll make it," AJ states, and the room goes silent. "What did I say?"

"You just called their wives hot." Blaze shakes his head. "Show some respect for the sanctity of marriage."

"I said no disrespect!" AJ defends. "I didn't ask how many times a day they get to lay hands on them."

Locke's face busts into a grin. "Let's just say, my pregame rituals have changed, and so has my batting average."

AJ chuckles then looks at Pope, expecting him to dish, too.

"Tereria"—he shakes his head as he scrubs a hand over his face then clears his throat—"my wife and I have five kids."

Grinning, AJ looks around the room. "See? That's what I'm talking about."

"You don't get married so you can stop beating off in the shower," Bennett scolds him.

"You get married because, one day, you're lucky enough to come face-to-face with the person who gives your heart an erection, not just your—"

"Momma Joe," Amias Steel gasps as his grandmother walks into the center of the gym.

"Good morning, Amias." She walks over and kisses each of his cheeks.

"Good morning," he says with a slight smile.

She turns and looks at Bennett, who is beet red. "As a mother of four boys, Grandmomma Joe to five young men, not including those by choice and by marriage, great-grand to eight"—she smiles bigger—"make that nine after last night when Gabrielle became a mother on Mother's Day—"

Claps, whistles, and congratulations pop off throughout the area.

"—and I can assure you that self-care in the shower doesn't end with *I do*."

Everyone, including Amias, laughs.

"I am sure Justice will be spending much more time doing just that in the coming weeks."

Bennett actually smiles.

"Any questions, feel free to ask me, after you've all come up for May's birthday cake."

"What kind is it this month?" Amias asks as she heads toward the exit.

"Cannoli," she calls back.

AFTER A SHOWER INVOLVING NO SELF-CARE, eating a piece of Momma Joe's amazing cannoli cake, where I heard Momma Joe thank more than half the team for Mother's Day cards, flowers, or gifts, I head out to my vehicle to wait for Bennett and Tereria.

I make a note in my phone to send Momma Joe a Mother's Day gift next year, hoping I'm still here, and check the app.

Grinning from ear-to-ear, I look at the pictures she's sent.

GoodTimesOnly:
How is it I still get shocked by things I see in the city?

GoodTimesOnly:
This or That *unicorn emoji* edition.

The pictures that follow are of different unicorn masks; two of which she is modeling. And yeah, she's beautiful. Long, thick, dark hair; big, pouty lips; and her eyes … well, what I can see of them with the masks on, are a stunning cognac brown.

SportsManSam:
Sorry for the delay, but I obviously prefer the one that doesn't cover your entire beautiful face. Those lips of yours look delicious.

GoodTimesOnly:
Perfect. That's what I'm wearing tonight.

SportsManSam:
That and nothing else?

GoodTimesOnly:
That and these …

I wait for the image to come through, and when it does, it's a pair of gold, Louboutin strappy stilettos.
Fuck me.

SportsManSam:
You just uncovered a kink I didn't know I had. Yes please.

GoodTimesOnly:
Not too much of a bad girl vibe?
And you've uncovered one for me. Good girl.

SportsManSam:
No, Little Miss Red Bottom, that mask, those shoes, they tick boxes on the good girl list.

I open my water bottle and take a drink as I wait for her reply.

GoodTimesOnly:
You like bottoms red?

I damn near choke and opt to let the mouthful of water spray out instead.

"Uyar, what the fuck?" AJ laughs as he opens the back door and slides in.

I throw the door open, hit the button to open the hatch, slide out, and then hurry to the back of the Audi to grab a towel from the pile of clean ones in a duffel and make quick work of trying to save my phone from water damage.

AJ's laughing his damn head off, and yeah, it would be funny until you're freaking out about losing the only way to contact the girl who sports the lucky nips.

After wiping it off and seeing it's still in working order, I hit her back.

SportsManSam:
*GTO, I had a mouthful of water when I "red" that last message. My phone got a bath. I'd have loved to redden that *peach emoji* if my phone was ruined and I had lost contact with you.*

GoodTimesOnly:
twerking GIF

GoodTimesOnly:
Hyatt Time Square. I won't know the room number until check-in. If by some chance we lose communication, I'll be the one in a *unicorn* mask with the red bottom … s.

"You texting your sister?" AJ asks.

I nod, even though that doesn't lessen the lie. It just feels better.

SportsManSam:
See you soon.

GoodTimesOnly:
Yes, you will. *unicorn emoji*

IF YOU HAD TOLD minor league, or even high school, me that he'd be driving an hour and twenty minutes for a hookup, he would have laughed in your face, probably even smacked some sense into you. But here I am, entering the Lincoln Tunnel to meet a woman with lucky nips, a killer sense of humor, is sexy, and wants nothing but a good time.

I glance in my passenger seat and second-guess the flowers and champagne. I won't be drinking because I've already decided I'm driving back tonight, ensuring I make it back in time to start my pregame routine.

At the light, I looked down at my phone to see if she had sent the room number yet, and she had.

GoodTimesOnly:
Thirteenth floor, room 1331.

I use voice to text to reply. "See you soon. Yeah, that shit's not gonna work. Well, hell, maybe it will. Unicorn emoji. If that reads wrong, forgive me. I'm using speech to text while driving in bumper-to-bumper traffic, rambling on like a moron."

A horn blasts behind me. "Fuck it. Full send."

5

JILLIAN

Ouch!

JILLIAN

THE FACT it was nine p.m. when I got to my room was enough of a delay in the game, so to speak. But now, my eyes are burning from the shampoo I got in them, and no amount of rinsing has lessened the effect.

Blinking, I lean closer to the mirror to get a better look. "I hope to hell my hair and makeup look decent, not that I can see them. Fuck, fuck, fuck."

My phone sounds off with a notification, and I blink rapidly as I look at the screen, hoping that minimizes the pain. It doesn't.

I tap the notification and the messages while leaning in to read it. When a voice comes from somewhere, I jump back and …

"*Noooo*," I cry as I slip on the wet floor, ending up on my ass—hard. "Shit, shit, shit."

I push up and slip again, missing everything he said but "*fuck it. Full send.*"

Eyes burning, vision fucked, ass aching, I know I should call this off, except his voice, deep and calm, a little bit commanding, I know I've picked the perfect hookup.

Eyes now hot because I'm super freaking frustrated and not in the head space I need to be in, I wipe away tears while leaning in.

"Oh my God, seriously?" I feel myself begin to spiral when I notice the mascara running down my face.

For a good ten seconds, I consider using the card Rome gave me for emergencies to get an Uber and head back to Jersey. There, I could hole up in the RV, eat my way through dubious amounts of those damn gummy nerds that CeCe has me hooked on, and binge-watch shitty reality shows, like *Real Housewives of Any-F'ing-Where But Here*.

I smack reflection, *I think*. "Get your head in the game, Hart. You fucking got this."

WITHIN TEN MINUTES, I've turned on the fake dollar store candles I bought, unscrewed lightbulbs on the bedside tables and desk, shoved drenched towels, clothes, and bags in the tiny hotel closet, and am ready to crash for a few minutes and rest my eyes when there is a knock on the door.

Taking in a deep breath then exhaling slowly, I step to the door, turn the knob, and open it, making sure to step back so he doesn't get the full effect of my devil eyes.

He's tall, dark, and blurry, not that I could see his face behind the flowers he's holding out.

"They're beautiful. You shouldn't have." I hold my hand out then pretend to smell them, but only so I can close my damn eyes.

"I …" He pauses, no doubt trying to figure out how to address the literal unicorn in the room. "You take the prize."

I walk over to set the flowers on the entertainment console. Then I turn and look over my shoulder. "Are you coming in, or …?" I leave it hanging but keep the flow going before he decides to run away, which he might, and I couldn't even be mad.

I must look like a lunatic with this damn unicorn mask on, but a girl has to do what a girl has to do. Which is why I am now pushing the hotel robe from my shoulders and shrugging it off.

"Fucking dream," he groans.

Groans.

It's incredibly hot. How hot? Hotter than ninety-eight point six degrees because I have goosebumps covering my skin.

Goosies.

My heart rate increases, my core is getting hot, my clit tingles, and my nipples are hardening. Burning eyes and blurred vision be damned. It's no longer just determination driving this sin train; it's desire.

I walk to the edge of the bed, bare except for the red bottoms, and bend down, ass pointed in his direction, not bending my knees so he gets a nice view of one of my best assets, even in this damn close to dark room, to remove the shoes.

"Allow me."

"Of course." I turn to sit on the edge of the bed.

His voice is thick, rich, and deep when he steps toward me. "Good girl."

Dear Lord, that's hot. Does that mean I have daddy issues? Probably, but who cares? I'm burning for this.

With his two huge hands on my knees, he begins to squat

down, spreading my legs apart to make room for his massive frame. He dips his head down and kisses the inside of each knee.

His hair is longer than how I pictured it in my filthy little fantasies the past several days, and it's soft against my now blazing skin.

His hand, rough and calloused, gently and slowly run down my legs. "Wasn't sure we should take these off, but it got me between your legs, and you smell"—he runs his nose across my inner thigh—"fucking delicious." Firm strong hands around my ankles, he lifts my legs, one and then the other, over his shoulders. "Lie back and let me fuck your sweet pussy with my tongue."

Before I have a chance to say *yes please*, his hand is between my legs, cupping my heated flesh. A finger slides between my folds and inside me, causing my core to immediately contract.

"So hot and tight." His open mouth slides down my leg, teeth nipping my inner thigh, sucking in my flesh, making sounds that I wish I could record to replay when I go solo on my next self-care night.

I whimper as he slides his finger slowly in and out of me. Whimpers, moans, sounds I don't recognize but are undeniably mine, escape me.

He growls as he pulls his finger from inside me, leaving me empty and wanting more, so much more.

I don't wait long as he shoves his arms under me, giving a deep, firm demand of, "Lie back." Then he spreads my legs and licks right up my seam.

I gasp then hold my breath, fisting the comforter as he licks, sucks, and plunges his tongue deep inside of me while holding my legs that are instinctually attempting to close wide open. Everything inside of me is going off. Hell, even my toes are tingling. *Toe-gasms.*

It's not long before I'm rocking, moaning, writhing beneath him.

"No, no, no, no." I reach down between my legs to play with my clit, knowing I'm right there and what it would take to send me over the edge, but his hand captures mine and pins it to the mattress, and then his tongue circles, flicks, and nudges it and he sucks.

"Fuck, fuck, fuck!" I cry then sputter nonsensical words and phrases as the mother of all explosions detonate inside of me.

"Gonna make you come again, and then I want you on all fours so I can fuck this hot little hole of yours and make that peach bounce."

"Oh my God, oh my God, oh my God," I cry as he does it all again.

SMS stands up and starts removing clothes. Then he removes a packet from his pocket and holds it between his teeth. "All fours."

Doing as he says, I glance over my shoulder and watch the muscles in his shoulders move as his hand works the condom over his cock.

"You good?" he asks, voice thick with need.

I clear my throat, not wanting to sound like I'm freaking the hell out that I'm going to lose my virginity doggy-style. It's not like I haven't fucked myself with plastic dicks for a couple years now. I got this.

"How about you tell me once you're inside?"

He chuckles darkly. "Mask is cute as hell. Eating you out and fucking you in it makes it feel"—he pauses as he grips my hips and pulls me to the end of the bed—"some kind of way. It's hot. But round two, it comes off. I wanna kiss those sexy lips of yours."

He lines up the head of his cock with my entrance. "Gonna ease in, stretch you out a bit so I don't hurt you."

"No one's ever died from getting fucked hard and fast, have they?" I quip.

He leans down and bites my ass lightly. "Don't know, but I don't wanna hurt you. We're not finished yet."

"I got two already; you take yours however you want. But round two, I wanna ride you like—"

I was fully unprepared for this, I think, unable to breathe as he moves slowly in and out, getting deeper with each stroke as he curses and praises, grunts and growls.

"Need to fucking hear you," he hisses as his fingers dig into the flesh of my ass. "Unicorn pussy," he grunts. "Magic. Fucking amazing."

"Amaz—" I force out but stop to bite the damn bed to stop from screaming when he pulls me back against him.

"Jesus, you're hot."

"Hot," I whimper.

"So hot."

I manage to mumble, "Uh-huh."

His hand wraps around me, and he pulls my body up so my back is against his hard as hell chest. One of his hands immediately finds my clit—thank God—and the other cups one of my tits, fingers immediately finding my piercing. "So hot."

"*Mmm* …" I moan as the immense pressure and discomfort between my legs eases, but only slightly. The pressure on my clit, though, and the way he's playing with my tits, feels so fucking good.

"Lips," he groans, and I turn to give them to him.

His mouth tastes like me and bubblegum. His lips feel

like cushions or pillows—whichever is softest—and he's good, so good at the kissing part, too.

He tears his lips from mine, sneering, "Fuck, I'm not gonna last much longer." His hand releases me. "Back down for me, all fours. We're gonna come together."

Highly unlikely, I think but obviously don't say.

"Your tits, your mouth, that ass," he says as he thrusts deeper, faster, harder, rolling his hips, gripping my ass, and …

"What are you—"

"Wanna fuck your tits, and right here, too." He presses his thumb more firmly against my asshole. "Not now, though. Your pussy is too good. So good."

"We're gonna come," he sputters, and then his hand is between my legs, and he performs a miracle.

I come, too.

It's a good thing I didn't tell him it wasn't possible because it would have made me a liar. I may be a lot of things, but a liar isn't one of them.

When he pulls out, I collapse on the bed, and he crawls in beside me.

"Ten minutes, and I'm good to go again."

"May take fifteen before the aftershocks subside in my—"

"That's so hot." He pulls me toward him. "Oddly, so is the mask."

I can't help but giggle.

"No judgment. To each their own," he says, and I hear a smile in his sexy, postcoital voice.

"Good. I don't think I'll ever take it off."

"No way. We had a deal." He sighs.

"Truth?"

"Always."

"It's to cover my face so I don't scare you away," I admit, because why not? Our one night is almost up.

"Calling bullshit. You're stunning."

"No bullshit. I was running late and showered after the show. Whatever soap the hotel supplies should be outlawed. It got in my eyes, and I couldn't rinse it out fully." I turn and face him, still not really able to see him, more due to the lighting now, but even so. "It was either cancel or wear the mask so you wouldn't freak out seeing a woman who looked possessed or high, maybe both. Oh, and demonic, too. I couldn't see to remove my makeup, so there's that."

His chest vibrates as he reaches over and cups my boob. "Between your perfect ass, amazing tits, and the robe drop, I'm not even sure I would have noticed. Fucking hot, GTO."

"Even partially blinded still, I can tell you're not so bad yourself, SMS."

"Should have brought my pole. You'd look fucking amazing dancing on it."

"New life goal." I yawn. "Gold medal pole dancer."

"You want me to run down the block and grab you some eyewash?" he asks, messing with his dick, and I realize he's taking off the condom.

"No, it's getting better now." *The tears I shed from your massive dick must have cleaned them out pretty good.* Probably should have allowed myself to cry.

"You sure?"

"I am."

"Ten-minute power nap, and then you can show me what you got?"

I OPEN my eyes and can tell he's asleep, so I slide out of bed to use the bathroom.

Quietly closing the door behind me, I walk to the sink and pull the mask the rest of the way off my face. My eyes are no longer burning, but they're still sore. I make quick work to remove the makeup so that I don't look like someone off of a horror movie going in to round two. Because yes, there will be a round two. I am not a quitter, regardless of the fact my vagina feels bruised and battered. I also brush my teeth because I will be kissing him again. He's a fantastic kisser.

I quietly pack up my makeup bag because I know myself, and I'm going to pass out, and we're heading back to Jersey at the ass crack of dawn. I can toss my hair up, throw on a ball cap, and shower with nontoxic shampoo at CeCe's place. Lesson learned the hard way, as per my norm. I will never travel without my own again, even if just for a night.

When I tiptoe out of the bathroom, I hear him softly snoring, or is that …?

I see his phone lighting up his pocket and decide to grab it for him. But when I glance at the screen and see a familiar name as the sender and a picture from O'Donnell's Pub with not just one or two but four familiar faces, I freeze and glance at the bed, afraid to fully take him in because this is a fucking nightmare that I *do not* want to come true.

What I do next is cowardice but necessary.

NOUR

Sex Coma

Nour

I WAKE up to an unfamiliar sound, butt-ass naked, and sit up. Rubbing my eyes, I look around, see a light coming from the bathroom, and grab my phone.

When my screen shows half a dozen missed messages and the time shows it's almost midnight, I toss it on the bed as I get up and run to the bathroom, wondering if something happened to my sexy little unicorn, only to find she's not in there.

Starting to freak out, worried about her eye issue, I rush to my phone and open the app to send her a message and find one from her.

<u>GoodTimesOnly</u>:
Sorry to jet on you, but one of the girls had a crisis and needed me. Feel free to stay in the room, but I'm not sure I'll make it back. Check out is automatic, so you don't need to do anything. Thank you for an amazing night. *unicorn

emoji* *eggplant emoji* *peach emoji* *raindrop's emoji* *two fingered peace sign emoji*

Unsure if I'm pissed or impressed that this self-proclaimed, semi-retired player just got played by a unicorn posing as a good girl … Nope, she was definitely posing as a unicorn.

SportsManSam:
Hey, hit me back when you get this. I'd like to see you again. *heart eyes emoji*

I get a message back immediately.

This user no longer wishes to communicate. Better luck next time.

Okay, seriously, it must be a mistake.
My mind starts doing some crazy shit, like telling me I'm going to be butt-ass naked on social media, passed out with a unicorn in bed.
Not today, lucky nips, not today.

SportsManSam:
Hey, hit me back when you get this. You left a credit card on the console next to your flowers. Don't worry; I'm not going to hunt you down. We had an agreement. One night. Just wanted you to know it's here. Hit me up, and I'll mail it to you.

"Take that, GTO." I laugh to myself, knowing damn well anyone would want the card back. I hit *send*.
The reply:

eye roll emoji *Warning Emoji*
Take the hint and move on or risk being banned from the
number one dating app in the US.
stop sign emoji

"You have got to be fucking kidding me." I flop back on the bed and groan.

My phone chimes, and I lift it up, hoping to see a message from her.

Nope.

AJ:

You wanna let us know you're alive?

I scroll back and see a picture of him, my sister, Bennett, and Rudy G at O'Donnell's with the message: *Busted.*
Fuck, fuck, fuck.
I send a message back.

ME:

Needed a few hours alone. Be back at CeCe's soon. Chill.

AJ gives it a thumbs-up.

I sit back up and hit the light switch on the nightstand table, but it doesn't turn on. I reach across and try the other. It doesn't, either.

I hit the flashlight app on my phone and look to see if it's unplugged. It's not.

I then check to see if the bulb's blown and quickly realize it's unscrewed.

"What the hell?"

I get up and try the one on the desk. Also unscrewed, and yeah, so is the other lamp on the other nightstand.

"You're a fucking idiot." I seethe as I screw all of them

back in then go take a much-needed piss, as I again remind myself, "I'm so fucked. So completely fucked."

When I walk around the room that is no longer dark, I see red. I step closer to the bed for further inspection.

Blood.

"Fuck, she's hurt. She left because you battered her pussy, you fucking idiot."

THE WHOLE DRIVE back to the city, I'm pissed at myself for leaving when she could be hurt and come back. I could at least apologize. In a blink, I even consider it since she blocked my ass. And I'm pissed right now, as I turn down our road, because I know damn well AJ and Blaze are going to ask a million questions, and all I wanna do is shower and go to bed.

When I pull into the driveway and see there are no lights on, I thank whatever spiritual being who ducked out on me today and didn't give me some sort of gut feeling that I was making a shit choice.

Who the hell am I kidding? This dry spell needed to be broken. The need to be in something hot and wet would have overruled that feeling. I'd have had to have gotten a flat tire, or the stomach bug, or explosive diarrhea to stop me from meeting her. Let's hope she felt the same and got freaked out by the thought of me seeing her face without the mask. Maybe she shaved off an eyebrow … or she's fucking married. That would fuck with my head.

If she is married, I don't want to know. Cheating is unforgivable. More unforgivable? The lies told to conceal the act or betrayal.

No, fuck that. I shake my head to rid myself of the

memory of what damn near ruined my fucking career. If I can block that out, I certainly can block out the memories of a red-bottom-wearing unicorn with pierced nips.

Fuck them and fuck the unicorn, too. I still have my first true love—baseball—and a whole new family—the Jags.

WHEN I WALK into the house, I'm greeted with the pup whimpering.

"They left you in the dark?" I huff as I flip on the light. "Sweet Jesus."

Lying in a pile of shredded toilet paper, paws covering her eyes as if she is ashamed of her actions, is CeCe and Rome's pup.

I walk over, squat down, and pet her head. "Bad choice, but it's the guys who should be ashamed of themselves for not putting you in your crate."

Her tail thumps on the pile, sending little pieces of the paper floating in the air like confetti.

I pull my phone out of my pocket, take a short video clip, then stand. "You need to go potty?"

No longer ashamed, she stands up and rushes to the door, leaving a trail of shredded paper behind her.

"All right, let's hook you up and take you out."

Outside, motion lights turn on as we walk around the perimeter of the property, her leading the charge. We pass by the RV that the Hart ladies stay in while here, ever since the fire. Still feels like a dick move sleeping in the house and them out here, but we've offered, and they seem to love it. I can't imagine my mother or sister would ever sleep in a camper, even one as nice as theirs.

After she's peed, we head back inside the house.

Although I should leave the mess for AJ and Blaze, I just can't bring myself to do that. Elle won't go near it, and it's where her food and water dish are located.

Once that's done and I have my prepped chicken, broccoli and rice heating in the microwave, I clean out her dishes and refill the water bowl, knowing this goes against the rules.

"A girl's gotta stay hydrated, right?" I ask, squatting down.

She paces back and forth, head hung down, peering at me with the saddest puppy dog eyes I've ever seen.

"Come over here. It's all good now."

Her ears perk up at good, but she doesn't come.

"Seriously, you, too?" I groan and scrub my hand over my face before I cave. "Come on, good girl. It's okay."

Her tail starts wagging.

"That's right, *good girl*; come here."

She barrels over to me, happy as can be, and laps at her fresh water.

Once she's had enough to drink and I've broken another puppy training rule by hand-feeding her a bit of chicken and broccoli, she lies down and starts to fall asleep.

I slide off the stool and walk over to grab her leash. "One more time?"

Outside, Elle does her business, and I bag it up then give her a scratch behind her ears. "Good girl."

Never cringed after calling a dog *good girl*, but now the unicorn has ruined it for me, I think as I walk to the back porch.

"Nah, fuck that." I squat down and give her more attention. "You're a good girl. Yes, you are. The best good girl, aren't you?"

"Get a room," AJ calls to me from somewhere.

"Probably blew his hotel budget today when he blew us off for ass," Bennett slurs.

I stand up as they round the corner of the house and come into view.

"You drunk, Bennett?" I ask.

"Your sister ordered shots." AJ chuckles.

"Doctor's orders." Blaze fucking Bennett grins.

I shake my head, a little bit shocked. "Holy shit, you do have teeth."

"Been smiling all night." AJ shakes his head as he walks past me and inside.

"Your sister is—"

"Nope, don't go there," I cut him off.

He huffs, "If I put moves on her, she'd be on my arm."

"Giving you a pass and gonna pretend you didn't just say that to me." I head up the stairs.

"Fuck that, I'm a good man. I know how to treat women."

Inside, I unhook Elle. "Holy shit, man, just—"

"No, fuck you, Nour. Don't judge me because my old man's a piece of shit, womanizing bastard"—he steps to me—"and I won't judge you because you've never once spoken of even having a sister. That's shitty."

"Okay, let's not do this shit." AJ walks over and gets between us.

AJ's move is unnecessary. I'm not fighting a drunk, not ever again.

I step back and head toward the stairs while Bennett continues running his mouth and AJ continues to attempt to diffuse the bomb that was never sparked to begin with.

In the bedroom, I grab a few things then head back down the stairs to take the room CeCe's sister, Chloe; her husband, Danny; and niece, Aggie, stay in when they're here.

"What are you doing?" AJ asks as he and Bennett start up.

I'm pissed off enough to tell him it's none of his business, but he's not done shit.

"Gonna crash downstairs."

"Because you're pissed at me?" Blaze accuses.

Calmly, I reply, "Bennett, I got nothing but love for you."

"You ditched us tonight." Blaze glares over his shoulder at me as he heads to his room.

"I took some time alone."

"I get that, but you lied. You fucking lied to us."

He's not wrong, I did. "Sorry, man."

Inside the room, I pull out my phone, feeling some sort of way, and send Amira a text.

ME:

You get home okay?

AMIRA:

Of course. Sorry I blew your spot. Next time, give me a heads-up so I can cover for you.

ME:

Nah, they assumed, and I let them. Bad on me. Sleep well.

AMIRA:

Any chance a girl can get a ticket to the game tomorrow?

I send back: *You got a ticket to any game you wanna come to, but don't feel like you have to.*

AMIRA:

I missed a lot while away at school. I'll buy a season pass, if that's okay with you.

ME:

No need. You've got them already. CeCe can give you the VIP entrance info.

AMIRA:

Thank you.

ME:

Glad to have you here. Just worried you'll regret it.

AMIRA:

You worry about winning games. I'm a grown woman.

ME:

Goodnight, Mira.

AMIRA:

Goodnight, no-no.

Smiling, I set my phone down and go open the door to the only good girl I need to worry about tonight.

"They leave you all alone again?"

She sits.

I nod toward the bed. "Come on in and chill. Gotta be up by seven, so we don't fuck up my groove."

After a quick shower, I slide into bed and pat the mattress. "Gonna have to wash them, anyway."

I DRAG ass out of bed, hit the bathroom, piss, brush my teeth, and then throw on some sweatpants and a tee-shirt. When I walk out of the ensuite bathroom, I can't help but laugh at seeing Elle, just a nose sticking out from the covers in the spot I was sleeping.

"Come on, you; let's go potty."

Outside, we walk around until she finds her perfect spot, but then something distracts her, and she starts barking and jets, causing me to lose my grip on the leash.

"Hey, get back here!" I call as I start running in fucking slides to catch up with her.

When I round the barn, I see she's at the RV, looking up at the window, barking. Thank God she didn't run the other way, toward the road. Even so, I need her to stay there and not run again. I can't lose Rome and CeCe's pup.

"That's a good girl. Stay right there for me."

When I get close, she runs again.

"Fuck, come on, Elle. We're buds. Hell, I didn't even get pissed when you all but buried your cold-ass nose in my armpit at three a.m.."

When I round the RV again, there's a chick in a tee-shirt that's not long enough to cover her extremely bruised ass when she's bent over like that, petting Elle.

She stands up and looks over her shoulder, sunglasses covering her eyes. "Got her."

"Shit, thanks." I look at the RV. "I didn't know the Hart ladies were back already."

"Just me," she says, looking down at Elle. "I came back with Cora. Rome and CeCe are on their way back. We did the house thing, so our mom's staying back for a week, or forever."

"She must have been over the moon."

"Yeah."

"Wow, that excited, huh?" I joke.

Her lip curls up slightly.

"Not a morning person; got it." I hold out my hand for the leash. "Thanks for the save."

"Morning has fuck not to do with it. You never speak, ever. Actually, you're kind of a dick."

Ever had the wind knocked out of you and never felt the punch? Yeah, me, neither. But before I have a chance to respond, she's throwing open the RV door.

"Be more careful with her, for God's sake."

"Yeah? Well, you be more careful, too."

She whips her head around and scoffs, "*Me*? I didn't—"

I walk the fuck away, calling back, "The giant bruise on your left ass cheek says otherwise."

Inside, I'm blocking out all the shit that's happened in less than twenty-four hours. I cannot be in this fucking headspace. I can't let my emotions get the best of me, or I'll fuck up.

I can't fuck up.

I look down at Elle. "We're sticking to our game day routine, cool?"

Her tail wags.

"Perfect."

The bacon is finishing up, the omelets are covered and staying warm, and the toast has just popped out of the toaster. "I'll feed you first, then me and the boys."

"You made us breakfast?" Blaze asks, walking into the kitchen.

"We don't deviate from the plan, especially when it's been working."

"I wanted to say—"

"Nope. We're good. It's game day."

"You heard the man." AJ smacks his hands together and walks into the kitchen. "Time to fucking chow."

JILLIAN

Flowers

JILLIAN

I WAS MINDING my own business, hiding out in here, waiting for the Jags to leave, when *he* had to go and lose my brother's dog.

Freaked me the hell out that he tried to have a conversation with me, because he *never* does. In fact, the most he's ever said to me, and it wasn't just to me but directed to both Cora and I, was "This either of yours?"

Holy shit, holy shit, holy shit. He knows. He knows I'm on that app, and he purposely matched with me.

Does that mean he thinks I'm hot, or does it mean he's a world-class asshole and decided it would be fun to bone his teammate's sister and then act like he doesn't know, when he actually knows. *He freaking knows.* Of course he does!

What a dick!

As Roman's sister, *and not the girl who got fucked by his teammate,* I should march over there and bitch-slap him for doing that to Rome. Fuck bitch slap. I wanna nut-chop him.

Clearly, he's psychotic. And he lives with them … sort of. But yeah, he does.

Oh my God, poor Elle. Was he trying to use her to fuck with my head?

I grab some shorts and a hoodie, because, bitch please, I'm not a girl you can fuck with, and neither is Elle. I have to get her to make sure he doesn't pull some more crazy shit and she ends up getting hurt.

I know CeCe's not here, but I give zero fucks as I throw open the door and march my ass inside. "Come on, Elle; you and I are going for a walk."

"Hey, Nour made breakfast," AJ calls to me as I grab her leash. "Want something to eat?"

Grrr, I think as I hook her up. "No, we girls have shit to do."

Before any of them can say anything else, we're out the door.

Once down the driveway, I glance down at her. "I know you may think I'm nuts. A little on edge, yes. Nuts no. Don't let that freak you out, though. Me and you, we're good. Your mom and dad will be home soon, and I'll come up with a plan to make sure we don't have another bat-shit crazy man to deal with."

Okay, maybe I'm losing it, but I think she just arched a brow at me.

"Look, I'm no Gwen York, but I was raised with two brothers, which means I'm a badass in my own right."

Still, she doesn't look convinced.

"Trust me; I've seen some shit."

We stop and make sure no cars are coming before crossing the road. "We have to act cool, and in order to act cool, we need to be cool. Are you cool? Of course you are. Elle's a good girl."

Her tail wags.

"You like that, huh? *Good girl*? You can trust it coming from my lips, but a man says that to you, it's best to tuck tail and run."

We walk for a few blocks, just looking around, and I give her some ear rubs. "I know this is crazy, but I have to tell someone, and since you don't talk, I'm pretty sure my secret's safe with you." I lean down. "I'm not a virgin anymore." I stand back upright, and we continue on our way. "For obvious reasons, I can't tell anyone else, so thank you in advance for being a captive audience." We stop and wait for the light to turn. "I wish I could say it wasn't all they say it is, and maybe more, but that only lasts for a few minutes, and then you're faced with the question: was it really worth it?"

She sits down and looks up at me, I shrug.

"In any other situation, it would be. Yeah, sure, two thumbs-up. All I have to say is you should follow your gut—if you think you should back out, then do it right then and there."

She lifts her nose in the air and sniffs, so I do the same.

"Smell that? I think it's lavender. Maybe there's a park around here."

She pulls to the right.

"Fine, I'll follow you."

I immediately realize where we are—just a couple blocks from Wags vet clinic and O'Donnell's Pub.

"Damn, girl, you have great instincts. Follow them, Elle Hart, and you'll be just fine."

As we pass O'Donnell's, I see CeCe's friend, Fawna, and wave as we walk by. I don't hang out and see if she waves back, because Elle and I are on a mission to find where the smell of lavender is coming from.

"Hey, Jillian, wait up," I hear from behind and turn to see Fawna coming toward us.

"Good morning." I smile.

"This is going to sound insane, but I got a text from CeCe last night that she'd miss coffee with us this morning, and somehow, it came up that you used to bartend?"

"I worked behind a counter at a snack shack through high school."

"But you're going to help out with some events in Blue Valley?" she asks.

"I am. Pretty excited to be back—"

"Any chance you're free tonight after the game? We had two call-outs, and I know it's going to be crazy in here."

"Yeah, sure, if you don't mind me flubbing my way through."

She squeals and hugs me. "Thank you, thank you, thank you."

"No problem." I smile. "What's the dress code?"

"Any chance you own any Jersey Jags attire?" She grins.

"I think I can find something."

"Perfect." She squats down and gives Elle some much-appreciated attention. "Your auntie Jillian is a lifesaver."

Then she stands up. "All right, see you tonight." And then she all but skips away.

As we walk away, I look down at Elle. "I'll take two of whatever she's drinking."

I expect that she'll lead me to cross the road and take us to Wags, but she doesn't. She keeps on trotting down the road and pulls me left.

As soon as we turn, I see the source of the amazing smell.

"Delivery day?" I ask Elle.

From behind the truck comes, "For another month."

I should know better than to carry on a conversation with

a strange man, but I don't. He's clearly having a shit day, and I can empathize with that.

"Let's hope not."

"The old man's closing the place down," the man with the round belly and white beard grumbles.

"You sniveling about it is not gonna change a damn thing, Frankie," an older man carrying a crate says. "Now move out of my way, or you'll be unloading this truck yourself."

He glances at me, and then down at Elle, then back at me. "You know the Hart fella?"

I smile. "He's my brother."

"Kid's been keeping me in business. He's gonna have to go elsewhere soon."

"That must be why Elle dragged me this way, and here I thought it was the lavender we smelled from down the street." I look up, see the sign, "*Etta's Beautiful Bouquets*," and know exactly why Rome comes here often. "Etta's a name you don't hear often anymore."

"Was my wife's name. She died. This is her shop." He glances at the driver. "Never was mine."

"I'm sorry to hear that."

He lifts his chin. "Come on, Elle; your treats are in here."

She stands up and follows him inside, dragging me along with her.

Inside, it's … messy, disorganized, and has clearly not been taken care of for some time. I would safely bet it was after his wife's death.

"Has Rome ever told you our grandmother's name?" I ask, following him.

"Nope, not interested. One love is it for me."

Oh my God, he thinks I'm trying to set him up. That has got to be the cutest thing in the world. "Our grandmother's name was Etta. I'm sure that's not the only reason he frequents here, but I bet it's what drew him in."

"Probably not. Just put her name back up," he says, walking back over to us with two giant milk bones. "Took it down when she left me."

Left me.

"Hoping she won't be as pissed I let it go if I put her name back up."

"You selling it or—"

"Nope. Place needs too much damn work. Isn't worth the hassle."

I look around. "It doesn't need anything more than a little organization and maybe a coat of paint."

"I don't have it in me after Mother's Day, and the kids all moved West. When the tenants upstairs move out, I'll let it go to auction." He looks around then back at me. "Now, what can I get you?"

"Some lavender and"—I look around—"jasmine if you have any."

"Not sure. Lena will be in soon. If you can get her to stop talking to the flowers, she might know where it's at."

Twenty minutes later, I walk out of Etta's with an arm full of lavender and jasmine that I found myself and an IOU because they don't take credit cards or anything other than cash and checks. Lena, a woman who looks to be be in her ate sixties, early seventies, did come in, and Burt was right; she totally ignored everyone except the flowers.

WHEN WE RETURN BACK to the house, I am elated to find the boys are gone so I can take a shower and make something to eat. I also decide to start documenting my personal research project.

Elle and I head to the RV to grab my bag and drop off half the flowers, bringing the rest to put on CeCe's island so when she comes back, she can enjoy the calm, too.

After putting the flowers in a vase, I grab a cup out of the cabinet to pour some much-needed coffee into and notice a note on the counter.

> *Elle has already eaten.*
> *Please ensure she's in her crate if you leave her.*
> *She tends to find herself in trouble otherwise.*
> *Nu*

I glance down at her. "Are you a troublemaker?"

Her little bottom shakes.

"Of course not. Boys are stupid."

Coffee in one hand, the strap of my bag still draped across my shoulder, I grab one of Elle's toys, and then we head toward the downstairs bedroom to take a shower.

I shut the bedroom door behind us and look around to make sure there's nothing in here that she could possibly get into before heading into the bathroom, determined to wash the feel of *his* hands off me.

While undressing, I catch a glimpse of my ass in the mirror and gasp at the size of the bruise. "You have got to be kidding me."

After a long, hot shower, I stand in the bathroom, brushing my hair, enjoying the ability to stand here naked, airdrying. I didn't grow up in a houseful of prudes, but I did grow up in a house that was always full.

I wasn't looking forward to being a way from my family, but I was excited about having a place of my own. It feels wrong to be bent out of shape about my rain delay.

I am so lucky to have a mother who never wanted for anything but for her kids to feel loved and be happy. Mom got pregnant at seventeen, had Rome before she was eighteen, had Hudson two years later, and me two years after that. She's lived more than half her life working to raise us and has never asked for a thing.

I hurry out of the room to grab my phone and shoot her a text.

ME

> Tell me how happy you are.

MOM

> The gift you all have given me was the sixth happiest day of my life.

I reread the message before replying.

ME

> Huh?

MOM

> 1 - Roman's birth, 2 - Hudson's birth, 3 - Your birth, 4 – Rome's, Hud's, and your graduation (both high school and college tie for fourth days), and 6 - this past Sunday.

ME

> I don't remember my birth, but I'm sure that was my favorite day.

MOM

> "Huh?"

I laugh as I reply.

> ME:
> I got to meet my role model, on the outside.

"Elle, are you …? Fuck, fuck, fuck!"

"Get out!" I scream as I run into the bathroom, grab a towel, hide behind the door, and peek out.

"Jesus Christ, I am so sorry. I was—"

"Everything okay?" Blaze Bennett's voice comes from outside the room.

"Yeah, Elle's in here. All good," Nour says, turning his back to me.

"Why are you still in here?" I whisper-hiss at him.

"Because I don't do drama on a normal day, and game day, it's all positive vibes."

"The hell does that have to do with me?" I snip out at him.

"Lavender and jasmine calm. You're stressed. Whatever I may have done to—"

"Ew, no." I grab a tee-shit, throw it on, and then step into the shorts. "I don't need to be shrinked by you or any other man, so"—I walk past him and point to the door—"kick ass, player. Now be a *good boy* and go find your Zen."

He shakes his head as he looks at me. "I don't know what your deal is, but you and I have never had issues before. If you're going through something and need help, you need to call someone you trust."

"You rattle off a hotline number, I'll nut you."

Elle walks over and nudges my hand, and I look down at her. "You got my back, right?"

He holds his big old catcher's mitt in the air, his fingers easily the size of an average dick. His dick? An anomaly. "Nobody needs to have anyone's back."

I sneer at him, and his brows shoot up.

"Sage, white sage."

I gasp, "How dare you?"

He pinches the bridge of his nose then opens his eyes and looks me over, brow quirking as they fall breast level then move quickly to meet my eyes. He clears his throat and turns, saying, "My apologies."

"Ba-bye."

As soon as he leaves, I look down and confirm that, yes, my nipples are wowing out.

8

NOUR

White Sage

Nour

AS FUCKED up as today has been, I managed to stick to my schedule. I ate my loaded omelet and two pieces of toast—one with butter, one with strawberry jam—before my shower. I damn near pulled my dick off, angry fucking my hand, to the memory of the picture now lost in the great abyss that showed the deranged unicorn's pierced nip.

After Little Hart left with Elle, the boys and I watched *Real Housewives of Beverly Hills* together, and I would have napped liked a champ, if I didn't lie there, mind-fucking what I did to have Little Hart all tipped over. The only thing I could come up with is Elle taking off on me, but how the hell could she not realize it was an accident and I wouldn't have let her get hurt? I did still manage to get some good sleep in.

Blaze and AJ decided to go to yoga with me, so I was still sticking to my routine and yoga did help … until we came back to find Elle MIA, and then another run-in with Jillian.

It's gotta be a full moon.

"Zoning out again," Archer mumbles to Cooper.

"He's considering his next move. Let the man think," Cooper whispers back.

"If a man's gotta think that hard during a game of Candyland, he shouldn't be allowed to have a driver's license," Archer says, shaking his head. Then he leans back, links his hands behind his neck, and man spreads like he's a grown-ass man and not still in elementary school.

"He's not grown; he doesn't have a wife yet," Cooper whispers to him harshly. "Can't be grown until that."

Archer rolls his eyes then looks up at the ceiling. "How are you even related to me?"

I look back at my card and move my gingerbread man to the black dot. "You two are killing me."

Archer sits forward, rubbing his hands together. "Darn right, we are."

After getting stuck in Molasses Swamp, it's over for me. Cooper won, Archer came in second, and I was called a loser.

"All right, Jags, go get suited up and hit the field. You owe the hometown fans some extra love this week," Coach announces.

WALKING OUT OF THE TUNNEL, I go through my checklist.

1 - Loaded omelet.

2 - Two pieces of toast; one with butter, one with strawberry jam.

3 - Showered and jerked off.

5 - Watched *Real Housewives of Beverly Hills.*

6 - Napped liked a champ.

7 - Yoga.

8 - Played a game with the boys.
9 - I'm wearing the tie-dyed jock.
10 - old Gold chain is on.
11 - Bracelets the kids from the center gave me, secured.

On the field, I look up and see Amira, who waves a big foam finger at me. I blow a bubble, and she throws her head back, laughing. I also notice Jillian. I mean, you can't miss all that hair and big tits, but I don't look at her; she's bound to go off on me for something else I've done and don't know I have.

"All right, listen up, men," Coach calls us, and we all gather around him. "Been brought to my attention that we're on game number forty-three of the season, and I haven't utilized our relief players nearly enough. Bennett and Nour, you're starting but coming out after four innings. We're climbing the ranks in the league, and we don't need one of you two going out mid-season because your bodies were abused."

"They don't make 'em like the used to," Chuck Turner jokes.

"You fucking kidding me?" Bennett mumbles.

"We're good," I say just to reassure him, using two of my eight words less than a minute from hitting the field.

"You're starting," Amias Steel says. "Still considered your game."

"Yeah, well, sitting on the bench half a game's still a joke."

Amias chuckles. "Try two years as designated hitter and rarely on the field."

Shut up, Bennett, I think.

Josh Henley, one of the relief pitchers, and Brady Masters, the other catcher, are standing there, looking down, but I know damn well they want to do fucking flips and shit, as well they should.

Masters looks at me out of the corner of his eye. I dip my chin, hoping he's reading that I'm good with it.

"Batting order's the same as last game. Now, go warm up."

I nod at Masters to follow me and start heading to do warmups.

AS SOON AS Bennett releases his first pitch, I know it's perfect, and not for us.

Happ rails it right between center and left, where both AJ and Locke are too far away to catch it, but AJ manages to scoop it and gun it to Rome, ensuring he doesn't get to second.

"Thought this kid was good?" Olsen says as he steps up to the plate.

Typically, I don't respond to shit talk, but this asshole deserves it.

"He is. That was a welcome gift; don't get used to it."

I signal to Bennett that this one needs to be taught a lesson, and he delivers a splinter. Olson's bat catches it, and it soars just above Bennett's head. He leaps in the air, catches it, then guns it to first, where Pope easily tags Happ out.

"Fuck," Olson mumbles.

"Welcome to Jersey," I call to him as he stomps toward the visitors' dugout.

I look at Bennett and give him a big ass smile. He bites back his own and rolls his neck before delivering three strikes.

I WALK in slow so Bennett can catch up.

"Killed it, man."

"Fucked up the first one," he admits.

"Being out half the game only means one thing."

"And what's that?"

"We win it in the first four."

"Sounds good."

"Bennett?"

He looks at me.

"We gotta dance for the fans before we hit."

He rolls his eyes. "You and your superstitions."

I point to his socks. "People wearing kitten socks from college under the ones issued shouldn't throw stones."

"How the fuck do you know that?"

"You're my pitcher, friend, and my brother, Bennett—I know every reaction before you even know you're going to react."

"I fucked up last night."

"You got drunk last night. Fuck last night. Last night was shit. Tonight, we play, we win, and we do it again the night after that, and after that, and keep this going. Wash, rinse, and repeat. We good?"

He nods. "Yeah."

I toss two fingers in my mouth and whistle.

Amias Steel glances over, and I hold up four fingers then tap the pointer to my chin—the ASL sign for talk—and then I grab my cup, because it's been a long time since I have signed and *dirty* has escaped me.

A big as grin spreads across his face as he looks up at his dad.

"Steel, Pope, Galleon, Turner, Uyar, Locke, Vander, Hart,

and Tereira," Coach T yells our lineup as I quickly take off my equipment.

When it's all off, the song begins.

Every one of us that was just on the field gets into position and starts off with a hand slap right before we get to shaking our asses.

The crowd even joins in, and that shit is why the Jersey Jags fans are the best in the country.

"All right, get your shit together, Jags." Coach T laughs. "Let's get some points on the board."

STEEL STEPS UP to the plate and allows a strike. The next pitch is a ball, and he lets it fly by. The third, he sends into the outfield and makes it to first.

Next up is Pope. He connects with a solid hit to right field and makes it to first, advancing Steel to second.

Rudy G strikes out, but those calls were questionable as fuck, and he's pissed. Can't blame him at all, but what are you gonna do?

Turner, they walk, which we all know damn well was purposeful.

"One out. Take your time, Uyar," Locke calls to me as I make my way out to home plate, flipping my bat and stepping over the lines as I catch the knob, tap the ground four times, before taking three swings. Then I step into the box, grind my left toe into the dirt, and nod to the pitcher.

The first pitch is way outside, but the umpire calls a strike.

I grit my teeth as I step out, roll my neck, and look up at the sky, inhaling a deep breath.

"Jesus ain't gonna help you, Rookie." The Cubs' catcher chuckles.

The next pitch is outside, too, but my arms are long as fuck and my mood has been on simmer all day. I decide to take it out on the ball.

Like last time, I feel an energy course through, but it's even stronger.

I drop the bat and jog as I watch the ball soar and keep soaring until the announcer yells, "Rookie Nour Uyar has just hit his first grand slam as a major league player!"

I round the bases faster than I have to, but it's unavoidable. I feel high as hell. So much so that when I hit home base, I ask the loud mouth catcher, "What was that you said a minute ago?"

When I head to the dugout, I look up to see Amira on her feet with the rest of them. My sister witnessed that, and I can't even begin to understand why that feels so damn good to me.

She yells something, and even though I can't hear her, I know exactly what she's requesting, and I give it to her. I do a flip, which apparently is even more appreciated by the Jags fans than a grand fucking slam, because the crowd hits an even higher decibel.

"Jesus, man, what got into you?" Rome grabs me and pulls me into a one-arm hug.

"I fucked a unicorn," pops out of my mouth before I even have a chance to think, but fuck it, it's the damn truth.

He busts out into a laugh. "Keep that shit up."

The Jags win by two.

In the locker room, we're all still amped up, and yeah, word's gotten out about my unicorn fuckery. The whole team thinks it's hilarious, all a big joke. Oddly, that eases the fear about what they'll say if a picture is ever leaked. I know how they'll react. I can play the role as team clown if need be. I just hope it doesn't come to that.

O'DONNELL'S IS PACKED from wall to wall, but the bodies part like the Red Sea when we walk in.

"Enjoy it, kid." Pope smiles. "You earned it."

Gwen and Locke are next to Pope, and I swear she's teary-eyed.

"You … were amazing."

"Are you"—I pause because Gwen doesn't cry, but yeah—"cry—"

She punches me in the arm. "Fuck no."

Locke throws his head back in a loud laugh, and she elbows him.

"You shut it."

Whitney hugs me. "I'll admit, I shed a tear. That was beautiful."

"Thanks, Mrs. Pope."

CeCe grins. "You the man!"

Rome chuckles as he looks down at her. "Someone's had a couple drinks already."

"I'm going to be so easy tonight," she says louder than I bet she realizes.

"I'm not touching that with a ten-foot pole." I chuckle.

"Oh, I am." Gwen laughs.

"Shots, man." AJ grips my shoulders and steers us up to the bar.

Abe O'Donnell, the owner's father, reaches across the bar. "That was one hell of a hit tonight, Uyar, and every other hit an RBI. You do know your batting average's in the top five percent of the Jags and the top twenty of the league, right?"

I shake his hand and don't even try to hide the grin. "Thanks, and no, but I do now."

"Wherever that came from, utilize it."

"He fucked a unicorn last night." Bennett chuckles.

"Bro." AJ shakes his head.

Bennett shakes his own head, clearly following AJ's motion. "He didn't."

AJ winks at him, and Bennett nods and looks at Abe. "He didn't."

Abe shakes his head, too. "No?"

"No," AJ answers.

Abe lines up a few shot glasses. "Well, whatever it was, keep not doing it."

AFTER A FEW SHOTS and a lot of selfies with Jags fans, I turn to order and see none other than Jillian Hart behind the bar.

"Can I help you?"

Okay, she's being normal. Well, at least, I think this is her normal.

"Tallest glass you have of H2O, please."

"Make that three," comes from beside me.

Smiling, I turn and see Amira and CeCe's little sister, Cora.

Amira laughs, eyes misty, and pulls me into a hug. "You are incredible."

"Not bad for a kid who wasted his parents' money on college, huh?" I hug her back.

After a minute, she and I separate, and she says, "Don't be mad."

"You never start a sentence with that." I shake my head.

"Well, it was more about me and less about you."

I motion for her to keep it coming.

"I sent a video to our parents of that hit."

I shake my head. "And what I'm about to say is more about you than me. Don't waste your time."

"I just wish it could be what it once was."

"They crossed a line and drew another. It can never be the same."

"One last request?" She pinches her fingers together, showing me *little*.

I nod.

"Could you let me send them a picture of your contract to show them you make much more than you would have had you—"

"No." I laugh as I shake my head.

"That's easy enough to find on the internet," Jillian says as she pushes three glasses of water forward.

I turn and look at her, eyes narrowed.

She shrugs. "I don't know yours; I know Rome's and Hudson's. And no, I didn't go looking." She looks at Amira. "When people find out who your brother is, you'll have more people wanting to be your friends, who know more about him than you. It's disgusting what lengths people will go to fuck with their life through you." She looks down, wipes the bar with a rag, and then peers up at me, brown eyes narrowed. "If you let them."

"I don't have a pro player in the family tree, that I know of, anyway," Cora says, holding up her glass of water, "but yeah, I'll drink to that."

"But look at how strong it's made you." Amira smiles fondly at her. "And you've bounced back and are peopling again, yes?"

Cora nods.

Amira continues, "Next time you and Jillian go to a Broadway show, I better get an invite."

"It was so good." Cora smiles then looks past Amira to me. "No offense, but Broadway over bleachers."

"What?" AJ gasps.

Cora shrugs. "I said what I said."

"Broadway's cool, but you're wrong," Blaze states.

Cora's face immediately catches fire. *Oh shit.*

I throw the poor girl a life vest. "What did you see?"

"Last night, it was—"

She's cut off when a drink is spilled all over the bar and her.

"Shit, my bad," Jillian says, making quick work of cleaning up her mess. "I'm so sorry, Cora."

Cora looks down at her soaked shirt and laughs. "First wet tee-shirt contest ever."

AJ damn near chokes on his drink but manages not to spill it all over her, swallowing it down. Then he grabs her hand and lifts her arm in the air. "Ding, ding, ding, we have a winner of O'Donnell's first post-game wet tee-shirt contest!"

I pull off my sweater as I move to hand it to her, glaring at him. "You want to sleep in your car tonight? Rome will have your ass."

"You mean *your car*? I still haven't decided on what I want." AJ laughs.

9

JILLIAN

No Accident

JILLIAN

ASIDE FROM BUSTING my ass the other night on a wet floor, I'm not clumsy by nature. Spilling that glass of water was to ensure that the conversation about NYC ended. Which it did.

Then I was asked if I minded driving CeCe's car and the boys back to the house once we closed. Of course I couldn't say no.

"You killed it." Fawna smiles, pushing a stack of bills toward me from the tip jars.

Having watched her combined the money from all four jars on the bar, cash in singles for larger bills, I know she hasn't spilt it between the four of us.

I push it back with the reminder, "You need to split it."

She crinkles her nose. "Please do not insult me. Owners who take tips are just gross."

"She's right." Her father, Abe, chuckles.

"It's over five hundred dollars in, like, four hours."

She looks at her sister, Dromida, who works at Mercy West hospital. "More than a surgeon makes."

"Game nights don't count."

She picks up the stack of bills, flips through them, then fans herself. "Oh, they count."

"Wait till she finds out we add twenty percent to the drink prices on game nights to ensure our staff gets paid for their service." Fawna's mom winks at me.

"No way!" I gasp.

"It won't be this good every night. Fawna normally has three on."

"We killed it tonight with just us," Fawna states. "You work, girl."

I will admit it was busy as hell, and I have to pee so bad I don't know how I'm still standing here, but so worth it.

"We did eight K in four hours, and this is nothing compared to what the next two nights will be. They win night one, two is busy, and three is insane." Fawna laughs at what I assume my expression must be. "You'll still average anywhere between five and eight hundred a night with three on."

"When Aria's on, take notes; she pushes top shelf shots. With the twenty percent increase, that's bank." Fawna shrugs.

"You're back here, too. It's only fair you—"

"I do just fine." She leans in and whispers, "Four to five hundred percent markup on liquor." She steps back and winks. "I'm not just a pretty face and hot bod."

"You're a fucking genius," I state.

She throws her hands in the air. "Right?"

"Why doesn't everyone own a bar?" I ask.

"Being self-employed has its perks," Abe states as he

dries off a glass, "and even more downfalls. Your business becomes your spouse and your children. This place could become your only social life. You also have to deal with nights like tonight when two people call out. Wouldn't matter what plans you may have had, you're working. You have busy seasons, like now, and months you may be lucky to get ten people through the door. Lot of people can't handle that. You have to be smart with your money. Servers and bartenders do, too."

"Invest in yourself, and you'll never go wrong." Nikki smiles. "Fawna's opening a restaurant this fall. Upscale, fine dining, catering to the local professionals. Her off-seasons here at the pub won't be as heavy a hit. Her new place will bring in a different cliental."

"That's amazing." I nod, head swimming with all the opportunities people like me never considered.

"All right, I think we're good here. The boys need their beauty sleep." Abe nods to the table where the boys, Cora, and Amira are sitting around, laughing. Well, all but Nour, who's looking at his phone. *Probably trying to find another pussy to bruise.*

"Same time tomorrow?" I ask.

"You can ride over from the stadium with me if you want," Fawna offers.

"Sounds great, and thank you so much for the job."

"BOYS TRULY DO THINK of sex every five seconds." Cora laughs as I approach the table.

"One, two, three, four, doggy-style." AJ laughs his ass off.

"One, two, three, four, the bus is leaving, kids," I say as I continue toward the door.

I glance back as I open the door to make sure they're following. They are, and they don't leave behind the conversation; it continues right on out of the bar.

"Gotta be careful who you're hooking up with now." AJ chuckles. "Biggest move from minors to majors is realizing it's quality over quantity. You mess that up, you could find yourself in a Turner situation."

"AJ," Bennett slurs, "you can't throw a teammate under the bus like that."

"I didn't throw him anywhere; them's the facts," AJ states. "He's not hiding it. Loves those kids of his, even if he doesn't love the women he made them with anymore."

"I believe the problem was he did love them," Nour defends Turner. "And he believed they loved him."

"Jersey chasers," Amira sighs. "You boys better wrap them tight."

"You wrap yours tight the other night?" AJ laughs, and my body tenses.

"Mind your business," Nour mumbles.

Amira laughs. "He always has."

"Amira," Nour grumbles.

"Until I can bring out the naked baby pictures, I have nothing else but stories."

"Spill them all." AJ laughs as I hit the key fob and unlock the door.

"This one lost his virginity in our mother's car." She laughs.

"How was your mom?"

I can't hold back a laugh, and not just because of what was said, but because two people said it at the same time. Those two people? Cora and Blaze Bennett.

"You're all assholes," Nour grumbles.

"Funny," Amira admits. "But the true story, even better."

"Are you seriously doing this?" Nour snarls at his sister.

"You bet I am," she says as she opens the door. "Mom found a pair of girl's panties in her car, and he told her that they were mine."

"Did you at least cover for him?" AJ asks as he climbs in behind her.

"Nope," Nour answers.

"I was in college—they couldn't have been mine. They grounded him until he admitted who he'd defiled. He refused. He was grounded for an entire spring and summer. His entire sophomore year." She laughs.

"When did you finally cave?" AJ chuckles.

"He still hasn't confessed. They caved before one of their trips to India."

Everyone laughs, except Nour.

Blaze gets in and looks at Cora. "You're gonna have to sit up front or on a lap."

"Front." She all but runs around the vehicle.

"Pop the hatch?" Nour asks.

"You're going to get in the trunk?" I ask, confused.

"He used to hide in the back of my car and scare me senseless." Amira laughs.

"Okay, suit yourself." I hit the button.

AS WE PASS through the light to take Amira to her place, red and blue lights flash behind me.

"Are you kidding me?" I look down, knowing I'm not speeding, for God's sake.

"You have a drink after your shift?" AJ asks.

"No, thank fuck," I grumble as I hit the signal and pull over.

"You're good then." He grips my shoulder.

"I've never been pulled over in my life." I search for my phone, knowing my license is in the case somewhere.

"You might want to put your hands on the wheel," Amira whispers.

"Why?" I ask, confused.

"You have two people in the vehicle whose skin tone sometimes causes issue."

I turn around and look at her. "Let a cop come at me like that, and I will have their fucking badge and their nuts."

The cop taps on the window, and I turn around and glare at him.

"Step out of the car, please, ma'am."

"Oh my God, just do as he asks," Cora pleads.

To make both Cora and Amira feel less worried, I hold one hand up and open the door with the other before sliding out.

"Aren't you supposed to tell me why you pulled me over and ask me for my license and registration before you just tell me to *step out* of a damn car?"

"I don't have to tell you a thing. Now put your hands on the hood. I'm going to have to pat you down."

"You fucking kidding me?" I gasp.

"Now, ma'am, or I'll be forced to—"

"She didn't do anything wrong. She's driving us home from the bar she works at," Cora cries softly.

"What bar are you leaving?" he asks.

"O'Donnell's," I snip.

"She's Roman Hart's sister," Cora adds. "I'm Cecelia Shaw's sister. She owns the—"

"I'd like you to step out of the car, too," he cuts her off.

"She didn't do anything! She's in the—"

"Step out of the car and walk around to the front," he speaks over me.

"Okay." Her voice shakes as she opens the door, holding her hands up.

"Who else is in the vehicle, miss?" he asks Cora as she walks over, visibly shaking.

"AJ, Blaze, Amira, who's also vet—"

Again, he cuts her off. "Could you all slowly step out of the car, please."

"One of you better be recording this shit, because I'm going to sue the Trenton Police Department."

He bends down and hisses in my ear, "What you're going to do is shut the hell up and remain calm until backup gets here."

"For what?"

"Oh God." Amira laughs as she walks around with her hands up. "Do you think there's a man hiding in the trunk?"

"Is there?"

AJ chuckles. "No seats left, and we're just around the corner. Nour, you wanna identify yourself to the officer?"

"You just did, jackass," Nour calls back.

"My brother, Nour Uyar," Amira says, hands still up, holding her phone. "He hit a grand slam tonight. Would you like to see it?"

"Jesus Christ," the cop mutters, grabbing his radio. "Cancel backup. We've got a Subaru full of drunk Jags, and a mouthy bartender with the last name Hart taking them back to Cecilia Shaw's house."

"Hold your place; we're in route," comes through his speaker.

"I said, cancel backup," he clarifies.

"While all that shit's going on, could one of you open the hatch and let me out?" Nour calls.

"You promise not to shoot me if I let the Jag out of the back?" I ask.

"I never put my hand near my weapon, Miss Hart. Yeah, let your Jag out of the back."

"Like cat out of the bag." Amira laughs as I pass her and hit the button, opening the back.

The backup patrol car pulls up to the scene … that they caused.

Two officers climb out of the vehicle, and the one who pulled me over calls to them, "I told you twice to cancel."

"We were already en route, and you mentioned drunk Jags." One laughs.

"Hoping to get a couple autographs without waiting in a line somewhere."

Amira flips her hair back then holds out her hand. "Fine, give me a pen and tell me where to sign."

"He said Jags, not cougars." AJ laughs.

Her jaw drops. "You *did not* just call me a cougar!"

"Why you gotta say it like it's a bad thing?" AJ throws his arm around her. "A twenty-three-year-old, hot as hell pro baller can dream, can't he?"

Nour smacks him in the back of the head. "Not in front of her brother, he can't."

"Does that mean I have permission to do it behind your back?" AJ asks.

Nour steps to the cop holding the baseball in his hands. "What I don't see happening between two adults is none of my business."

"Hell of a hit, kid," the older, rounder cop says as he hands him the ball and then a marker.

Another smiles at Bennett. "I don't care what they say, you're better than your old man ever was."

The cop who pulled me over comes back from his cruiser with a Jags' ball cap. "My kid plays center. You're his favorite."

"Fuck, man, that's cool to hear. What's his name?"

"Little T works. His name's Tony."

"JILLIAN," Rome sighs.

"Grown-ass woman with a job," I remind him.

"Love that for you, love that you stuck up for the fam, but you ever hear the term *don't bring a knife to a gun fight*?"

I lift my arms and make muscles. "I bring the guns everywhere." Then I step back and raise my hands in the air. "Goodnight, everyone. It's been fun, but I'm going to head back to my little tin can and pretend you all don't exist until the sun comes up and we do this all again."

Rome rolls his eyes. "There's room in here."

I turn and head to the door, reminding him, "Grown-ass woman with a job, and a taser, and pepper spray."

"Oh shit, I forgot to tell everyone. Three days, and we can move back into the townhouses."

"Seriously?" I hear one of them ask.

"Seriously." Rome laughs.

"It's about damn time!" AJ cheers.

AFTER A HALF-ASS SHOWER, I'm sitting in the middle of the bed, surrounded by a pile of money. Five hundred and ninety-seven dollars, all mine.

I do the math, and even being conservative with the numbers that Abe suggested, I'll have close to thirty grand by the end of the season. That's a nice little nest egg for grad school without touching the stupid amount of money both Rome and Hudson gave me for college graduation.

When my phone buzzes, I look down and frown when I see the name *John Smith*. I don't wanna deal with him, but I know he won't go away until I do.

I hit *accept*. "Hi."

"That all I get from Daddy's little Jill?"

I roll my eyes. "It's late."

"I know that, but I caught the game tonight and saw you looking like a million bucks on the big screen and had to call."

"No, actually, you didn't have to."

"Don't be like that, Jill."

"How should I be to the man who squatted in a house and—"

"That is my mother's house. My mother who Linda and those ungrateful bastards turned against me."

"They didn't turn—"

"I couldn't go see my dying mother in fear that they'd attack me. They stole that from me, Jill. They stole that, and I simply took back what's mine."

"Your thinking is as skewed as ever." I sigh.

"It's the damn truth. You know it is."

I say nothing because there's no sense in arguing with a drunk.

"It's okay. I'm not like them. You don't have to pick sides with me, Jill. I love you too much to put you in that situation."

"Yeah, so much you decided to show up before I could even graduate college like a normal kid."

"Don't feed into their rhetoric. You were never without a home. Trust me; I know what it's like to be un-homed. You haven't a clue. None of you."

Because our mother made sure of that.

"It's almost three in the morning. I'm going to bed. Goodnight."

"Wait. I just had to pay taxes, and I'm out of money. I just need a little scratch to get me some food and maybe toilet paper."

You have got to be fucking kidding me.

"My mother, your grandmother, wouldn't want me to go hungry. She used to help me out when I was in a tight spot."

"You've mentioned that. I still don't believe you."

"Don't be a little bitch, Jillian."

I hate when he calls me by my full name. Took me forever to stop hearing it in a sneer, no matter who said it.

"Not a little bitch anymore. I'm a big bitch now. You've missed a few years."

"Then you leave me no choice. I can sell my story—"

"You sell whatever you need to. You'll get the most from selling the house you waited to squat in until we were gone, screwing me out of having a place to live so I could maybe finish classes in person."

"You don't want that kind of trouble for your precious brothers, now do you? Think about that. Think about how that will feel to them, to that whore mother of yours, to you."

"Look, old man, I've got a hundred bucks in my account; will that get you whatever fix you need and stop the calls until you get your check?"

"I need three—"

"Cheap booze, Dad, not top shelf. Get a job, function as an adult, then go for the gusto, but—"

"You suck off them like a little whore and call me out?"

"I have a fucking job. I—"

"Then three hundred shouldn't be that hard to come by for the man who gave you life, now should it? And before you answer, it'll be enough to stop me from selling my story."

"This is the last fucking time."

I hit *end*.

10

NOUR

Broken Horns

Nour

STANDING OUTSIDE OF THE RV, I am livid over what I just heard.

Jillian slides the window open and asks through the screen, "What do you want?"

I simply hold up the mask. "Elle dropped this on my stomach when I was lying in bed."

She rolls her eyes. "Then maybe she wants to play dress up. What does it have to do with me?"

"You know damn well what it has to do with you."

"I'm tired."

"You've been raging mad at me for a full twenty-four hours; I deserve ten minutes of your time." I hold the mask up again. "You get this in New York City on your girls' trip?"

She opens the door and hisses, "Will you shut up? There are cameras everywhere."

"Holy shit, I'm right." I point at her tits. "Pierced."

She grabs my wrist and pulls me inside before walking as

far away from me as she can, *which is about ten feet.* "You can stop acting like you didn't know." She turns around and holds up a little can of pepper spray. "I'll use this if I have to, you fucking weirdo."

I shake my head and toss the mask onto the counter. "First, we're in an enclosed area—we'd both be effected. You're better off with the taser when you're inside" I pick it up and toss it to her. "Second, you're calling *me* a weirdo? I'm not the one who likes to play dress up when getting railed."

"Fuck you!" she spits. "My eyes were almost bleeding, and you're the one with the unicorn fetish."

I'm gonna get sick.

"Oh my God." I squat down and scrub my hands over my face. "Holy shit. I fucked Rome's sister."

"Which is probably some part of a plan to ruin his career or get more—"

I stand up and throw my hands in the air. "I play better when I get laid, okay? With the fire and all the shit going on around here …" I groan. "Then Turner's story being weaponized and used as a cautionary tale, my batting average sucked. I needed to get off and get someone off to bring it back around."

"Oh. My. God." She laughs … at me. "You really think—"

"I don't think; I know. And tonight proves my theory."

She starts laughing even harder.

"Nothing about this is funny, Jillian." I pinch the bridge of my nose. "Rome asked me to be in his wedding when he marries CeCe. He's my best friend on the team."

"AJ and Bennett—"

"Are great guys, family even, but Rome is solid, dependable, and has been since I met him. He doesn't flip out when

I'm not holding his hand." I hold my hand on my abdomen. "Oh Jesus, I'm going to get sick."

"*Aw*," she coos. "It's those seven words every woman wants to hear from the guy who was last inside of her."

I sit on the tiny-ass sofa and bury my face in my hands. "Right, sorry, kind of like a chick thanking you for popping her cherry after the fact and—" I snap my mouth shut and look at her.

"Don't." She shakes her head and points to the door. "If the soap wasn't in my eyes, or I wasn't trying to keep it dark so SMS didn't think I was some crackhead, I wouldn't have let you in the door."

"I fucking wouldn't have come in." I look up as she rolls her eyes then looks at the ceiling. "You know I wasn't saying it for any other reason than you're Rome's little sister. You know you're beautiful, funny, and some guy who isn't me—"

"Ew, stop."

"Right." I blow out a breath and look up at her. "Feels wrong to say I'm sorry, but I am."

"Okay, let's not."

"You weren't a virgin, right?"

"Again, we're not doing this."

"Fuck me. I should have known from the first lick you were too damn sweet—"

"La, la, la, la, la—"

"Okay, okay, okay. But—"

"But nothing. You were proving a theory, and so was I."

I shake my head. "Now don't do that."

She stomps toward me, phone in hand, taps on the screen, and then shows me something in her notes. "An actual scientific theory, not a superstition," she clarifies.

Thesis

I AM COMPELLED to investigate a recurring pattern observed among the American females in their teens and twenties who have a tendency to prioritize romantic pursuits over personal dreams and aspirations.

(They chased boys and not dreams.)

Through a self-directed research project, I aim to uncover the underlying societal, psychological, and physical factors that influence this choice, seeking to understand its implications on their personal and professional development.

My hypothesis: It's sex, not love.

SUBJECT ONE: *SMS*

Thorough, great banter, focus on giving pleasure.
Possibly to ensure his ego stays well inflated.
Sexually deviant.

"INFLATED EGO? SEXUAL DEVIANT?"

"Ego, yes. Deviant, I suppose I can let that go, but you did seem to like the mask. And yeah, now I don't believe you knew who I was and that you were trying to ruin my brother's career." She holds out her hand. "See? We're good."

I scroll down.

"*Subject two*? No, fuck that, Jillian. You're lucky the guy you met wasn't a sicko."

"Oh jeez, thank *you* for being such a gentleman."

"You're welcome, you sarcastic little shit." I roll my eyes. "I was lucky, too. This whole time, I've been waiting for some freak in a unicorn mask to post a selfie of me passed out naked in the background."

"Not yet, but that could totally be used for bribery," she jokes … I think.

"You actually take a picture?" I ask.

She quirks a brow. "A lady never tells."

"*Lady*?" I joke, and she tries to jack her phone away. "Grown-ass woman with a job, a taser, and pepper spray—your words."

"Phone."

"Only if you promise not to send that piece of shit money again."

She's back to glaring at me.

"I was outside, you had it on speaker. Wasn't trying to be a creep."

"Yet, here you are." And pissed, super pissed.

I wish it wasn't turning me on.

"You were privy to my family shit tonight, with Amira's storytelling."

"Oh, please, don't compare being grounded over panties to our fathers' deplorable actions."

Was deeper than panties, but … "Fine, you win. Does Roman know he hits you up for money?"

"No, and he better not find out."

"Then you better not give him anymore." I stand.

"You don't get to tell me what to do because we boned."

I need to get the fuck out of here.

"Not telling you what to do. I heard you tell him you wouldn't. So, be a good girl, and—"

"Get out." She steps up to me and pushes on my chest. "Go."

"We still have to discuss how to handle the Rome situation."

"There will be no Rome situation, if you go—now."

She's fucking cute, but … "My loyalty's to him."

What she does next blows my fucking mind.

She grips my sac—pretty fucking hard, too—as she leans in and says, "You more loyal to him … or your balls?" She releases them and steps back. "You tell him, I'll find a way to rid you of them. I tell him, I won't have to find a way—he'll do it."

I swallow down a golf-ball-sized lump in my throat then rebut her statement, "He's a reasonable guy; he'll understand."

"You wanna bet your balls on that?"

"Not tonight. I have a game to prepare for."

"White sage?" she asks.

"No."

She glances down at my growing erection. "Might wanna take care of that. You could end up rolling over in bed with that, you might breaking it right—"

"That's so fucked up," I hiss, balls tightening up.

She reaches past me and opens the door. "Then make sure you watch your step. It's not a pogo stick."

"Your concern for my dick is unsettling."

"So was your concern for subject two," she says, and I know she's itching for me to volley it back.

"I don't have time for this debate. I have a game to prepare for."

"So you've said." She nods toward the door. "Ba-bye."

SITTING IN THE DUGOUT, with Bennett silently stewing beside me, we're up by two in the eighth when he breaks the silence with, "They're going to fuck this up."

Not any more than I did.

"That would mean a good night's sleep."

"I think it's dumb we don't go to the bar after a loss. Isn't that when we need it the most?"

"If we were alcoholics, but we're not, and we're not going to become one."

"The other night, when you dipped out on us."

I don't respond. It won't change how he feels regardless of what I say.

"Yeah, I think I need to get laid, like soon."

"You do what you need to do, man," I reply, trying not to laugh.

"My experience with real women is limited."

What. The. Fuck?

"Might need some clarification on that, Blaze."

"I wasn't allowed to date."

"Are you talking limited, as in blowup doll, or are you a virgin?"

He looks at me like *I'm* the idiot. "I lost my virginity at fifteen."

"Not to a blowup doll?"

He rolls his eyes dramatically. "Professional women."

"Your old man hired you hookers?" I ask, greatly needing clarification.

He nods. "They were part of my regimen."

"And now they're not?"

He shakes his head. "No. I left that all behind. My old man is on staff, so I don't have a choice in the matter."

"Never been on a date?"

He shakes his head.

"Never had a girlfriend?"

"Clearly not."

"You wanna get laid or meet someone?"

"Both, but separate."

"You want to date someone and fuck someone else?"

"Yes, but respectfully."

"You understand that dating someone and fucking someone else is, in fact, disrespectful."

"That's a problem. It's also a problem that I'm attracted to different types of women for each role," he states then continues, "You know that game marry, fuck, kill?"

I nod and brace for whatever is about to come out of his mouth.

"I'd marry a girl like Cora. She's sweet, funny, and has great child-bearing hips. I'd fuck Fawna or Amira."

I stand up to walk away, but he keeps on talking.

"Both together if they'd—" He stops. "Where are you going?"

"Not to jail."

When I round the corner, I see Turner and Coach T silently laughing their asses off.

"I hate both of you."

STANDING IN THE HALL, waiting for press with Roman and Amias, neither is saying a thing, but I can feel their eyes on me.

"So …" Ranger chuckles.

"Gonna ask that you not," I cut him off.

Rome starts in next, "He mentioned CeCe's sister, too."

"He did."

"The man has no filter, so whoever he fucks, marries, or kills will know what he's thinking." Roman laughs.

"He's pissed you didn't hang out," Amias says, trying to keep his shit straight. "He told me he changed kill to friend because, if he went to jail, he'd never have sex again."

"Thanks for giving me even more information I do not need to know."

"Who's he friending?" Rome laughs.

"Too much respect for Linda to say *your momma*, but you get the point, yeah?"

He laughs as Brisa pops her head out of the press room and waves for us to come in.

The last time I was on press, Blaze brought the room to a low that even had me feeling myself. *That's not happening this time.*

I head in first, needing to distance myself, if even briefly.

Upon entering the room, I realize I've made a huge mistake because, before my ass even hits the chair, they start firing questions my way.

I smile. "Bear with me for a minute while I try to familiarize myself with you all."

"How are you gonna do that?" a man's voice booms through the room.

"I'm going to look at your passes and match your names and faces to your network. By the end of the season, I should know most of you. You're ESPN, Stan Fierce, the man whose voice is louder than the whole press room."

This garners a laugh as I shift to the reporter next to him, who's wearing a cowboy hat.

"Fox Sports, Bobby Johnson, Fox, all American. Got it. Giddy up." Next to him. "MLB Network, Robby Freeman. Stats man, you carry that clipboard like it's your best friend."

"Gotta keep everyone straight."

"Grateful for that." I look past him. "You with the glasses, I can't see your press pass."

He holds it up. "NMC Sports, Bob Wiseman."

"Professor Wiseman, NMC. Glasses. You take them off, I'm

going to be lost." I lift a chin to the man to his right and already know who he is. "CBS Sports, Tony 'Touchdown' Romeo. I got you. Next to you, SportsNet, Mike Maple, magic on the mic."

They all laugh.

"One more, and we'll save the rest for next time in here with you all. TBS Sports, Timmy O'Leary, the tallest man in the room, let's start with you."

"That was one hell of a hit last night; what held you back today?"

"Game's always a little off when I'm too deep in …" I pause because I see Rome sit forward, and all I can think is "your sister." *Fuck!* "Yeah, just like that, in my head. We'll watch reels tonight, fix what we can, and be back tomorrow to win a third game."

I nod to the professor.

"Practically mid-season, and they just started giving you and Bennett a break. Was there a reason for that?"

"Yeah." I nod. "They probably didn't wanna hear both Bennett and I complain about being on the bench."

"Giddy up?" I nod to the Fox guy.

"You happy catching, or do you miss the field?"

"I'm just happy playing ball. They can put me wherever they want me." I look at Rome. "You wanna take a few?"

11

JILLIAN

O'Donnell's

JILLIAN

"WAS I RIGHT, or was I right?" Fawna calls over the crowd.

"You were right," I call back.

"You doing okay? Need a break?" Abe asks.

"Harts don't take breaks." I smile as I hurry to the end of the bar where a group of guys are waiting.

"What can I get for you?"

"Your name, number, the promise that you'll be the mother of my children?"

"Coming on a little strong, but I respect the game," I joke. "You gotta respect the hustle, though. There's a whole bar full, waiting for drinks to be served."

"Five shots of whatever you and I'll be drinking on your next night off."

"Better get him a straw with whatever he orders," comes from behind him, and I look up to see Hudson. "He's gonna need it to drink out of when his jaw's wired shut because he's talking to a fine young lady like that."

"You better have backup, man," the hottie who just asked for my info and womb says as he turns around and is face to chest with my brother. The idiot stands on the rungs of a barstool to get eyeball-to-eyeball with him. "We cool?"

Hudson shakes his head. "Why did God make men your size with brains two sizes too small?"

"He's a black belt," one of his friends pipes in.

"Yeah, the bigger they are, the harder they fall," another needles.

Hudson ignores them. "Can I get a beer, barkeep?"

"We were here first," the seriously cute, average size … idiot says as I pour Hudson a beer.

"Then order your drinks, little buddy." Hudson smirks.

I hand Hudson his beer, and he hands me a hundred.

"Keep it."

Little buddy turns and asks me, "Who is this asshole, anyway?"

"You a sports fan?" I ask, setting two bottles on the bar.

"Jags for life," he answers with a wink.

"Favorite player?"

"Cody Vanders."

"Shot fired, and he misses." Hudson laughs.

Little Buddy starts to turn back to him.

"Hey, let's get you those shots." I hold up one of the bottles. "Boss Hog. One fifty a shot." I hold up another. "Tequilla, ten bucks a shot."

"How much for a body shot?"

"If you have to ask, you can't afford it," AJ states.

The Jags have arrived, I think, glancing up into dark brown eyes that heat up my insides, only proving my theory more. I'm not even hating on it since we've cleared the air.

"We'll take ten Boss Hogs." Nour reaches over the guy's head and hands me a card.

"What the hell, man? Can't you see I'm working an angle?"

Nour leans in and says something to him that causes his eyes to grow comically wide then steps back. "Now order your shots and let her do her job."

"Five Grey Goose, chilled," he mumbles.

"Fifty bucks." I smile as I scoop ice into a tumbler.

He pulls out a wad of cash in a money clip, peels a hundred off the top of it, hands it to me, and winks. "Keep the change."

"You're the best—"

"Jay V."

I pour his shot and push them over. "Here you go, Jay. Enjoy."

"Who's drinking the Boss Hog?" Fawna asks.

I nod toward Nour and hand her Jay's and Hudson's hundreds. "Five shots of Grey Goose and a draft; the rest goes in the tip jar."

"Cool." She walks to the register.

"Nour, as in Nour Uyar?" Jay V swings around. "Holy shit, man. I just got my life threatened by the Jags' catcher?"

Nour glowers at him.

"Fuck, man, let me get a selfie."

"What am I? Chopped liver?" Hudson asks, ducking into the frame while Nour continues to glare.

"Give me your phone, Jay. I'll make sure to get you all in." I laugh and hold out my hand for it.

He winks as he hands it to me. "I knew we had something going on between us. You and I are destined to end up together."

"Watch it," Hudson says, perfect smile in place.

"And who the fuck are you? The bodyguard?" Jay, who clearly gives zero fucks about Hudson's size, asks.

"Yeah, Jay." Hudson pats him on the head. "Now smile, you idiot."

Smiling like he's having the time of his life, Jay fires back, "I don't much appreciate you talking to me like that, you walking fucking tree."

"I don't much like you coming on to my sister when she's clearly uninterested, Jay, yet here we are, celebrating a Jags win like old friends," Hudson says in the way that is too sincere to actually be, which throws the Jays of the world off.

"Things good?" Fawna asks as I laugh and hand Jay back his phone.

"We're good." I look at Nour. "You really want ten shots?"

"Yeah, line 'em up."

"They're for sipping," Fawna says, taking Nour's card as I hold it out.

"Where's Mom?" I ask Hudson as I pour the ridiculously priced whiskey into a jigger to measure it before dumping it into rocks glasses.

"She's never leaving the house." He smiles. "She's made friends with a couple of the Blue Valley matriarchy, and they're planting a garden."

"Blue Valley, as in the Knights?" Jay snorts. "Fuckers pissed off the whole NFL."

AJ shakes his head in shock and asks, "Do they know you've escaped?"

"The hell you talking about *escaped*?" Jay looks back. "You the centerfielder for the Jags?"

"I am, and I'm a Knights fan."

"How you gonna live in Jersey and root for the Knights?"

"I'm a Knights fan, too, Jay," I say, handing a group of men their beers as I pour them.

"Jesus, I may have to rethink this. You got a good—"

"I will make good on that threat if you continue," Nour cuts him off.

"Yeah, no shit. Show some respect," Bennett adds.

He doesn't bother looking back as he slides another hundred across the bar and says, "Five dark ales when you get a minute, future ex-wife."

"That lasted a long time." I laugh as Fawna steps in to deal with the money.

"You lost me at Knights fan." He shakes his head.

"Used to be an Eagles fan."

"Jesus, even that's a step up from the Knights. What made you jump ship? Don't tell me … it's that Kelce clown."

"Nope, but my favorite Knight has a brother who plays for the Jags."

"Fucking Hart boys." He waves me off. "Those bastards must have been born from a gilded vagina. That Rome was overlooked and lucked out that the Jersey's Jags were watching the NFL draft and …" He stops and looks back at Hudson with recognition in his eyes. "You big bastard, you let me go on and on about the Knights; played me like a fool." He pushes his phone across the bar. "Take another picture for me, will ya, sweetheart?"

Hudson holds his hand up. "Take it back about the Knights."

"You're damn right I'll lie to you to get a picture, ya big bastard."

Hudson laughs and, yes, I take the picture.

FAWNA INSISTED on dropping me off instead of taking a

cab, and when we pull in, we notice lights flickering behind the barn near the camper.

"Is that a fire?" she asks as she throws it in park, and we bother hop out, hurrying to check it out.

I hear Hudson laugh and say, "You're fucked, Tereira. No one over the age of eighteen is emotionally stunted enough to date you."

"You telling me it's possible my future wife may not have been born yet?" AJ jokes.

"What are you fools doing out here?" Fawna asks.

"There were strange noises coming from inside, so Hudson built us a little fire to keep us warm and cozy." AJ pats the blanket next to him. "Come on; sit down. Let us make you two ladies a drink for a change."

Blaze blurts out, "Fuck, marry, or friend?"

"Jesus, not this shit again." Nour stands up.

"Grab me a beer?" Hudson asks.

Nour nods.

"Nour, you can't be pissed at me. You're the one who got me thinking about sex with all that unicorn talk."

Fawna laughs as she sits down. "I need the story behind this."

"Nour's pissed at me because I said I'd marry Cora, fuck his sister and you, and then left the dugout before I could tell him who I'd friend."

"Oh, wow, I'm flattered?" Fawna bites back a laugh.

"See? She's cool with it. She owns her sexuality," Blaze slurs out.

"You remember that talk we had about not becoming drunks?" Nour asks.

Blaze flops back on the blanket he's sitting on and groans. "I'm twenty-one; everyone's an alcoholic for a minute when they're twenty-one."

"Bennett's speaking the truth." Hudson chuckles.

"You need a sweatshirt?" I ask Fawna.

She nods. "Sure, if you're getting one."

"You mad at me, too, Jillian?" Blaze asks.

"No. Are you mad at me?" I ask, amused.

He sits up. "No way. You, Gwen, and CeCe are my friends."

"Damn right, we are." I hold out my fist to him, and he taps it. "Be right back."

When I walk into the camper, Nour is looking around frantically.

"The cooler's outside by the door."

"Fuck the cooler. Where's the mask?"

I shake my head. "What?"

"The mask. Blaze is out there talking about, you know." He scrubs his hand over his face. "I left it here, and it's gone. Do you think—"

"That I tossed it in the trash? I wheeled it out to the curb this morning. Yeah, I think." I walk past him to get Fawna and I sweatshirts. "Chill."

"*Chill*?" he huffs. "How am I supposed to chill?"

I open the tiny closet and dig for two sweatshirts. "Deep breaths, mindful mediation, book a massage, listen to some soothing music." I grab the sweatshirts, turn around, and smile. "Jerk off. Any of those methods are known to greatly reduce stress."

"How can you be so calm?" he whispers.

"You really wanna know?" I ask.

"If you mention getting yourself off, I'll lose my shit."

Smiling, I walk to the door. "Then don't open the bottom drawer in the bathroom during your little freakout. *That* may put you right over the edge."

Walking out toward the fire, I hear Fawna laugh and ask, "Sexual rock, paper, scissors?"

"Don't tell me you've never played." AJ sighs dramatically.

"Okay, I won't." She smiles at me as I walk toward her. "If this is how it is every night, I'm moving in."

"I'm not sure what the boys do in there," I say, pulling the sweatshirt over my head.

"So, you've never played sexual rock, paper, scissors?" she jokes.

"She better not have," Hudson grumbles.

I sit next to Fawna. "Roman and Hudson have been the guardians of my virtue since the day I was born."

"Damn right we have." Hudson nods.

"Double standards much?" Fawna scoffs.

Blaze chimes in, "Double the double standards, because there's two of them."

"You sure there's not four?" Nour asks as he hands him a bottle of water, and then Hudson and AJ a beer.

"Fuck water," Bennett grumbles. "Fuck everything and everyone."

"You ready for bed, man?" AJ starts to get up.

"No, I'm not ready for bed. I'm ready to"—he inhales and exhales slowly—"breathe. Just breathe."

"He's so fucking cute," Fawna whispers.

"I heard that," he says.

She palms her face as Nour holds out two beers for us. I take them and mouth, "*Thanks*."

He responds by narrowing his eyes.

"I'm cute until you get to know me. Then I'm either an asshole or the fucking man. No in-between."

"Cheers for knowing yourself, bro." AJ grins at me and Fawna, and we both stifle a laugh.

"Since I'm not getting any action, I think I'll get my dick pierced like Locke and Jase Steel. How long do you think that takes to heal?"

"All right, Bennett." Nour walks over and holds out his hand. "You're spilling state secrets in the company of ladies. Let's get you tucked in."

Blaze bats his hand away. "I'm sleeping out here. The stars are beautiful."

I look up and see not one single star, but fuck it. "You're right; they're stunning."

"I love the stars."

"Who doesn't?" Hudson asks and looks up. He cocks his head then looks at me. I shrug, and he smiles. "Favorite constellation. Go."

"Any of you say the Big Dipper, and you're kicked the fuck out of the astronomy club," Bennett warns us.

"Canis Major," AJ answers.

"Why?" Bennett asks.

"Because everyone else says Orion." He shows us his phone and winks.

"Fair." Bennett yawns and sits up as he looks at Hudson "Yours?"

"Virgo."

"Why?" he asks.

"I feel like we should be studying," Fawna whispers, and AJ slides his phone to her.

"Two of my favorite things—virgin goddesses and justice."

"Hmm," Bennett mumbles.

"Yours?" Hudson asks.

"I could never pick just one." He reaches out his hand. "Help me up, man. I'm tired."

Nour stands from his squatted position and helps him up.

"Sleep good, man," Hudson calls to him.

"You, too."

As soon as they're out of earshot, AJ mouths, "*What the fuck?*"

"He's going through some shit." Hudson nods. "Like, yeah, y'all need to keep an eye on that."

12

JILLIAN

Blooms

JILLIAN

LYING IN BED, scrolling through the family text chain with dozens of pictures and videos Mom has sent since she began her gardening projects, seeing just how happy she is, it makes me miss her but not in a summer camp kind of way; in a way that lends hope to the fact that being benched for a year isn't the end of the world. It's what I do this year that matters most.

There's also a part of me that questions if my decision to pass on Montana was a mistake. It wasn't shocking, per se, to see Hudson show up here and Mom staying back in Central New York, but it was more a thought-inducing revelation. If Mom can have her own space, peace, time—whatever you may call it—then it makes me feel less guilty or selfish about wanting that, too. Kind of a Harts-won't-break-when-they're-apart discovery.

We're all happy at the same time. I'm no longer a virgin and have quickly realized that my theory is correct—sex and the desire for that feeling with a partner, and not solo, is some kind of voodoo shit, for sure. I can see how it may fool people who have been manipulated by society and its norms that you need a man to truly be happy. I'm living proof that it's not.

The man who punched my V-card is ever present, right there within arms' reach, and I'm not pining over him. I'm not lying in bed, wishing he were next to me. I mean, yeah, I'd like him facedown between my legs again, but that's a physical desire. I may not be the most experienced girl in the world or have been in love myself, but I've seen the good and the bad caused by the diluted view some have about it. I would take an orgasm over a man bringing me flowers any day. I can buy my own damn flowers, but I am not flexible enough to do what Nour Uyar did with his tongue to myself.

I'm no different after having a real dick inside me. I'm me with a new life experience under my belt. More knowledge and insight. I'm Dorothy at the Emerald Castle, having just unveiled the Wizard. But, unlike her, I'm not surprised that I'm not all twisted up about my discovery. I'm further liberated.

Knowledge truly is power.

Mom started a new chapter and is living a new experience. She's in her home, in an empty nest situation, and she's happy, thriving, growing ... flowers and vegetables, something she always wanted to do.

Rome has his true loves—baseball and, even though it's new-ish, it's clear CeCe and he are the real deal. The fact they met at a time in life when they had already attained their goals and their dreams had been realized, they came to the table whole people and have already overcome some really bad shit together. I know they're more than capable of combating anything that comes their way. Hell, Rome's even mentioned marriage to Nour, so I know it will happen and have no doubt they will work together as partners and have a beautiful life.

Hudson has made amazing friends in his football circle, no doubt happily tearing through the ladies, but with a gentle smile and leaving behind as little carnage as possible. Out of all three of us, he's the one whose heart I worry about the most.

From the other end of the RV, I hear, "Fucking kidding me." And then, "That piece of shit doesn't deserve a girl like that."

"You okay?" I ask, sitting up.

"I'm fine. All good."

"Obviously not."

"Nothing to lose sleep over. Sorry I woke you. Go back to sleep."

"I wasn't asleep and—"

"No, fuck no," he hisses.

"It's like watching a show with subtitles but backward, which is arguably worse."

"And this is like watching a fucking montage of our parents beginning, knowing how it ends."

"Okay, I'm hooked. Spill."

He sits up. "Riley Brooks' boyfriend."

"The guy you called a tool?"

"Yeah. He proposed, she said yes, and he doesn't deserve her."

"And you like her?" I guess.

"Fucking adore her, but not in the wanna fuck her way."

"Okay, so what do you want to do with her?"

"Put her on a shelf high enough that some little shit's not going to break her."

"Oh my God, you like her like her."

"Just said that, Jillian," he grumbles.

"No, you said adore. But you really mean—"

"Never gonna happen."

"Why?"

"Aside from the fact her mom's a Ross and part of that whole owner group?"

"Aside from that."

"Might have met her sister, Lauren, at a bar far the fuck away from Blue Valley, and neither of us knew who the other was."

"And you fucked."

He repeats, "And we fucked."

"Did she want more?"

"Nah, she's a cool chick. I was a revenge fuck. Her ex started seeing someone and …" He stops. "Doesn't matter. We're cool. No one knows, but I was fucking terrified, and I'm not doing that shit again."

"What if it was something more?"

"It's not. I've had plenty of women I should have fallen head-over-heels for, but it's just not there, Jillian, you know? Like, I think he broke something on the inside, too, that didn't heal, like a nose."

"No, I don't believe that." I climb out of my little bunk and make my way back to him.

"You don't believe in love." He forces out a laugh as I lie down beside him and grab his hand like he used to do to me when things were bad.

"I do. I just don't believe we all have to have it to be happy, and I don't believe it's something you search for. I think it's something you should allow yourself to fall into, if and only if it's the real deal."

"He's just like him. I see it coming."

I squeeze his hand. "How so?"

"Wasn't good enough to be drafted to play college ball; walked on, didn't play unless 'Cuse was ahead by enough in the last couple minutes that it wouldn't fuck up the win. More than likely kept on as a bench, riding a GPA boost."

"Not so much like Dad then."

"Except the part he's an insufferable dick when he drinks."

"You're friends, you and Riley, right?"

He nods.

"Tell her your concerns."

"Not my place."

"Then tell her it's not your place, but maybe show some vulnerability in telling her you see the parts of him you know he's hiding from her."

"Yeah, maybe."

AFTER HUDSON IS SNORING SOFTLY across the room, I fluff my pillow and set my phone on the shelf. I am about to fall asleep when I get an alert from the app that I was sure I snoozed for a week to allow for the feels to set in, if they were going to.

I reach up, see the notification, and tap to open it.

SportsManSam:
Hear me out before you block me again. You and I are in the same boat. Both of us testing a theory by using this app. First RBI in my career after the nip selfie. First grand slam after fucking the unicorn. Tonight, I hit for shit because 1 - as much as I can detach, my head's a little fucked up that the unicorn is distantly related to my ball fam, or 2 - I need that rush that you gave me, or 3 - I'm getting kicked in the balls by Karma for all of this and might as well finish out this contract, tuck my tail between my legs, and head back to school, proving my parents right, that this was a horrible lapse in judgment on my part.

His dot is moving again. To stop his spiral, I quickly type back.

GoodTimesOnly:
I'm not going to ask how you got unblocked, or into my phone. I'm just going to assume that you're a sneaky little bastard and a few seconds with my phone in your hand was enough to do all that. So, if I'm reading this right, you have more than just a unicorn kink; you're into far more deviant things and may have an incest fantasy. Ew. Because you're obviously in your feels and spiraling, I'll bite.

I send it then sit up, lift my shirt, push my boob up, maneuver her in a somewhat painful position that allows me to grab the end of my barbell with my teeth, and take a selfie, making sure my face doesn't completely show. Then I hit *send*.

GoodTimesOnly:

> ***If that doesn't work, you're on your own, kid. Kick ass tomorrow. Goodnight.***

> **SportsManSam:**
> ***You know, if this works, I'm gonna need more.***

> **GoodTimesOnly:**
> ***This completely contradicts the man losing his shit about my brother(s).***

> **SportsManSam:**
> ***For the love of the game, and lucky nips, I may be able to separate the two.***

Lucky nips? I laugh to myself.

> **GoodTimesOnly:**
> ***I didn't start this project to become a bow to the man kind of bitch. It's give and take *woman shrugging emoji****

> **SportsManSam:**
> ***And I'm not the guy who will ever send random dick pics without a request.***

> **GoodTimesOnly:**
> ***I'll take an IOU, close quarters and all …***

He sends a picture of … my vibrator.

> **GoodTimesOnly:**
> ***You stole my vibe!***

> **SportsManSam:**

Compulsive and out of character. I'll overthink that later, but not tonight. Sleep well. *zzz emoji*

I have so many things to say, scream, rage about, but that's counterproductive to Nour's game and could affect Rome's, too. Plus, it's not valuable information for my little research project.

"I'M NOT FEEDING into his superstitions; I'm treating myself," I tell Elle, who's been eyeing me suspiciously since I dog-napped her when the boys all left for their morning workout, or wherever they go after breakfast, showering, watching *Real Housewives*, and napping.

"CeCe gave me the play by play; I wasn't asking for it," I quip as I turn the corner. "And you of all … animals shouldn't judge them because, hello, you clearly have a routine if we're ending up right back here and you're the one in the lead."

I open the door and walk in. "Good morning, Burt. Elle dragged me along to—"

I stop when I see him sitting on the floor, leaning against the counter, his hand over his heart.

My own heart starts beating at a scary pace, but I remain calm.

"Are you in pain?"

He manages to groan out, "Phone."

"Okay, but we need to get you on your left side first, okay, Burt?"

I make quick work to help him into position then call 9-1-1.

Within two minutes, they arrive, and they all seem to know him. Apparently, he's a retired firefighter.

When they wheel him out, he's still conscious and able to give me some instruction.

"Treats, behind counter. Lena will be here soon. Funeral prep for Willie."

"You get better. Elle and I will hold down the fort."

"Thanks, kid."

Standing in the middle of chaos, I feel all that adrenaline start to fade as my phone rings. It's Mom, and she's using FaceTime.

When I answer, "Hi, Mom," tears start to fall.

"Oh, Jillian, what's wrong? Do you need me? Are the boys—"

"Rome's good, Hudson's on his way back to you, and I'm fine."

"Well, what is it, sweetie?"

I tell her what happened with Burt, and then I walk out and show her the sign. "Etta's mom."

"Etta's." She sighs.

I briefly explain how we found this place and that it's closing down.

"But that's not why you called. Tell me something good."

I smile.

Her concerned pause is brief, *she knows I need this*, and flips the camera. "We have a vegetable garden. It's bigger than I expected." Which is putting it mildly. "Ten rows of raised beds with four across. They're eight feet long, Jillian. We're going to have beans, and peas, and cucumbers; tomatoes, and all different kinds of squash and zucchini; onions, and garlic, and a whole box of herbs." She moves the camera. "This is the salad box. All different kinds of greens. We can come right out here and snip what we want off whenever we want it, and it's all organic, Jillian. I played in aged horse manure for two days." She laughs. "There's lots more to do, but isn't it beautiful?"

"It's perfect." I smile as she turns the camera back to face her. "You're glowing."

"And you've just been through an ordeal."

"I hope he's okay."

"We'll pray for him."

The little bells ring, and Lena walks in.

"Mom, I have to go. Lena just walked in."

"Call me, text me, and most importantly, you need me, don't hesitate to ask me to come to you. These are planted, and it's not like they need me to be present to grow."

"I've heard that plants do better if you talk to them," I tell her, hoping my words are heard by Lena, and that she may talk to me today.

We end the call.

"Lena, do you remember me?"

She nods.

"When I came in, I found Burt sitting on the floor. He's on his way to the hospital."

She doesn't react at all.

"Do you understand what I'm telling you?"

"Karma," she huffs. "Damn fool, that man." She walks around, speaking in Spanish, which I am familiar with, but textbook familiar and never having truly used it i'm far from fluent. What I do know is Lena's pissed. "Etta angry," she says, shaking her fist to emphasize her statement. "No sell. No. Sell." She puts her hand to her chest. "Her heart, right here." She points upstairs. "My home up there. Burt angry bastard." She throws her hands in the air in frustration. "She no want to go; the angels call. No choice."

"Was she your friend, Lena?" I ask quietly.

"Only friend." She holds her hand to her heart. "I come here for her. Now no home. No job. I go? I no want to go. I stay."

"I'm so sorry. I wish I could help."

"You buy. I stay. I work. You help."

Holy shit. "I'm going back to school soon."

"You buy. I stay. I work. You help," she repeats.

"Lena, I don't have money."

"Flowers money. Make pretty sell. Money." Her eyes shine with unshed tears. "I help. I work hard. Make beautiful. You give rent money, flower money to bastard." She holds her hand to her heart again. "I help."

AFTER TAKING Elle and the flowers back to the house, I drove back to Etta's, not wanting Lena to be alone. I was probably more a hindrance than a help, but we got the order finished and delivered to the funeral home in plenty of time.

When we came back, I asked her how long she had before her visa expired. Lena led me up stairs to a large apartment that was nearly spotless but needed a lot of work.

"Too big." She cringed. "Too much." She then gave me a file. "You take."

Knowing one of CeCe's friends is a lawyer and could possibly help me, I take it.

She then showed me the empty shell of another massive apartment across the hall and pointed upstairs. "Two more. Loud. Smoke. Kick out. Make nice. Get new." She holds her hand up and rubs her fingers together. "More money for you."

Exhausted from spending the day at Etta's. I napped like a champ and would have been late for the game if CeCe hadn't come and woken me up.

"You feeling okay?" she asked when I came out of the downstairs bedroom from my shower.

"Yes. Why? Do I look like shit?"

"Not at all. You've just been"—she shrugs—"distant?"

"Distant?"

"You should stay in the house." She pouts. "We have room. The best room in the house is free."

"You and Rome are nuts not to move down here."

"Makes more sense to save it for when Chloe, Danny, and Aggie visit."

"That's sweet."

She looks at her watch. "You ready to roll?"

"I am. Is Cora coming?"

"She and her father are in the city again."

"Damn, they really do love Broadway."

CeCe gives Elle smooches before sending her into her crate. "Did you not enjoy it?"

"I love any new experience, but I'd never choose theater seats over bleachers."

"A girl who knows what she likes," CeCe states as she hits the key fob, unlocking her car. "Rome aside, if we met in the wild, you and I would become friends."

I don't know why that gets to me, but it does. And as I slide into the car, I try to hide my emotions, but CeCe Shaw is too observant.

She takes my hand and gives it a squeeze. "You're incredible, Jillian Hart."

"I'm so glad he found you."

13

NOUR

Winner Either Way

Nour

AS IS tradition when we lose a game, we go home, binge-eat Taco Bell, and sulk as we watch the highlights.

I have a hell of a time sulking after I hit a triple tonight, with bases loaded, and hit two others in the five innings I played. I suppose I can play up my annoyance for the one grounder I hit that I was out at first before I was even halfway to the base.

My head wasn't in it. I had glanced up at the stands, saw Jillian on her phone, and immediately wondered if she was setting up a meet with subject number two.

That can't happen. It's clear that her nips are, in fact, lucky.

When two thirty hits and I've seen no signs of her coming back from O'Donnell's, it's not subject two that most concerns me; it's the phone call I overheard the other night from her old man and the fact she is a grown-ass woman and can do as she pleases with her money. But the vile things he said and the tone he used, he's clearly fucked in the head.

Rome walks down the stairs and looks around. "Boys in bed?"

"Yeah." I sit up and try to mask the worry when I ask, "Everything okay?"

"Jillian's car stalled out at a light a couple blocks away. I'm going see what I can do or tow it home."

"Need some help?" I ask, standing up.

"If you're offering, I'm not gonna say no."

Once in his truck, I decide to feel out how receptive he'd be talking about his old man by cracking open the vault and letting some of my ancient history out.

"Cool you know cars. My old man's idea of teaching me anything about them was giving me the number to AAA when I got my first flat."

"Mom taught us all how to change the oil, tires, jump a car, basic maintenance."

"I taught myself to change a tire with a YouTube video after that." I smirk. "He was so pissed."

"I wish mine was pissed. He tried to find ways to monetize that shit." He nods forward. "Glad she called and didn't catch a ride with whoever that is."

"Who the fuck is that?" I ask, leaning forward and seeing the license plate on a red Stingray as we pass by. "Master? That's—"

"Your backup catcher." He drives past her and does a U-turn.

"*Your* backup catcher," I toss back.

"Thought you were good with him?" He puts his truck in park.

"You good with that?" I ask, seeing Jillian smile and hand his phone back to him.

"Not one bit, but Mom's riding our asses about giving her room to … breathe."

"Hudson get that message?" I call after him as he opens the door.

"Jay V?" He chuckles. "Not her type. Google him."

"You think Masters is?"

He narrows his eyes and shrugs. "I know where he works. One step out of line, my mission is to make his life hell."

He gets out, and I sit here, shocked, stunned … pissed?
Get out and help, you idiot.

SportsManSam:
He was flirting with you in front of Roman and lived through it.

AND IT PISSED me the fuck off, almost as much as waiting ten minutes for a reply.

SportsManSam:
You want me to be real? Fine. He and you fucking will mess with my game.

Still nothing.

SportsManSam:
More real? I'm a guarantee *rainwater emoji* so the obvious choice for the "it's sex, not love" project.

Nothing.

SportsManSam:

I should have started with thank you for supporting my own research and sending me the HAF pic last night. Happy to return the favor.

What the fuck is wrong with me?

GoodTimesOnly:
You've got two minutes to bring me my vibe or I'm blocking you again.

It takes less than one, and it only takes that long because I have to bring Elle with me.

When I get to the RV, she's not in it.

I pull my phone out of my pocket to send her a message when I hear a whistle, and then Elle tugs on her leash, heading toward the townhouses.

"You get me yelled at again, and this thing you and I have going on is over." I hiss at her.

"Did I type out the wrong message? I said vibe, not my fur niece."

I look for Jillian and see her standing in the open doorway of my townhouse, stepping back into the foyer, scratching the top of Elle's head.

Eyes trained on hers, the warm light from the artificial candles she has scattered around casts a soft glow over her body clothed in just a threadbare tee-shirt that. It hangs to her knees and has a faded football on it.

"You snap your fingers and make this happen in the two minutes it took me to get out here?" I ask, kicking the door shut behind me.

She shakes her head, a smirk playing on her thick, soft lips. "It was after the squirt emoji and the reminder that it's been a few days since I've gotten off. You bring my vibe?"

I drop the leash, grab the back of her neck, pull her close enough to crash my lips over hers, and I devour her mouth. Hands skating up her body, pushing the shirt higher and higher, tracing her curves, groaning at the discovery that she's completely bare beneath it.

I have to break our kiss to pull the shirt over her head. "The sweetness of your mouth makes me crave the taste of your pussy. I want you on my face."

Clearing her throat, she straightens her shoulders and steps back. "I'm going on a date with him."

Fists clenched at my sides, I pray it helps keep the tension there and out of my voice so I at least sound calm. "When?"

"Tomorrow."

Teeth clenched, jaw muscles popping, I tell her the truth. "Then I'm going to mark your pussy; make sure you're still feeling me. It'll be like I'm right there with you, chaperoning."

I peel off my shirt, causing whatever smart-ass thing she was going to stay to stick in her throat as she eye-fucks me.

I grab her up, and she squeals.

"That was so un-GTO-like."

"Then put me down." She wiggles slightly.

"Perfect," I say before nipping at her tit and giving her piercing a slight tug as I squat down on the newly refinished floors, with her naked body straddling my abs.

I reach between us and cup her pussy, sliding a finger inside. "You're wet already."

"Uh-huh," she so squeaks out, and it's cute as fuck.

I pull my finger out of her and grip her hips. "I wanna drown in your cum."

"You what?" she asks as I drag her up my body.

"Get that sweet little pussy up here."

She straddles my face like she's done it a million times. Her confidence is sexy.

I grip her hips and pull her down on my face, burying it in her pussy. "Fucking amazing."

"Oh fuck," she whimpers.

"While I tongue-fuck you, I want you to ride my fucking face like you've never ridden anything before."

She leans forward, placing her hands on the hardwood floor, and I pull her back to where I want her, spearing her with my tongue over and over until she begins to ride, sliding back and forth, soaking my face with her slickness.

I reach around her and slide a finger up and down the crack of her ass, rubbing circles around her puckered little hole with my pinky. When she begins rocking, my cock grows so hard it's almost painful when I press in, just a bit, and she cries out, pressing into my touch. I swear I could come in my sweats.

I don't go much deeper, and it's not because she's not loving it, because she is. It's because I'm a greedy bastard, and the taste of her, the smell of her, the feel of her, is euphoric.

Her body is spasming as she curses, crying out my name, and then everything tightens.

"Gonna come. I'm gonna come so fucking hard," she cries.

I flip us over, needing more control than she's able to give me in this position, and continue licking, sucking, and finger-fucking her until she's limp beneath me.

She's soaked, I'm soaked, it's messy, and it's fucking beautiful.

"I'm gonna fuck your tits, and then your mouth. If I can't get off like that, I'm gonna fuck that tight, wet, pretty little cunt of yours."

Between pants, she says, "Okay."

After removing my pants, I straddle her body, bend down, and kiss her forehead. "Good girl." Stroking my cock, I then realize, "Fuck, no lube."

She grabs her tits and squeezes them. "Spit between them."

"Fucking dream girl," I groan as I spit in my hand and start rubbing it up and down my shaft. Then I lean down, spit between her tits, and position my cock between them.

"I need these." I move her hands away and push her tits together, rolling her nipples as I slide my cock between them.

On the first inward stroke, her tongue darts out, and she licks my crown.

"Fuck yes, do that shit again."

She does, every damn time, and when my balls draw up, I know I'm gonna come soon.

"You ever swallow or no?"

"Come on my tits," she damn near begs.

"You want my cum on your tits, dream girl?" I tug at her piercing.

"Yes," she whimpers.

"All over your sexy fucking nipples?" I ask.

"All over," she says.

The first burst covers one nipple as she watches intently.

"Now the other."

"Yeah?" I groan and give her just that.

Panting, I move and drop beside her, pulling her close to me. "That was so fucking hot."

"How long before you fuck me?" she asks.

Smile creeping up on my face, I answer, "I'm not fucking you when you have a date tomorrow night."

"Lunch date. Don't make it weirder than it already is."

"How am I making it weird? I'm not the one going on a date. I'm good with what we're doing."

She yawns. "And what are we doing?"

"Proving theories and giving each other orgasms." I turn my head and look at her. "You catching feels, dream girl?"

"No, but you seem to be getting jealous over a date I accepted just to see how Rome would react."

I smile. "As soon as we rolled up, I knew any kid who drives a red Vette with vanity plates wasn't gonna give a fuck that the sexy as hell chick he'd be beating off to later was his teammate's little sister. I asked Rome before we got out how he felt about that."

"What did he say?"

"He said your mom told both your brothers to let you breathe, and that if Masters fucked up, he knew where he worked."

"Oh my God, you're taking that as a green flag for this." She motions between us.

"This"—I motion between us just as she did—"is different. We both have theories to prove. And this"—I motion between us again—"didn't start with the expectations that comes with a date."

"What is that supposed to mean?"

"He's a major league ball player, asking a girl on a date?" I shake my head. "He has an agenda." I curl up into a seated position. "You might as well get a collar with an engraved tag that says 'WAG.' A guy like that sees how a hot little number like *you* fits perfectly into *his* life, Jillian."

"Do you think that's what I'm looking for?" she asks in a way I know I've pissed her off.

I grab my shirt and bend down to clean my jizz off her tits, and she bats my hand away.

"Is it?"

"There's no base I could stand on that would be far enough away to mistake you for a convenience, Jillian Hart." I grab my pants and step into them. "You're trouble with a capital T." I snag a candle off the floor and start looking around.

"Where are you going?" she asks, getting up.

"Checking out the place. I haven't been in here since the fire."

"Are you serious?" I hear what I think is a foot stomp.

Yep, I've pissed her off.

"Be pissed all you want; you know I'm speaking the truth."

I feel something hit the back of my head. "There's your jizz shirt."

I can't help but smile and stop when I hear her walking away. "Where are you going?"

"To sleep."

I hurry toward her, and when she turns to no doubt yell at me, I bend down, press a shoulder to her center, and lift her up.

"You asshole, put me down!"

"Not yet," I say as I jog through the house and up the stairs, straight to my room, where I set her on her feet in front of the back window.

"What is wrong with you?" She shoves my chest with both hands.

I grab them and turn her to face the window, pulling her back hard against me to keep her in place. "I was standing here one day and saw this bombshell brunette climb out of a car and stretch out, telling me she'd driven for a long time. She then grabbed a backpack and slung it over her shoulder.

It was so heavy that her shoulder slumped. I could tell it was loaded up with books. In that minute, I knew that girl was a strong, smart, independent woman on her way to make whatever it was she wanted to out of herself. She was not the kind of girl a guy who's on the road or at the stadium more than half the year could possibly do any justice by consuming her life."

I let go of her and stand back. "I'm not saying love doesn't exist—we see it every day. But your theory isn't wrong. There are people who know that love is the greatest thing in the world, and they want it so badly they press for it, force it. That's not real, and that doesn't last. Trust me; I know."

"You've been in love?"

Fuck.

I close my eyes and nod. "Thought so. It ended badly."

"Because of baseball?" she asks.

"Yeah, because of baseball."

She shakes her head, telling me she doesn't understand.

"We dated all through college. My parents and her parents had expectations of what our lives should look like. I chose what I knew mine was supposed to be. Their approval meant more than us to her. Add to that, a minor league player doesn't make shit, so her lifestyle would change drastically."

"I'm sorry."

I shake my head. "I'm not."

"I bet she's dropping into your DMs now."

"Nah, she was married three months later. They have a kid, one on the way, a dog, the perfect house—exactly what she was told she wanted, and she accepted that life gladly. My head was fucked up about it for a very long time."

When we hear Elle whine, we laugh.

"Guess it's time to go."

Downstairs, we gather up the candles, toss them in the bag that she brought them in, and head out.

"You ever gonna start sleeping in the house?"

She shrugs. "Yeah?"

"Bet Rome and CeCe would like that."

"Fine."

14

JILLIAN

Inside

JILLIAN

I WAKE up later than I'd hoped and blame it on the comfort of being inside the house.

I take a quick shower and hurry out to the kitchen as Rome is heading out the door.

"Hey, where you going?"

"Car shopping," he answers.

"Something happen to your truck?"

"Nope," is all he says, and I know that means he's hiding something.

I quickly realize what it is. "No."

"Oh, you think I'm getting *you* a car?"

I set my fists on my hips. "I have a job. I'll get my car—"

"Blown motor, transmission's shot. It would cost ten grand to make her safe."

My heart sinks, but I'm not going to get all sentimental about it when the boys are all here.

"You know what doesn't cost ten grand?"

He rolls his eyes. "What's that?"

"Nike sneakers and public transportation."

"CeCe and I are going to look for a new car for her. She wants a bigger SUV." He pulls a set of keys out of his pocket and tosses them to me. "I bought hers for you. Paid what the trade-in was going to be. We're scrapping yours."

"We can't." I hold my hand to my heart.

"It's either that or take it to West Virginia so he can have that, too."

"What?"

"Yeah, got papers at eight this morning, demanding the return. So, he gets it and scraps it, or we scrap it at a place that doesn't input it into a database."

"What do you mean *you got papers*?"

"He wants money."

I feel eyes on me and know it's Nour. I glance at him, and he crosses his arms and leans back against the counter, brow arched.

"Spill it, Jillian."

"Spill what?" I ask.

"You're a horrible liar. Your face gets all pinched up, and your voice raises about three octaves. Did he call for money?"

I shrug, which is more than enough of a confirmation.

"Tell me you didn't give him the fucking cost of a phone call."

Nour clears his throat, and I glare at him.

He bows his head and walks past me into the other room, calling back, "Come on, guys; let's give them some privacy."

"How much?" Rome asks.

I hold up three fingers.

"Three grand?"

"No," I huff. "Three hundred."

"Jillian, that fucker doesn't deserve an answered call, let alone three hundred bucks."

I look down like a shamed dog.

"He tell you he was gonna write a tell-all?"

Taken aback by the fact I never considered our father would be working all angles, I ask, "A what?"

"A book. Don't say a word to him, but the bastard got Hudson for ten grand a year ago with that bullshit. You know who he doesn't call and ask for money?"

"You," I mumble.

"Damn right. You know why?"

"Because you do everything right?" I smart back.

He does me a solid by not gloating. "He hasn't called Hudson in six months because he called his bluff and told him that he wasn't sure he could stay sober long enough to tell a story, let alone write a book. Be done with it. His threats are empty."

I nod.

"Cool. See you—"

"How much do I owe CeCe for the car?"

"Nothing, Jillian."

"I have a job now. I've made over fifteen hundred dollars in three days. Let me make payments."

"You made fifteen hundred dollars bartending for—"

I nod. "Eighteen hours."

"That's more than I made teaching school in a week. Hell, maybe two."

"Not a bad gig."

"Make sure you take taxes out of—"

"Fawna's taking them out of my paycheck."

"You made that in tips?"

"Yeah."

"That's great. Good for you."

"So, let me make payments for the vehicle."

"We'll talk about it later; I have to go grab CeCe."

"Rome," I call after him, "thank you."

From the next room, I hear, "Happy dance starting in five … four … three … two … one!" AJ slides into the kitchen and grabs my hands, jostling them around. "You've got a new car. You've got a new car. You've got a—"

Laughing, I join in, "New car!"

Bennett walks out and crosses his arms. "You taking it on your date today?"

I scoff. "How do you know?"

He lifts a shoulder. "Walls are thin at CeCe's house. When the sex has been had, the talking begins. Sometimes, the conversations are too riveting and I can't fall asleep."

"Whose ass are we kicking?" AJ asks.

"Rome's allowing it, so no one's," Bennett answers.

"Allowing it?" I arch a brow. "I'm a—"

"Grown-ass woman with a job," he and AJ say together.

"I'm older than you"—I point at Bennett then turn to AJ—"and only a year younger than you." I turn and look at Nour. "You wanna add your two cents?"

"Sure. He has the smallest dick on the team."

"True," the other two agree.

I cross my arms and ask, "Whose is the biggest?"

All three of them answer, "Me."

Knowing that would be their answer, I shake my head as I head to the door. "Have a good day, boys."

"Where are you going?" AJ asks.

"To do grown-ass woman shit."

I STAND when I see CeCe and Fawna's friend, Francesca, walk into the hospital cafeteria. "Thanks for meeting me."

"Not a problem at all." She gives me a hug then sits down.

I push Lena's file across the table. "These are the originals."

When she doesn't reach for them, I feel all hope dwindle.

"No, no, no, that doesn't mean I don't want to help. I need you to hand me ten or twenty bucks."

"Okay?" I reach into my bag, pull out my wallet, and grab a twenty, setting it on the table.

She looks up from her tablet and smiles then pushes it across the table toward me. "As soon as you sign, you have retained me as a lawyer." She holds up the twenty. "And this acts as a retainer."

I sign with my finger then push it back to her.

She flips through a screen and pushes it back to me. "Gabrielle Steel just had a baby, but she's agreed to look at Lena's case. She doesn't know it's you who has brought this to me, but you sign this, and she's all yours. Immigration law is her specialty and her passion. Trust me when I tell you that she's the best. And she's going to take it on pro bono."

"Are you serious?"

"As a heart attack." She cringes. "Poor comparison given the reason we're here."

"You think it's possible?"

"If he's going to let it go to auction so he doesn't have to deal with it, I guarantee he'll agree to hold the mortgage long enough for you to show equity to get the loan, especially if it's all wrapped up in a pretty little package." She reaches into her bag and pulls a file out, setting it in front of me. "Which I happen to have right here."

"In one night?"

"Not my specialty, but it's a simple contract. A phone call to a realtor friend and getting comps only took a few keystrokes. Just make sure he understands it's pending an inspection."

"To make sure it's structurally sound?"

"Exactly. And if it is, and you're willing to do the work, you're going to have a ton of equity and will not have a problem getting a loan. Which, again, as a friend and lawyer, I think you're nuts not to ask your brothers, but I know it's a sticking point for you."

"It is."

"Stubborn and independent. I like it."

AFTER LEAVING the hospital where I left the contract with Burt and told him to take his time considering it and that I was in no hurry, I went straight to Etta's to help Lena with whatever she needed. I didn't tell her I was considering buying the place, because getting her hopes up and not being able to deliver was not an option. I would have told her that Gabrielle Steel was looking into her case, but running late to start the day messed that up. I want to be able to take time with her to do that, and because I agreed to meet Brady Masters for lunch, I decided to wait.

Brady Masters is a ten—black hair, blue eyes, perfect smile, and a hot body. But the entire time I sat across from him, all I could think about was his small dick. It's awful, I know it is, but it's the truth.

Halfway through my chicken club sandwich, Nour, AJ, and Bennett walk into the bar. Passing by, they all say a cordial hello and proceed to sit at a table behind ours, where I have a clear view of all of them, but Nour fully.

Brady is completely unbothered, which I give him props for, but when the table is clear, he begins telling me how he can't wait to get married and have a bunch of kids so he has something to look up in the stands to. "You know, my people, my reason."

Someone coughs out the name, "Turner," and I manage to shoot daggers at them without getting seen by Brady. They all titter like teenage boys. Well, Nour doesn't. He looks to be standing on the line between angry and annoyed, like a small breeze could send him in either direction.

"Imagine how I felt when this gorgeous brunette turned my head a few weeks ago, only to find out she's a teammate's sister."

"Imagine." I smile politely, wanting to crawl under the table and out the door.

"But then I saw you on the side of the road, and I reminded myself I was the Master"—he winks—"of my own destiny, and I had to shoot my shot." He reaches across the table and squeezes my hand. "I am so glad I did."

Thankfully, I get a text.

"Oh, shoot, excuse me for a minute." I pull my phone from my pocket and look at the screen. It's a group text, and the name of the group is "*We Got Your Back*."

> UNKNOWN:
>
> Tereira *running man emoji*
>
> UNKNOWN:
>
> Bennett * baby and an eggplant emoji*
>
> UNKNOWN:
>
> Uyar I didn't ask to be added to this, you assholes, but yeah.
>
> UNKNOWN:
>
> *man pointing up Gif*

"Is everything okay?"

I shake my head. "I hate to do this, but a friend needs me."

I send a text to Fawna and play it up that I'm gravely concerned.

> ME:
> I'm escaping this shitshow of a lunch. Can you please tell him the check's been covered after I leave? I don't want him to think it was a date.
>
> FAWNA:
> Girl, he's *fire emoji*
>
> ME:
> Feel free to *tag emoji* in.

I shove the phone in my pocket and stand. "I'm so sorry."

"Are you sure you should drive?"

"I didn't drink anything that—"

"You're upset. You shouldn't—"

"I'm honestly good."

"Can I walk you out?"

"No, no, finish your drink."

I exit as if I'm in a hurry with no further explanation.

IN THIS CAR, it's impossible to ignore the notifications sounding off with my phone automatically connecting. I'm sure it will be a convenience at some point, but right now, it's annoying as fuck.

I hit the screen to stop it, and am startled when …

"*Unknown says: you ran out of there like your ass was on fire. Woman running emoji*

"*Unknown says: laughing face emoji, skull emoji, rolling on the floor emoji, laughing crying emoji*

"*Unknown says: queen move emoji*

"*How would you like to respond?*"

"Can you block them?"

"*Sending: can you block them?*"

"No, it was a fucking question, you idiot."

"*Sending: no, it was a fucking question, you idiot.*"

"Oh my God, make it stop!"

"*Sending: oh my God, make it stop!*"

Does it stop? No, dozens more come in.

"Fuck off, you toddler emojis, and lose my number."

"*Sending: fuck off, you toddler emojis, and lose my number.*"

"Of course you are," I grumble.

WHEN THE BELLS to the shop's door jingle, I look up and see Rome and Elle walking in. The fact he looks like he knew I would be here, I have some explaining to do and an ass to kick.

He doesn't walk to the counter; he begins a slow perusal, and he's not looking at the flowers, either.

"Before you go all Rome on me, let me call my lawyer and fire her."

"Wasn't a lawyer," he says, still looking around. "I stopped at Wags to bring the ladies lunch, and Cora mentioned her dad was hired to do the assessment. She was worried you were upset with her, and that's why you hadn't mentioned you were buying a flower shop." He shrugs. "Told her not to worry about it; neither had I."

"I—"

"Then I got a call from Burt."

"Of course you did." I reach down and grab a treat out of the box for Elle, who is sitting there, waiting patiently.

"He said you saved his life."

"I dialed 9-1-1."

"I think I'm more upset you didn't tell me about that. That's not even a grand slam moment; that's a world series win, Jillian. You saved a life." He walks over and finally looks at me. "The fact you didn't share that with us so we could at least celebrate with you by sending text confetti in the group chat is—"

"There's more involved"—I glance around—"but Lena could be back any minute, and I don't want—"

"You at least give me a jog-through?"

I counter with, "Sprint?"

He smiles. "I'm good with that."

"Should we FaceTime Mom and Hudson?"

"Mom doesn't know?"

I rub my temples, trying to remember everything that's gone on this past week. "She FaceTimed me right after they took Burt out on a stretcher, and I was waiting for Lena to show up, so no, not about me wanting to buy it." We move through the back where more refrigeration systems hold flowers and tables line the walls. "This is where arrangements are put together."

"Looks more put together than the storefront."

NOUR

Family Dinner

NOUR

ONE NIGHT off between two back-to-back home series is a luxury. A perfect time to chill and rest your mind, body, and spirit. That is exactly opposite of how we've spent our day. Aside from our well executed lunch break, we haven't stopped.

"Last load," AJ says, leaning back in the seat of the U-Haul that we rented to make driving back and forth from the storage unit that we rented after the fire to store the new furniture we bought, not wanting it to end up waiting longer to get set up than we had to.

"And then we set up," Blaze groans.

"Rome wants us for dinner," I remind them. "We can do beds after. The rest can wait."

"Sounds like a fucking plan."

We pull in and park the U-Haul, heading right over to CeCe's place.

When we walk in, Rome, Jillian, CeCe, and Cora are all sitting around the island with a large paper spread across it.

"What are we eating tonight?" AJ asks, rubbing his stomach.

"A takeout buffet is on its way." Cora laughs.

Blaze does something completely out of character and ruffles her hair. "You should be a poet."

Everyone looks at him, including Cora, whose face is crimson.

"What? Is it not okay to do that? It's not like I groped her ass."

"Right?" she agrees. "Like, seriously, not a big deal."

My eyes catch Jillian's, and she smirks.

"Moving on," Rome mumbles then stands up straight. "Cecelia has asked me to move in, so I wanted to give you guys the option of—"

AJ grabs my hand and raises our arms. "We call Rome's pad."

"Is Locke keeping his?" Bennett asks.

CeCe smiles. "No, he's happy at the beach."

"So, you have two freed up?" AJ asks.

"Rudy G. wants one of them, and both Masters, Henley, and Cody Vanders have expressed interest. I wanted to see how you guys felt."

AJ is the first to throw in his choices. "Rudy G. and Vanders have my vote, obviously."

"Vanders getting divorced?" I ask.

"I didn't ask," Rome states.

"All of them have three bedrooms; everyone could fit," Cora offers.

"Not opposed to a roommate, but I'm not moving in with any of them," Blaze mumbles.

I look at AJ, and he nods. "You could move in with us."

"You sure?"

"A hundred percent."

"Aw … look, the family is staying together." CeCe smiles. "That makes me so happy."

"Now that that's settled"—I point to the paper—"what's this?"

"Jillian's buying a flower shop," Rome says proudly. "Made the move with none of our input but has a solid plan to—"

"Do more grown-ass woman shit?" AJ asks.

Jillian smiles as she looks down at the paper. "We're just drawing it out to see if what I want will actually work."

"So, no more graduate school?" I ask.

"Definitely not in Montana." She smiles at Rome. Then looks at me. "The two schools I wanted the most, I was waitlisted, which was a kick to the ego."

"Sucks," I tell her.

She lifts a shoulder as she looks back down. "Maybe it all happened for a reason."

The fact I want to believe it has something to do with me is fucking wrong on every level, and yes, I will be checking to see if my balls have been removed ASAP.

Cora chimes in, "She's taking classes online from both schools toward a different degree as a backup, and we're going to be roomies someday."

"Damn right, we are," Jillian agrees.

Cora points to the paper. "We're going to have the penthouse, with exclusive roof access for our party pad."

"It sounds so much better that we're going to have walls and a running toilet and have to rough it out until all the other apartments are done and rented out so we can afford to upgrade our air mattresses."

"The Harts are buying up Trenton. I like it. Fucking real estate tycoons." AJ claps his hands and rubs them together.

"And Jillian can join the very exclusive, nepo baby club." Blaze looks at her. "We meet the first Monday of the month."

"Oh no, she won't have that. No help from us," Rome states.

"Get over it." Jillian hip-checks him.

"You changing the name of the shop?" I ask.

"Not a chance." Roman chuckles.

"Actually, I *am* changing it."

"What?" Rome asks, seeming offended.

"I mean, can you blame her?" AJ laughs. "*Etta?*"

"Oh, AJ ..." CeCe whispers.

"What?" he asks.

"That's our grandmother's name, and it stays." Jillian laughs as AJ slowly sinks down until he can't be seen behind the island. "It'll be *Etta Harts*, with no E like our last name, and flowers."

"That's beautiful, Jillian."

"Thanks, Nour."

I READ over the message Jillian sent again, trying to figure out how to reply, because after the past couple days, she's become more real to me.

GoodTimesOnly:
You have a *baseball emoji* game tomorrow night and ur not soliciting. What gives?

GoodTimesOnly:
OMG, please tell me you're not being a bitch *baby emoji*

about a thirty-minute date that you were basically on and actually saw me leave, alone.

What does one say to that? *Yes, Jillian, it did actually piss me off.* Or, *Actually, Jillian, I orchestrated us showing up at O'Donnell's because after your call with your old man, it became a safety concern, and I shared your location with me and defend that with the fact that now that Roman knows, I don't feel like it's my responsibility, so I will again be stealing your phone to remove myself from your find a friend app, so I do not show up on every date you will inevitably be going on in the future ... until I can convince myself it's not your tits that bring me luck, of course.*

SportsManSam:
Truth, I'm not interested in any game aside from baseball, which I take very seriously. The thought of being with someone who another guy thinks he has a shot with, not my thing.

SportsManSam:
Even if that guy is a fucking tool.

GoodTimesOnly:
crying baby emoji

Jesus, good luck to the man who falls for her and tries to be "vulnerable." I call bullshit that women actually want that, and now I have proof.
GoodTimesOnly:
screen shot
The photos are of a text message between them, with him

asking if she's okay, and her thanking him for his concern. Then him asking her out again and her telling him …

GoodTimesOnly:
screen shot

Another picture comes through with her reply.

I realized that you and I are looking for two completely different things. You want love; me a good time when I can squeeze it in. Best of luck, truly.

SportsManSam:
Straight and to the point, but still …

GoodTimesOnly:
eye roll emoji *zzzz's*

SportsManSam:
*On a completely different *music note* congrats on the new venture.*

GAME ONE AGAINST THE TWINS, no RBIs and only one run in.

SportsManSam:
So …?

GoodTimesOnly:
I send you a titty pic, you better make sure my vibrator's in my room at Rome and CeCe's tomorrow.

SportsManSam:
finger emoji *left arrow emoji* pinky promise.

GoodTimesOnly:
titty pic

Game two against the Twins, 2 RBIs, made it home twice, zero outs.

I SNEAK away from the boys and belly up to the bar, hoping to get Jillian's attention before they notice.

Walking toward me, she holds up a hand for me to give her five? Whatever, fine.

I tap her hand.

"Good game, Uyar."

"Gonna grab a round, but really wanted to tell you that I got busted trying to sneak your little buddy into your room today."

She arches a brow. "Really? Is that going to be your story?"

"One hundred percent truth, and the fact I know your RV is locked because I was trying to put it in there—"

"Okay, fine, but I want it back."

"Meet me out back after your shift, and I'll put it right in your hot little hand."

"I think you can be more creative than that."

I look at her sexy, red glossy lips. "Yeah?"

She shrugs. "You, maybe not. But SMS, he most definitely has the capability."

THE SKIES LIT the fuck up at two in the morning, and the rain began coming down in buckets. The forecast, it's not letting up until dawn.

Vibe in my pocket, umbrella over my head, and blanket tucked under my arm, I make my way into the larger of the two barns and up to the second floor, set on being creative.

I watched her dot move from the bar all the way to our street, and when she pulls in, I send her a message.

<u>SportsManSam</u>:
Look up.

16

JILLIAN

Rain

JILLIAN

LOOK UP...

The rain is falling harder, and between the wiper's intervals, I see him standing in the open barn door.

He's there, he's gone, he's there. He's gone. Lightning flashes and awakens me from a mini trance.

I pull the hood of my raincoat up, grab my bag, and throw the door open, squealing as the raindrops flood my face.

Inside, there are tiny little tea lights glowing from the back of the barn, ascending the stairs. The fact he's up there and not meeting me down here makes the little wings that carry the millions of baseballs soar through the air, all gathered in my belly and moving me forward.

Heart pounding with anticipation, I float to the stairs and up them. Seeing him standing here in absolutely nothing with the storm lighting him up from behind is a sight to behold. I feel it so deep inside of me that my body tenses, tightens, and … aches with need for his touch and the desire to touch him.

Standing in front of him, he makes quick work of ridding me of my clothes, and when our lips meet, I feel so connected to everything around me, but mostly him.

When he touches my hand, it feels as if lightning surges from my fingertips to the bottom of my feet. When he palms my breasts, lightning courses through them and pulls at my core. When he pinches my nipples, every ounce of blood pools between my legs, and my clit, it catches fire.

I cry out into his neck as my body shakes when his fingers enter me, that fire burning hotter.

Rubbing his crown between my slick folds does nothing but make me want him even more, want him closer, as close as he can possibly get.

"Tell me you want my cock."

"I … I … want …" I moan as he hitches my knee up.

"Tell me now. Tell me you want me to fuck you. Tell me how bad you want my cock."

"Jesus," I whimper.

"Tell me," he insists.

"I want you to fuck me."

"Tell me you want my cock," he hisses.

"I want your cock." I nip at his neck.

"That's a good girl," he says as he moves to rub his lips across mine. "And you're going to get it all damn night."

I nod.

"Say it."

I swear my pussy spasms. "I want your cock inside me all night."

"Good, because you're going to get fucked so good, so hard, that you won't give a fuck about a goddamn thing but my cock making you come for the three weeks we're on the road."

He lifts me, and I wrap my legs and arms around him,

kissing him. And when he pushes his lips against mine, I dig my fingers into his shoulders and bite his lip.

He opens his mouth as he bends down and lays me out on a blanket. Then moves so he's kneeling between my legs. I can't stop myself from rubbing against him, whimpering at the heat growing inside of me.

Leaning forward, he grips the back of my head and pulls my mouth to his. His tongue rushes in and takes control of my feeble attempt at a kiss. He licks inside my mouth, strokes my tongue with his, and doesn't stop.

He pulls me up against him harshly, one hand cupping my ass, still licking and tasting me just like he does between my legs. It's all-consuming, and I wouldn't want it any other way.

He reaches between us, lines his cock up to my entrance, and slowly, so fucking slowly, pushes in while laying me back down.

"Fuck," he groans, throwing his head back when he's seated so deep that it's almost impossible to inhale, and it feels so … full, so good. I don't know if I care.

He moves, placing his elbows on either side of my head, stroking my hair as he whispers, "You are so much more beautiful without that mask."

"Hard call," I exhale, and he smiles.

That smile, it does something to me. Everything clenches. Hell, my soul does. And in that moment, I get it. I get how people can mistake this for love and want so badly for it to be real that they'd give up everything, even their dreams to stay just like this forever.

We both begin to move. Our hands are everywhere, our mouths greedy to steal the next kiss and give the first, the next, and yes, the last orgasm. And yes, we fuck just like that, all night long.

Two Weeks Later...

"THIS PLACE IS FABULOUS!" Francesca says, taking in the apartment. "Two weeks is all this took?"

"Two weeks of sixteen-hour workdays. This was the one Burt was going to use as an Air BNB because we're so close to the stadium. Meaning, it was a gift. The others, they'll need to be totally gutted," I explain.

"So, when are you moving in?" Fawna asks.

"Oh no, this will be Lena's place." I shake my head. "I can't believe she's eighty and taking those stairs a dozen times a day."

"That's probably why she looks like she does." Fawna laughs. "Note to self: take the fucking stairs."

"I'm sorry, I'm a selfish bitch, but *I'd* live here, and I'm admittedly a diva."

I wipe my hands on my pants. "Okay, I'm ready to sign my life away."

"Sweetheart, your life's worth a hell of a lot more than a quarter of a million dollars." Francesca rolls her eyes.

"I'm here. Sorry I'm late. A little chihuahua came in, looking for a home, and I couldn't tell her no. Give me a sledgehammer." Amira shrugs off her coat and looks around, eyes landing on the TV. "Wow, I'm very late. This is stunning, and it even has cable already hooked up."

"Four more upstairs," Fawna explains, grabbing her bag. "All right, ladies, I'm heading to the bar."

I grab the pen and start signing on the dotted lines, deciding to break the news to Amira. "You're actually not late; you're a day early."

"Oh my, I am terribly sorry."

"Don't be sorry. Stick around. You're about to witness one of those moments that you'd never see on the evening news." She nods to the door. "Justice and Gabrielle just showed up. You should go get Lena."

"WHY YOU STILL HERE? It's late," she asks as she opens the door.

"I wanna show you something. Will you come with me?"

"I come with you, yes. But right back. My shows." She brings the hammer down like the umps do when they call an out. "No baseball."

I love her sense of humor, and I really love that I figured out that she isn't speaking to the plants to nurture their growth; she's mostly talking shit about everyone who pisses her off.

I respect that.

When we walk into the apartment, her eyes light up. "You make beautiful. Big monies. Burt never sell."

When she spots Gabrielle Steel, in person and not on a video call, her eyes mist, and so do Gabrielle's.

They hug, and they talk in a language that I am excited to be able to use what I know and learn more from this amazing woman.

Gabrielle waves me over. "You're one hundred percent sure this is what you want? Because after this, tu eres mi familia."

"One hundred and ten percent."

Gabrielle explains that I have bought the business and property. She explains that this apartment we're standing in is part of her employment and retirement package, and then she tells her that, together, we're going to make sure she becomes a citizen of the United States.

She cries, I cry. Hell, I think Justice Steel may have shed a tear or two.

STANDING in the middle of a now wide-open room, panting and exhausted, we wait for the dust to settle.

I look at the time, and then to Amira, who has removed her mask, a stunning smile spreading across her face.

"You won't be smiling tomorrow. It's two in the morning."

"It's two in the morning sounds horrible. It's two in the morning, and the entire flat is wide open makes it sound far more appealing." She holds up a hand, and I give her a high-five. "No gym for me tomorrow."

"No yoga?" I ask, knowing how much she loves it.

"I'll find the time and space for yoga." She smiles. "One day, I'll get you to join me."

"When this place is done, I'll take you up on that."

"Then fencing."

"You fence?" I call back as I walk to grab a bottle of water.

"My brother got me into it."

"Nour fences?"

"Not Nour. Alton, his twin."

I'm standing here, trying to keep my jaw from hitting the floor as she unzips her Tyvek suit and pulls out her phone.

"Alton, his wife, and son, Burak, was named after our father."

"Not identical," I casually observe.

"Not alike at all, actually." She smiles as she continues to scroll through the pictures of her family, and she doesn't stop; she goes all the way back to pictures of Nour at a college formal.

"Oh my God, tell me he wasn't a frat boy."

"Of course he was. They both were."

"Same university?"

"All of us attended undergrad at Brown. Our parents are alumni."

"Your brothers have the same taste in women."

"Ah, yes." She nods then shakes her head.

"Wait. Can I just see that—"

"You can, or you can ask the question you want to ask."

"Sisters?" I ask, even though I fear that's not the truth.

"That would have made things much easier."

Oh damn.

"The way No-no looked at her, he was in love. This hurt him a great deal."

"No-no?"

"I swear to you, when our parents were away, which was often, and I was tasked to watch them, chasing him, that was all I had time to say to him. He's always been wound up tight."

She stares at the picture for several seconds then shakes her head. "Look at the way they both look at each other, with such love. I will never understand where love goes when it dies."

"I'm sure it becomes part of the walls we all build to try to protect ourselves, stopping from that kind of pain."

"Or perhaps it's like the fireflies that dance all summer long, that we marvel over until, suddenly, they're gone again. Then, suddenly, they're back, lighting up the darkest of nights."

She shows me another picture. "Look how unfeeling he is in this, and this, and this. That light was gone for so long that I didn't think I'd ever see it again." She shows me another picture. "Look at this one from right before they left. It's coming back. I think my No-no is returning."

"Of course he is, and I bet it's because his sister is now living here."

ME:

> You boys almost lost it tonight. You better get your heads back in the game.

ROME:

A win's a win. We'll take it.

AJ:

We're missing the Hart cheering section.

I GET a FaceTime request from Blaze and hit *accept*.

"Congrats Jags!" I hold up my foam finger and cheer. "Whoop-whoop."

"Look at this place?" He turns the camera and scans the crowd in the bar they're in. "More Jags fans than Pirates."

"They know what's up!" I wave my finger at him again.

Rome and CeCe pop on.

"You're coming to New York for one, right?"

"Damn right, I am."

AJ leans into the screen. "If we win the first, don't come to game two; come to three, okay?"

I give him a thumbs-up as I look around the screen, trying to catch a peek at SMS, who hit a triple tonight, no doubt partially due to the pink vibe between the tits pic with my new piercings and the custom-made baseball bat barbells that just came in.

But when I do see him … I really wish I hadn't.

I end the call and send a text.

ME:

> Shitty service. You guys have fun tonight. Wrap 'em tight.

17

NOUR

New York was a Bust

Nour

NEW YORK WAS A BUST. I get Jillian hadn't seen her mom in a month, but from what I gathered, that was some planned force separation. We didn't hook up in the City, and I was looking forward to it. Sucked. But what sucked worse was the realization of how badly I wanted her.

Something changed for me that night in the storm. I knew it then but tried to deny it. The only way to prove the theory that storms heighten the experience is to do it again, right?

Night one of our first home series in three weeks against Chicago, we lost. I struck out for the first time in months. Game two, Coach started Masters and Henley. When Bennett and I went in at the top of the fifth, we were down by four. We managed to tie it up. Game three, Coach waited too long to put us back in, and we lost by one.

Three nights home, and we didn't hit O'Donnell's once, so there was no good excuse to take it off the app. But I tried. I shot my shot, and she shot it down, reminding me that my batting average was now in the top twenty-five of the entire league and raised the question: why ruin a good thing?

With one day off until we played Arlington and the Shaw/Hart house full of … well, Harts and Shaws, I was desperate to get my hands, along with other appendages, on and in her, but Slugger Row wasn't an option, as we were now at max capacity. Rudy G. was now next door, Cody Vander's next to him, and Henley and Masters at the other end. Hell, I even thought of testing fate with another barn meetup, but that was thwarted when I woke up to the sound of work crews in the backyard.

"What the fuck is going on out here?" I ask absolutely no one as I walked out on the back deck.

"Morning, neighbor." Rudy G.'s voice startled me, but that was nothing compared to the shock I felt when I noticed, with the exception of a worn-out ball cap, he's butt-ass naked and worse—sporting morning wood.

"G., what the fuck is that?"

He looks down. "It's like a dick, only bigger."

"There are ladies around here," I hiss. "You can't be out here like that."

Hudson Hart makes a surprise appearance and yells, "My eyes! My fucking eyes! Put that shit away!"

Chuckling, Rudy removes his hat and hangs it on his dick. "Gonna need to get the 4-1-1 on who else is an early riser on The Row and the lay of the land so I can adjust my schedule for non-game days." He nods to the back. "Hart building another row?"

Then comes a sexy morning rasp. "That's CeCe's property. They're putting in a pool." Jillian walks past Hudson toward his vehicle, smiles at me, and nods. "Morning, Uyar. Morning … Jesus, Galleon, that's an awful place to put a hat hook."

"Look away, Jillian, look away." Hudson grabs her shoulders and moves her forward.

Laughing, she yells back, "And a privacy fence!"

"It's early morning in June, Mr. Galleon," Linda Hart says, eyes on her kids and not over here. "You may catch a chill and drop your hat."

"Mom." Jillian laughs.

"Athletes shouldn't play with their health in season," she responds.

"G., put on some fucking clothes," Roman says as he follows behind his mother. "Didn't realize I needed to put that in the fucking lease agreement."

"It's part of my off-day routine," Rudy G. calls to Rome.

"Needs to change," he calls back.

"Where you all heading?" comes from way down the row. Masters.

"Hart family counseling," Hudson calls back as he slides into the driver's seat. "Going to bust down some walls."

"That's ... healthy," Masters replies.

I hear my phone spout off and turn to head back in and grab it.

"Just me asking why we weren't invited."

I look up and see Bennett leaning out the window.

Hudson slows to a stop beside the back deck, and the rear window rolls down.

Jillian leans out and looks up at Blaze. "Trust me; you don't want to be part of this. It's messy and dusty, and you could wake up sounding like me."

"So, we can come if we want?" he asks.

"Of course you can," Linda calls out. "She's just advising against it."

"Can I come, too?" Rudy calls.

"I'm sorry, Rudy. This not only requires clothing, but Tyvek and masks. I'm not sure it's your scene."

"Your dick dropped your hat, G.," Blaze says right before closing his window.

"Dinner tonight. We're grillin'." Rome winks.

"What should we bring?" I ask.

"Yourselves," Linda answers. "Rudy, clothing is not optional for dinner. Pants are a requirement, dear."

They all laugh as Hudson throws it in drive and pulls out.

Inside, AJ is bent over and facedown on the island. "I need coffee or sleep."

"We'll get coffee on our way to grab Tyvek and masks," Bennett says. "Now, get dressed; we're going to family therapy."

"You sound way too excited for—"

"Begged my parents for years to go, so you bet your ass I am."

THE SIGN on the door reads, "Etta's is closed on Sundays, Mondays, and Tuesdays. Wednesday through Friday, they're open from eight to five, and Saturdays from nine to noon."

The one below is a Help Wanted sign with a handwritten addendum added to it:

Long-haired freaky people, please apply.

"Someone loves 90's rock." AJ laughs as he opens the door and steps in.

"You here to help?" a tiny woman asks.

"We are," I confirm.

"Follow me. Don't touch flowers, or I touch you with broom," she says then hurries past the counter. "Chop, chop."

We follow her through an area where they obviously make arrangements to a door she opens that spills into a hallway. She points to a closed door that reads, "Lena's Home."

"Stay out," she warns, shaking her fist at us. Then she points up. "Two floors. Follow noise."

"Yes, ma'am."

The music stops as we start up the stairs.

"Jillian wins," Linda says.

"Damn right, I do. I choose Rome on drums, Mom on the electric guitar, and Hudson on vocals."

"Obvious choice." He chuckles.

"I'm on acoustic." Jillian giggles, and I like that sound too much.

"What the fuck are they doing?" Blaze whispers.

"Shh, just listen," AJ replies.

"They have a band?" Blaze asks.

The music starts, and Hudson laughs. "Fuck you, Jillian."

"Uh, uh, uh," Linda says. "It's Jillian's choice, fair and square."

We all fall into line and creep up the stairs as guitar music plays. When we reach the top floor, there's plastic hung. Through it, we can see four figures lined up, backs to us.

AJ pushes the plastic aside, and we all fight back, laughing at seeing Jillian play air guitar.

Blaze grins. "Tesla's 'Love Song.'"

Linda starts playing the electric air, and Hudson, well, he's on lead, but he's actually singing.

I realize I'm vaguely familiar with the song when Rome enters with his … air sticks. This is so fucked up, but oddly entertaining.

When Linda's big solo begins, she turns around and sees us, but she doesn't stop. Instead, she nods for us to come in.

They all turn around, and although surprised, they don't stop. They just laugh.

"Can't stop once you start—those are the rules." Rome rolls his eyes. "Enjoy the show."

"Could use some backup singers," Linda says, not missing a beat.

AJ holds out his hand. "Throw me a mic."

Hudson tosses him an imaginary one, and Blaze looks at me. "I don't know the words, but if you do—"

"Throw me one, too."

I watch them all acting like total fools, looking completely ridiculous and having a great time.

When the song ends I clap, and cheer, and whistle while they all laugh and high-five each other.

"Okay, break's over," Jillian announces. "One wall down, a shit ton left to go. If you don't wanna get messy or don't know what you're doing and could screw up the brick behind the sheetrock, that's cool; just stay out of our way." She grabs a sledgehammer and heads toward a wall.

Hudson points to her. "Center walls don't have brick behind them, but there are wires. The electricity's off, but we're salvaging what we can. Shit's expensive." He stops when she sings, and it's hot as fuck watching her.

"Support beams, don't fucking touch them," Rome says. "Wire's nothing compared to a roof coming down." He swings and smashes through a wall.

"If you don't mind getting dirty"—Linda picks up a fallen piece of sheet rock—"and have descent aim"—she leans out of one of the open windows and throws the arm load of sheetrock out—"and can hit your mark, the dumpster is down there."

"Crew votes on who did the most every thirty minutes. Winner gets to choose the next song," Jillian adds.

The three of us suit up and jump in. I make damn sure not to win the round.

"AJ Tereira, you're the winner!"

"Load up 'Walk This Way,' Run DMC's version." He points to Linda. "You and I on lyrics."

"Jillian and Hudson on acoustic, Nour on bass, Rome on drums. Bennett, you get boards."

I scrub a hand over my face and mumble, "Fuck me."

If I wasn't ready for that, nothing could have prepared me for Bennett's pick.

"I see where this is going, Bennett. And, although we've promised Mom we'd let Jillian do her grown-ass woman shit, I will suffer her wrath if you do this, you sick, filthy bastard."

Bennett smirks. "Oh, dang, you think I'm picking Jillian for lead?"

"You pick Mom, and I will throw you out the window, into the dumpster, and gladly do the time," Rome threatens.

"You two are way off base. I'm doing lead."

Everyone busts up laughing, and then … then Bennett's song begins.

"Oh, baby, baby, how was I supposed to know …"

THEY KICKED us out by noon, and all four of us hit yoga, and then did some PT.

When I walk out of the shower, Blaze is showing Zandor the video of his performance, proud as hell.

"Looks like the Jags need to add a new dance to the set list, huh?"

Blaze shrugs, now trying to act cool. "I mean, what would it hurt to mix it up, right?"

"You get mine?" AJ asks.

"Sure did." He smiles.

"You guys moonlighting as contractors or putting together a band?" Amias asks.

"Rome's sister—Jillian—bought a property. Just helped out a little."

"Good of you. What did she buy?"

"Flower shop. Has a few apartments she's fixing up." I grab a pair of cargo joggers, drop the towel, and step into them.

"Hart's sister's a romantic." He nods. "Guess you gotta be with a name like that."

I laugh. "Not sure that's true. She was swinging a sledgehammer all morning."

"My girl, Georgie, will play in mud puddles wearing princess gowns." He laughs. "I was so quick to put girls in a box growing up."

I nod. "Barbie. *You can be anything.*"

Laughing, he snaps his fingers. "And change in the blink of an eye."

We finish dressing, and he sighs loud enough to grab my attention.

"You good?" I ask.

"I am. You?"

"Of course."

He turns and grips my shoulder. "You sure?"

"I'm not catching what you're throwing."

He chuckles. "Got it."

I narrow my eyes at him, and he winks.

"You need an ear, I have one to lend." Then he walks away.

I see Pope eyeballing me and Locke, too.

"You two good?" I ask.

"Damn good. See you tonight."

"Tonight?"

"Barbeque at the Shaw/Hart home." Pope winks.

"Texas in Jersey, baby." Locke laughs.

"WELL, SHIT," AJ says as we pull into the driveway. "The landscapes changed since eight a.m."

"You think that's a less than subtle hint they don't want us next door?"

I point. "The gate right there literally says otherwise."

We park and get out, hearing CeCe's niece belly laughing.

"Elle, be gentle or your freedom will be short-lived." CeCe laughs.

"She's giving you kisses." Chloe, CeCe's sister, laughs, too.

"Howdy, neighbors," Danny, Chloe's husband, calls from the back porch. "Want a beer?"

I nudge Bennett. "See?"

His lips twitch up. "Yeah, yeah, yeah."

LINDA HART, CeCe, Rome, AJ, Bennett, Cora, Locke, Gwen, Marks, Pope, Whit, Danny, Chloe, and Aggie—the little fam that developed when the fire and shit went down with the Shaw girls—are all here. But that's not all; the newbies from Slugger Row—Rudy G., Vanders, Henley, Masters—and CeCe's friends—Fawna and Francesca—and my sister, Amira, which is an added surprise—are also in attendance.

Twenty plus people in the now fenced in backyard where Elle and Aggie take turns chasing one another in circles, all laughing and having a great time. Twenty plus people, and I'm waiting on one.

Roman got a text from Hudson not to wait for him and Jillian to start dinner. They stall for a while, but eventually, they place platters of the meat Danny barbequed on the tables.

The back porch and picnic tables are all overflowing with great food and drinks. Music is playing in the background, and they've hung a movie screen on the back of the barn. People slowly start to fill their plates and sit down.

CeCe and Bennett are laughing when the screen lights up, but it's hard to see what's on it since the sun has yet to fully set.

"Oh shit," AJ coughs into his fist as the videos Bennett took at Jillian's place start to roll.

"This is what we walked in on," Bennett announces.

"He's coming out of his shell," Amira notes.

"I didn't sign a waiver, did you?" I turn around as Hudson and Jillian open the gate from the driveway and walk in, both fresh from a shower.

"You get a lot done?" Linda asks, walking over and hugging each of her kids.

Jillian nods in our direction. "The apartment we started is done."

"Please tell me there's more. It was an invigorating workout. Better than any Orange Theory class I've taken."

Amira was with Jillian?

"We'll have a sign-up sheet for the second floor's sessions soon." Hudson nods to the screen. "We've added to the structure of the program. So, BYO instrument."

"The side we worked on?" AJ asks.

"Finished." Jillian smiles. "Cora's dad's working on the electric this week, and then I get to start the fun part."

"We'll help, right?" Amira nudges me.

"Oh." Jillian shakes his head. "Nour doesn't play an instrument, so—"

"Nonsense. He's a classically trained pianist from the age of four all the way through college."

"Amira," I grumble.

"So, you think you're too good to play in an air band then?" Hudson nods. "Well, let me tell you something, Mr. Classically Fucking Trained …" He pauses and then laughs. "You're probably right."

18

JILLIAN

Of Course He Is

JILLIAN

NOUR UYAR IS DEFINITELY a fuck boy, but he's a different kind of fuck boy than I was expecting—the most lethal of all kinds. The kind even a grown-ass woman like me, Jillian Hart, could even fall for.

"You okay?" Cora asks, sitting beside me on the double chaise lounge.

"Exhausted, but yeah." I turn to my side and ask, "You?"

"I got in."

"You got in?" I ask, confused.

"Rutgers, I got in."

Squealing, I sit up and pull her into a hug. "Congrats!"

"You're not mad?"

"Mad? Are you freaking insane? I'm ecstatic for you."

"I have to live on campus the first year, and that means I won't be able to live in our fabulous penthouse until a year from now."

"Don't even worry about that. Our fabulous penthouse

probably won't be done for a year, anyway." I pull her into a tighter hug. "And if you love college, stay, immerse yourself in it. Enjoy every minute of it. Kiss all the frat boys and frogs until you find the Prince Charming who lets you be the most fabulous version of Cora Parker."

"Are you crying?"

"Maybe a few tears, but trust me when I tell you that it's not you; it's me. Every muscle in my body is screaming at me." Laughing, I sit back. "How do Chloe and CeCe feel about their little sister going to Rutgers?"

"I told you first." She shrugs. "It's not a big—"

I throw two fingers in my mouth and whistle as I stand up. "Cora has an announcement to make." I reach down and pull her up.

"Oh my God, it's not a big deal."

"It totally is."

She reaches into the pocket of her little skater dress and pulls out what I assume is the envelope containing her acceptance letter. "I got in!"

"You what?" Chloe covers her mouth.

"Rutgers pulled me off the waitlist. I can go to school if I want."

"You want!" CeCe laughs. "You so want."

I hop down as CeCe and Chloe run over, and then it's a Shaw sister hug, cry, celebrate, and snuggle fest.

"You okay?"

I look over my shoulder and up, finding Nour Uyar's dark eyes filled with concern.

"I'm great. You?"

"You look like the walking dead."

"Another one of those things every girl wants to hear from the major league player in the top fifteen now for RBIs and one of the top ten catchers in the league."

"Fuck him." He chuckles. "SMS does better with the ladies."

Keeping my eyes on the crowd, I reply in a neutral tone, taking care to hide any inflection of emotion, which is easier due to the fact I actually feel like the walking dead. "I don't know about that. You did okay in Pittsburgh."

He moves to stand beside me and lifts his beer to take a drink. "I'm not sure what you're talking about."

As he takes a swig, I remind him, "Bennett FaceTimed while you all were having a good time at a bar?"

He swallows down his drink. "We hit bars after wins in every town, just like we do here. Part of the routine. And you know how I feel about my routines."

"I do." I smile up at him, and he smiles back. "I did notice something, though."

"Do tell." He looks down at my lips.

"I mean, it's nothing scientific, but you played better that night then the next day."

"Didn't get a picture that night."

"No, that's not it. There have been plenty of nights you haven't gotten one and played your ass off the next day." I look away.

"Okay, I'll bite. What was it you noticed?"

"During Bennett's call, you were behind him, standing at a table, leaning down, face buried in blonde hair. My theory? Blonde's not your color."

I begin to step away, and he grabs my elbow, stopping me. "Is that jealousy I sense?"

"Not at all. Just an observation." I pull my elbow away and head toward the girls.

"Hey," Fawna calls to me, and I gladly head in her direction.

"Hey yourself."

"What was that?"

I look around. "Did I miss something?"

"You may have, but Hudson's shooting daggers at Nour, whose eyes are glued to you."

I glance at Hudson and, sure enough, he is.

"Girl, I got it, but you and I are gonna have a real talk about this soon."

She walks over to Nour and whispers in his ear, and then she throws her head back in a laugh as she hooks her arm through his and pulls him in the other direction.

I look at Hudson, who exhales and shakes his head, laughing as he heads toward me.

"I was two minutes from throwing down, thinking you and Nour were doing some shit behind the scenes."

"Not for nothing, but who I do behind the scenes shit with has nothing to do with you or Rome."

"Jillian, you're kidding, right?"

"I'm not a little girl anymore. I'm not a virgin. I have a favorite position, and—"

He covers my mouth with his big paw. "I never want to hear the words favorite position out of your mouth again."

I roll my eyes, and he moves is hands.

"Fine, it's not our business, whatever. But teammates?" He shakes his head. "That's a line you can't cross. It fucks up trust and makes you question loyalty."

"I'm too tired to debate why that is some backward thinking bullshit—"

"That's because you've never been in a locker room, listening to your boys talk about the chick he fucked the night before in graphic detail."

"I really hope you know I'd never be with a man who shares details like that with sixty of his closest friends." I shake my head. "I'm going to bed. I love you, even though you're a fucking neanderthal at times."

<u>SportsManSam</u>:
New series, I need a new pic.

THIS MOTHERFUCKER.

<u>SportsManSam</u>:
And an apology.

Oh, hell no!

<u>SportsManSam</u>:
Sending a voicemail, which is above us, but clearly, you need it.

A blacked-out video comes through.

"So, that blonde in Pittsburgh, did you exchange numbers?"

"Yeah, no shit, Bennett, we haven't heard a damn thing about your first time."

"Don't be daft. It wasn't my first time. No numbers were exchanged, and she won't be sliding into my DMs."

"That bad?" Nour asks.

"I require more of a show, I suppose."

"Probably best you do your own introduction then." Again, Nour.

"Or you could just do better," Bennett states. "I'm going to bed."

A few minutes later, I hear AJ chuckle. "You think he's got, like, split personalities?"

The video ends, and I reply.

GoodTimesOnly:
My mistake.

And yes, I send a picture, knowing it's the last one.

SportsManSam:
I think we need to talk.

GoodTimesOnly:
Not tonight, and not tomorrow night, unless you win.

THEY WON.

The bar is packed, the money's rolling in, and I'm doing one hell of a job pretending Nour Uyar's not here. Thankfully, it's so busy there hasn't been time to be questioned by Fawna about that, and I didn't have to have the conversation at closing due to an influx of online orders for the flower shop that gives me the perfect excuse to duck the hell out. Not that I was in any yank to do this part, either, but it's unavoidable, just like the end is.

He and I are meeting here at Etta's when he can sneak out. Secretly, I hope he doesn't get the chance because it's going to be … uncomfortable as hell.

Sitting on a stool in the back, the doorbells chime, and I know he's here.

I look up as he walks through the shop, around the counter, and enters what we now refer to as the studio.

"Good game tonight, number ten."

He pulls out a stool, sits across from me, and smirks. "White sage."

"A hundred online orders for tomorrow. I suppose I have you to thank for incorporating that in your opener."

"Not sure you should thank me since it's you who is stuck doing the work." He nods to the red thread. "Baseball stitching?"

"-ish." I shrug.

"How many more to go?"

"I shut off the online order, so until we run out."

"Worth it?" he asks, watching my hands.

"Fifty to seventy percent profit on everything we sell. Two hundred orders covers Lena's pay and lots of items needed for the projects upstairs. So yeah, of course." I raise my hand and wiggle my gloved fingers. "I prefer not to spread my bad juju to others."

He shakes his head, a slight smile on his perfect freaking lips. "You have a lot of projects going on right now."

"Which brings us to why we're here." I set down the finished smudge stick and meet his eyes whioeI remove my gloves.

"We got off course with your project, I think." He acknowledges.

"Diving headfirst into the deep end of the pool," I joke.

His lips twitch in a two-second smile. "Not gonna work without trust."

"Not gonna work without getting irritated by the unwelcome appearance of that little green monster. My bad."

"Pretty sure I brought him onboard when Masters entered the scene." *He's not wrong.* "You and I fucked around and found out, little Hart."

I smile and laugh out, "That we did."

"Did what, exactly?" he asks.

I shake my head. "We did a lot."

"Oh, I see." He chuckles.

"You see what?" I ask, tossing it right back at him.

"Okay, okay." He leans across the work table and grabs both my hands. "I'm man enough to admit I don't dislike you as much as I did the day after."

"Fine." I roll my eyes. "I will admit I don't think you're an evil genius set out to destroy Rome's career."

He shakes his head. "That's crazy thinking. It would ruin mine, too."

I pull my hands back and nod. "And that's why we can't anymore."

He scrubs a hand over his face. "Saw that coming. Didn't expect it to—"

"No need to say it. Makes it … weirder."

"Fawna question you tonight?" He asks.

"Too busy, thank God." I smile, thankful for the shift in subject. "Stupid for me not to ask you what you said so I could corroborate the story."

"Well, I, uh … I wasn't thinking that quickly at the moment."

"Oh man, what did you say?"

"Told her that I was interested in you, and you weren't reciprocating."

My jaw drops. "What the hell were you—"

"I wasn't. I wasn't thinking. A few drinks, and yeah, I fucked up." His fist clenches his shirt, and he tugs at it, his irritation evident and so un-Nour-like. I don't like it, not at all. "I've been fucking up a lot lately."

"Just stop, okay? Just shut up and, like … stop. It's okay to feel and be unprepared and wing it. She won't say anything, and whatever. Just shut up."

I'm not sure when I got up or when I moved around the table. I don't know who kissed who first or how I ended up laid across the countertop. I don't remember my clothes being removed or removing his. I don't remember the details at all.

But I will never forget the sound of the thunder, the rain against the windows, or the feel of him inside me. I will never forget following his taillights all the way back to CeCe's, the sound of the wipers swishing back and forth, and wondering why the fuck they didn't work, why I couldn't see, and the realization that it wasn't the rain or the wipers. It was tears. And I will never forget that is when I knew I had fallen in love with Nour Uyar that night in the barn, in the rain.

Nour hit his second major league grand slam the next day and has hit a home run in every game since.

One Month Later…

WHO WOULD HAVE THOUGHT that me, of all people, would owe everything to a superstition.

White sage, wrapped in baseball stitching, has kept me so busy I can hardly breathe, let alone pine after Nour Uyar, who is killing it his first year in the majors. Bonus, I have zero hard feelings toward the guy I gave my virginity to, and I'm not losing myself because I fell in love or suffered heartbreak.

Etta Harts now has two part-time employees and the sweetest marketing student doing her internship here, and she is so trustworthy that I am taking a week off to go to Blue Valley. When I return, Lena is taking her first trip to Mexico in thirty years to visit her sister who is still alive at eighty-nine.

"You sure about me staying in your apartment? You've only stayed two nights," Helene —my right hand— asks.

"Of course, I am," I answer, throwing clothes into a bag.

The bathroom wasn't supposed to be done until I got back, but I'm not complaining about it. I'm stoked I had the money to hire someone to get it done.

"Use the tub. Soak, enjoy, drink, and read in it. Life changing." I hitch my bag over my shoulder and give her a hug. "Don't forget the last order goes out—"

"By ten. I know." She opens the door. "Go, go, go. Your mom's waiting."

19

NOUR

Play-Offs Bound

Nour

WE MADE THE PLAYOFFS, and I should be as high on it as the rest of the team, but I'm fucking exhausted and looking forward to the season ending, and not just in terms of baseball.

In July, at a pool party celebrating Rome and CeCe's engagement, surrounded by couples, I had a fucked-up breakdown. Drunk and angry, I was pissed at myself for betraying Rome's trust and could never make amends.

All these months later, I'm still pissed that I can't tell Jillian her project led me to realize I could one day trust a woman again. Because I do, I trust her. And now I love a woman I can't have.

I may be the selfish prick my parents painted me to be for loving this game, but it didn't mean I couldn't love it and a woman the right way, too. This had nothing to do with the game. It was all about them and their fucking perfect image.

Fuck Alton and his opportunistic charades, his manipulative ways, and my ex for buying into it all.

The right woman wouldn't leave me knowing I was walking away from a multimillion-dollar trust fund. Money wouldn't mean shit.

My anger peaked that night at the pool party. Thankfully Leland and Gwen Locke got me the hell out of there before I broke and confessed to Rome.

The next day, hungover, I went to the gym, and Xavier and Tris were there talking about music. And, for some reason, I told them I played piano.

One was in the clubhouse the next day, a day in which we had a rain delay. Patrick and Xavier Steel played, Tris and her boys, Nico and Nash, and Brand and Cooper Falcon played. Xavier whispered something to Cooper, and he came over and dragged me to the piano.

It had been ages. I'd avoided it because it'd been expected of me, something for my parents to boast about. As a joke, I started playing "Raindrops Keep Falling on My Head." It started a whole thing. Xavier followed it up with CCR's "Have You Ever Seen the Rain." Tris played and sang "Purple Rain," which they live-streamed on the stadium's monitors for the Jags diehard fans out there waiting it out. Brand Falcon played and sang G&R's "November Rain." Then I played "Kiss the Rain" by Billy Meyers, which Tris sang with me because, yeah, she's good. Me, I can just get by. The clouds cleared, and my first time at bat, I hit a homerun. That song and playing, it's now on my game day list.

That trust fund I lost may have been nice, but I've surpassed that with endorsement deals over the past three months. One is with Steinway. They're designing a baby grand, white with red stitches. A limited-edition piece. A playoff win ensures they'll sell; a series win would make sure it sells out and guarantee me another year.

Aside from realizing my playing wasn't an extension of them, that it was all mine. There is no one happier that I'm playing again than Amira. We have a dinner date at least once a month at her place. She has a piano, and that's the only place, besides the clubhouse, I play. I will have to step out of those confines when I shoot the commercials for the endorsment deal

But not yet.

TRENTON IS CELEBRATING THIS WEEKEND, and the Jags are booked for appearances every day for the next week around town or doing interviews on shows and podcasts.

Tonight, I'm doing a two-hour meet-and-greet at O'Donnell's, and the press will be present.

When I walk in, I'm greeted by the cheers of a packed bar and fans who deserve the best I can give them. So, I smile, showing them the gratitude they deserve, and I keep my focus off the bar because I don't want to know if she's here and I cant be in my fucking feels right now.

I see Xavier and Patrick Steel, Amira's with them, and Tris is hiding underneath a baseball cap, which is a pleasant surprise. I will focus on them. When I see that my new agent, Drew Daniels, is also here and walking toward me, I have no idea what to think, but with her comes money, so I'm good.

"Today's a bigger day than planned, so just go with it."

"I'm going with it."

"Steinway called me last night with a wild idea. They weren't sure they could pull off. I called you three times, emailed, and sent you texts. You didn't answer," she whispers as she moves us through the crowd.

"I turned off my phone." Which I do now to stop myself from reading old messages, or checking her location. Pathetic, I know, but it is what it is.

"I figured. Zen and shit. So, again, just go with it."

I realize we're heading toward where they sometimes have a band set up and force a smile as I ask, "Are you fucking kidding me?"

"Great smile. Keep that in place. Hopefully, the joy of seeing this will shine through."

Standing in front of velvet ropes, a Steinway rep nods at me before he pulls the black fabric covering off unveiling the baby grand.

"Drew, it's—"

"Stunning, gorgeous, so much more than I ever imagined, incredible. Those are your choices. Do not veer, for fuck's sake."

"This is incredible." I continue smiling. "More than I ever imagined."

"Thank fuck," Drew says before stepping away.

"Come play us something."

"It's stunning up close. The details are incredible." None of which is a lie.

I shrug off my sports coat and toss it to Xavier, who catches it.

"'Kiss the Rain,'" someone in the crowd yells as I step over the rope and walk around the piano.

I look to Tris, whose eyes are glued to her phone, no doubt playing some game.

"I'm not here," she mumbles.

I sit down on the bench and stretch a bit, before opening the fallboard exposing the keys.

After a few more stretches, I glance at Amira, who mouths, "*Impromptus, Schubert.*"

I play a few bars and quickly realize I'm playing the wrong song for this crowd. I continue until I find as natural a transition as I can into "Piano Man" and end up playing the entirety of the song because everyone is singing along. Hell, I quickly join in, too.

When I finish, they erupt into applause.

I notice them looking behind me and glance back to where Xavier and Patrick are strapping on guitars.

"Mind if we join you?" Xavier winks.

"You know I don't mind at all."

Xavier strikes the first chord of the song requested. I join in and glance at Tris as I start singing, "*Hello, can you hear me?*"

She smiles and starts shifting in her seat, which tells me I won't be making a fool out of myself for long; she's bound to jump in.

When she does, she doesn't take the lead; she comes in on the chorus and sings harmony.

Fuck it, I think as I sing a little louder and with more confidence than my voice deserves.

The beginning of the second verse, I catch sight of Jillian and can't look away. In this moment, I don't care if she hears the words of the song stuck in my mind on repeat, accompanied with images of not her tits, but of the way she looked at me that night in the barn and that night surrounded by flowers and white sage with rain coming down outside.

When the song ends, Patrick is turning from her direction to me, and when I don't look away, he dips his head slightly. It shouldn't feel good to have possibly shared my feelings with him, but it does.

The Steinway rep walks over as I stand and shakes my

hand. We pose for a few photos, and then I head out to answer some questions.

During the question-and-answer session, I see Amira and Jillian outside on the street.

Amira has an arm around Jillian's waist, holding her back.

I stand up. "If you all would give me a minute, I need to visit the little boys' room."

I pass through the crowd and start toward the door when Fawna snatches my arm. "Bathroom's this way, Billy Joel."

"What the hell is going on?" I stand, unmoving.

"You can deal with it, but you're going out the back so this whole night isn't sullied."

"Sullied?" I ask as she drags me toward the bathroom.

"It's a word. It's in books. Pick one up."

We pass the bathroom and end up in the kitchen. Patrick and Xavier are standing by the door.

"What the hell's going on?"

"Some chick and a dude who looks a lot like you showed up. Jillian asked them to leave. Then she showed them the door." He pushes open the kitchen door. "Let's not blacken the eye of a great night."

As soon as I step out, I hear Jillian say, "You put your hands on me again, and I will fuck up your face."

"Yeah, there's going to be blackening and shit's getting sullied."

I jog toward her voice.

He doesn't even see me coming when I grab him, yank his ass back into the alley, and shove him against the brick wall.

"You put hands on her?"

"Well, hello, brother," Alton taunts.

"He didn't touch the bartender, Nour." The ex, Alara,

grabs the back of my shirt and pulls. "Get your hands off of my husband."

I don't even acknowledge her. "Jillian, did he lay hands on you?"

"He didn't put his hands on me; he tried to walk through me. This little twat put her grubby-ass, brother-fucker hands on me."

"Amira?"

"Yes, Alara did, in fact, put her grubby-ass, brother-fucker hands on Jillian," Amira says, sticking her nose in the air.

Alara screams, "This is a public establishment. She has no right to—"

"Amira," Alton says our sister's name as if it's repulsive, and I lean in just a little harder. He doesn't shut his fucking mouth, though. "The way you spoke of my wife will have consequences."

"Tell them to take my trust fund. Give it to your children," she huffs. "They'll need it to buy friends. Burek's behavior is deplorable. Perhaps Demir will—"

I watch as Jillian catches Alara's hand mid-swing.

"Do not hit her because she's speaking of something you can't handle. Face it, and fix it."

"And do it off of my property," Fawna adds.

I let go of Alton's arm and step back. "Ms. O'Donnell told you both to leave."

Alton turns and straightens his suit jacket. "We came to make peace, to attempt to fix what you broke in our family."

"You fucked my girlfriend." I laugh.

"You dirtied her name." Alton bares his teeth at me.

"Sullied," Fawna corrects him, which would be funny in any situation but this one.

"You wanna do this right here?" I ask.

"These people of yours should know who they are defending."

"I didn't dirty her name. If I wanted to do that, I'd have given graphic detail."

"You questioned the legitimacy of my son's paternity."

"You married her before I even knew we broke up. She was pregnant in a blink. You bet your ass I questioned it. No way in hell I'd let a child of mine be raised by you."

"We are the same in every way."

"Clearly not. Your vision's seriously impaired if you see Nour in the mirror," Jillian quips, then looks at Alara. "How hard do you have to squint to make *that* resemble Nour during sexy time?"

"Whore," Alara spats.

"Brother-fucker," Jillian taunts.

"I'm done here." I look at Xavier. "I have obligations inside. I hate to ask, but—"

"It's not a hardship. We'll see that the trash is taken out. You and the ladies get inside."

"*Trash?*" Alara waves her hand toward Xavier, her judgmental face pinched. "You're nothing but a painted freak."

"Love my ink and getting freaky." He winks at her.

"He owns the Jags, you twat," Jillian yells at her.

"Part-owner." He shrugs. "But don't get it twisted. To the soul, I'm painted and freaky."

"Dad, don't give this basic bitch another word." Patrick steps forward to Alton. "Get you and your wife off the property, or I'm gonna kick *your* ass."

"Fuck, man." Xavier holds his hand over his heart. "No matter how many zeros you add to your net worth, I've never been prouder of you than right now, kid."

Inside, Jillian is all but bouncing off the walls. "Fucking love them." She looks me up and down, noise scrunched up.

"You kissed that? Put your dick in her? Oh God." She covers her stomach. "You ate her pus—"

"There's a bar full of people waiting for drinks and conversation. Can we not ever finish this conversation?"

"Fine." Jillian rolls her eyes.

"Are you okay?"

"I'm not sure." She shakes her head.

"Physically?"

"Oh, hell yes. Bigger men have pushed me around," she jokes.

"I want names."

"Oh my God, the two of you should just wake the fuck up already," Fawna mumbles as she leaves the kitchen.

"You have fans waiting, pretty boy." Jillian walks by, then turns, looking me over. "Seriously, that bitch needs an eye exam."

"Are you hitting on my brother, Jillian Hart?" Amira asks, amused.

Jillian waves a hand up and down, "This guy? The major league, piano playing, trust fund baby? *Pfft*. Way out of my league." With that, she turns and leaves.

Amira crosses her arms. "That, brother, was the equivalent of a woman answering the door in the buff." She shoves me. "What is wrong with you?"

"So many things."

20

JILLIAN

Playoffs

Jillian

IT'S BEEN two weeks since O'Donnell's and my failed attempt to be cunning and sexy. I openly flirted with Nour in front of Amira, knowing that she'd tell CeCe. If I didn't want her to, I would have to specifically use the words, "Please do not tell a soul I flirted with your brother," to ensure she didn't.

That isn't because she's a gossip, nosey, or a person who loves being the first to tell others something; it's because she is passionate about people, animals, life, … everything.

So, yes, she told CeCe, and it just so happened to be in front of Rome, who has just shown up at the flower shop and asks me, "Did you come on to Nour at O'Donnell's the other night?"

"Come on to him? Ew. Phrased like that, it's like I whispered I want to ride you or let me drop to my knees and suck your—"

"Jillian, fuck." He covers his ears. "I don't want to hear that shit."

I pull his hands away from his ears. "Then don't ask stupid questions."

"It's a stupid question to have to ask, yet here I am in a situation that calls for me to straighten this shit out."

"If me flirting with a hot guy is a situation for you to straighten out, you may want to sit down and grab a notepad to take names because you're going to have a whole lot to do other than your fiancée during the off-season."

He looks like a deer in the headlights, and I can't help but laugh.

"Oh my God, Rome. I'm not a virgin. I've had sex. I've had things done to me that you yourself have probably done to CeCe. I have kinks. Being called 'good girl' is a huge turn on. Yes, that screams daddy issues, but I'm smart enough to know I happen to have them. And so what if I do?"

Still nothing.

"That list? Put Nour Uyar at the top. He's hot."

"I can't even talk to you right now. My teammate?"

"Is he too good for me?" I ask.

"Fuck no!"

"Okay, now take your time with this one and think before you *fuck no* it. Am I too good for him?"

He opens his mouth to respond.

"Think, Roman, because if not Nour, who, by the way, hasn't even looked in my direction since I flirted and came on to him. But is someone like him such a horrible thing?"

"He's my teammate, Jillian, so yes, me wanting to rip his dick off doesn't make for an ideal situation."

"Okay, so you couldn't handle it. How do you think Hudson is going to react when I'm in Blue Valley, bartending, and I see one of his teammates a few times and think, *damn, he's hot*, and, *oh, wow, he's actually a great guy*."

"You've got a better chance with me than you do Hudson, and you know that."

"All right then. I guess it's back to the dating apps and hoping I don't match up with a married man or serial killer." *Take that, brother.*

"Can't you just …" He stops then sputters, "Fuck."

"You had no issue with my date with Masters, but my failed attempt at being cute with Nour, and you're willing to push me back in the dating app closet to—"

"Masters?" he huffs. "He's no match for you. I knew you'd chew him up and spit him out."

"And you think I couldn't do the same to Uyar if I wanted to?"

He crosses his arms. "No."

"And why not?"

"Because." His jaw tightens so hard I swear he may break a tooth.

After a few moments of silence, I look up from the arrangement I'm murdering. "This is about you, and it's about Hudson, and you're making it about me."

"You really use dating apps?"

"I graduated high school, never having been kissed. I went to college and …" I shake my head. "I love you and Hudson, the best brothers a girl could ask for, but you've got to get over your shit."

"We don't want you to end up with some shitbag who's going to lay their fucking hands on you."

"And I appreciate that. But real talk? I hooked up in a hotel after messaging with a guy for a week because I wanted to get rid of my virginity and prove to myself that I can have sex, just like you guys do, and walk away if it's no longer healthy for me." I lean in a bit. "And to feel desirable, and sexy, and all those very normal feelings I knew I was missing out on."

He opens his mouth to speak, and I slap away a tear. "No. There was no question in that. And don't run to Mom, either. Let her fucking breathe and live. And Jesus, Rome, let her find her CeCe."

Again, he starts to say something.

"Rome, I love you, but I need you to leave. I'll see you after the game."

"That's not for three days."

I shrug. "I know, and I hope you really think about what I've said. I'm not going back to wondering what is wrong with me that men find so repelling. Am I that ugly? Do they only want to fuck me to get close to you and Hudson."

"That was never our intention, and you know it."

"I do know it. And I know if I had said these things to you both all those years ago, we wouldn't be doing it now because you'd understand the depth of my words, or you'd have still been trying to twat block me, but that would be real hard to do if I was in Montana, where I would have been free to be me. I'd see you all on holidays and—"

"Are you—"

I walk past him and into the store. "Helena, I'm going for a walk. Are you good?"

"We're good, boss."

I walk outside and start heading down the street.

"Jesus, Jillian, wait up."

I turn around and wait for him to catch up then give him a big hug and step back. "Three days, Roman. I need three days."

"I love you. Hudson and I fucking love you."

"That's never been in question." I smile, turn around, and walk.

Twenty minutes later, I'm no longer getting messages; my phone actually rings. It's the shop, so I answer it.

"Hello."

"So, your mom called and said you're not answering your phone. What should I tell her?" Helena asks.

"Tell her I love her and will call her when I am done taking a mental health moment."

"You good with me closing up?"

"Oh shit, is it—"

"You left right before five. No worries; I just didn't want you coming back and—"

"Go, go, go."

"Love you, Jillian Hart."

"Love you, too."

My phone rings again, and I assume she forgot to tell me something. "What's up?"

"That all I get from daddy's little Jill?"

"I am not in the mood to deal with—"

"All I want is to see my son play in the playoffs. I don't care if it's nosebleed seats, but I want them, and I damn well deserve them."

"Feel free to purchase a ticket online, like everyone else."

"Don't be a little bitch. That boy wouldn't be the athlete he is if it weren't for me."

"That *boy* is the man he is because Mom raised good men. You fucked money out of Hudson and me. We've compared notes. We're done. Bye."

"They're not the only ones who's capitalizing off of me. Your little flower shop has my mother's name on it. I know you make enough money off of your little snake oil sales to get me into the game. If you don't get me those tickets, you'll be sorry."

"I'm already sorry—sorry I answered the phone. Fuck off."

Am I freaked out? No. He can fuck off. But is it going to be getting dark, which makes everything a little freaky? Yep.

So, I turn around and start hoofing it back.

I decide on Mexican takeout, so I can go home, watch shitty reality TV, and eat my feels. Lena's favorite place is just around the block, and she's been a little down since returning from her trip, so she will appreciate it, too.

While waiting, I scroll through my emails and see one from Montana. I open and read it.

I decided to defer my acceptance instead of rejecting it all together. They want to know if I would like to start in January.

After Rome and my argument, I am taking that as a sign. The deadline is a short one, and they apologized. They shouldn't. All I need is three days.

Head spinning, I walk home, my home, one I poured blood, sweat, and tears into. Would I give it up to follow my dreams? Are my dreams the same? Could I have both? Would Helena and Lena be able to run the show without me? Would I be able to start my mornings without hearing Lena trash-talk to the plants?

Have my dreams changed because they were supposed to, or did they change because I fell for a guy?

I won't know until I sit down and make a couple charts, spreadsheets, and lists.

Laughing at myself because I am giddy with anticipation to get home to do just that, and the reality that dick and love, neither changed me.

I'm Jillian fucking Hart, and I'm a grown-ass woman doing grown-ass …

"What the fuck?" I turn to see what it is that hit me in the head, as dots spot my vision until everything goes ….

"I NEED A DOCTOR! I need a fucking doctor!"

"SHE HAS A CONCUSSION. Her pulse is strong. Her vitals are fine. She'll wake up soon."

THE BACKGROUND SOUNDS ARE UNMISTAKABLE, and so is the fucking headache.

"Did someone hit me, or did a giant bird drop an egg on my head, or worse—shit an actual brick?"

"What's your name?"

"Jillian Hart."

"Date of birth?"

"If I say today, do I get cake? Because I'm hungry, and I'm pretty sure I dropped my tacos and enchiladas."

"She's good." I feel a hand squeeze mine, and I totally recognize that voice.

"Did the Jags win the Super Bowl? The Knights win the World Series? Am I covered in bird shit?"

The sound of his low laughter makes me attempt to open my eyes, but …

"Oh my God, that light is blinding. What is wrong with all those people who walk toward it?"

"You're full of questions, Jillian," a female says, sounding amused.

"Yet, here I am, with no answers."

I feel lips on my knuckles and hear a deep inhale before Nour Uyar answers, "I can tell you that if you got tacos and enchiladas—they were gone when I found you. So was your purse and—"

"My keys." I start to sit. "Lena is—"

"She's good. Helena is there."

"How long have I been out?"

"Not long. Helena called your phone. I answered. Apparently, your mom called her cell."

"Oh God, Mom's going to freak."

"Helena told me not to call anyone unless you were going into surgery or dying."

"Someone give the girl a raise. I love her. She deserves it." I turn my head and squint up at him. "They'll show, anyway. My location is—"

"Off."

"Someone give *you* a raise." He squeezes my hand gently. "Doctor?"

"It's Dromida, Jillian."

"You can't tell Fawna. She'll tell CeCe and—"

"You're covered by doctor/patient confidentiality."

"Cool. Can I leave?"

"Hell no. You're staying at least a few more hours, and that's only if you have someone with you for the next twenty-four."

"Lena is always there."

"I'll hang out with her."

"Don't you have an interview to do or a piano to promote?"

"I'll check back in a couple hours. If you need anything—"

"Dark, a pain killer, that birthday cake."

Dromida laughs. "I'll see what I can get for you."

"You're the best." I turn toward Nour. "You're busy. Playoffs and—"

"I have a full two days off. Just have to get a workout in. I can do that anywhere."

"Nour?"

"Yeah?" He gently brushes my hair from my face.

"My dad called me half an hour before whatever happened, happened. He's—"

"You should call Rome and—"

"I'm on a break from him and Hudson for three days."

"Oh, I heard."

"What?" I snap, then cringe because snapping hurts.

"He's pissed I didn't flirt back because his sister is a—his words—fucking smoke show, and then he was pissed because you flirted with me."

I open my eyes just a little and see he's tapping on his phone. "What are you doing?"

"Telling Gwen you need her to look into some things and that it's not to reach your family."

"She's pregnant; don't bother her."

"Then you have to give them a heads-up," he says, brushing his fucking lips across my forehead.

"Can you get a hold of Marks without tipping off Gwen so she's not all stressed out?"

"I could have tried, but I may have already sent the message."

"Dude," I sigh.

"Did you just call me *dude*?"

"I mean, yeah. Is that an issue?"

"I prefer *major league, piano playing, trust fund baby*, unless me not picking up on that as you flirting, and thinking you just were trying to make me not feel like a fucking shitbag after you met the twin and the—"

"He has every right to hate you."

"I'm sorry, what?"

"You drained all the hotness out of him in the womb and kept it for yourself."

"Question?"

"Shoot."

"Was that flirting?"

"Yeah, SMS, it was."

"Good. No, not just good; great. Thank God."

"Can I go to sleep for a while?"

"Of course."

"If I say anything sexy in my sleep, or even not sexy, it's flirting."

I'm not sure I slept, but whatever it was felt peaceful.

The peace was interrupted by the police, who took my statement, and Dromida gave me a bottle of pills, which I would not need for another six hours, and then I was wheeled out and picked up at the curb.

I fell asleep surrounded in a heated seat in a vehicle that smelled like leather and Nour, both things which remind me of sex, which I would not be having until Dromida cleared me. She offered to do a house call if I paid her in enough white sage to get her through the playoffs.

Lying in my comfy bed in the dark, the only light coming in is from the doorway, and the twinkling lights of the Trenton skyline. It all seems so peaceful. But my head is aching and outside the room I hear Nour on the phone, I know it's anything but.

NOUR

Concussed

Nour

"You've got to be fucking kidding me, Gwen."

Leland Locke chimes in, "You're on speaker, *Romeo*; watch your tone with my wife, or I'm gonna call our second baseman and let him know you're obsessed with his sister."

"Do you know what a fucking position you're putting me in?" I hiss.

"Oh, we do." Gwen snorts. "We've recently been put in quite a situation ourselves."

"Except no, you haven't. My shit didn't involve hiding the fact either of your mothers was getting railed by Marks, and … no, I can't even remotely connect these situations."

"Hold up. Marks is railing *my* mother?"

My spine straightens, and I look back over my shoulder.

"Can you pretend you didn't hear that shit, Jillian, and I can maybe club myself over the head hard enough to forget it, too? For real?"

"Jesus, kid." Leland snorts, and then my phone does some shit, and I look back to fix it.

"Did you FaceTime me?"

"He did. I didn't," Gwen says. "But did we, or did we not, just hear Jillian in the background?"

"Yeah, I'm here. Concussed and curious."

"I am so fucking sorry, Jillian. I—"

"Shh, stop talking and walk it over here." She sits on her huge-ass chair that's more like a freaking … well, it is a huge chair.

"I hope you're happy," I snarl at the phone.

"Sadly, we are. This is the best entertainment we've had in—"

Jillian snags my phone. "I'm not entertained. I'm confused and—"

"Concussed, we heard." Leland chuckles.

I lean into view. "You remember warning me about being a dick to Gwen? Well, I'm giving it back. Go easy with her, or I will …" I groan as I grind my teeth together when I realize I have not even one leg to stand on.

"Yep, exactly."

"Okay, let's back things up here," Gwen says. "Jillian, a black BMW is sitting outside your place. He arrived ten minutes after Nour called. He checked out the place, checked on Lena, and checked back in with me, telling me all was good."

"Okay."

"There's a car at Rome and CeCe's, too, but that's just to make you feel better. Marks and my company handle the surveillance there; all is well."

"Thank you."

"She forgot to tell you, when Romeo had his meltdown in July over you, Gwen knew before he fessed up that he was tripping over you. Marks, he knew you two were meeting in the camper and doing the barn boogie long before we did. They're professionals. That shit's on a need-to-know basis." He grins. "I'm not, so I find this all fascinating."

Jillian looks mortified.

"Jesus, Locke." Gwen smacks him. "What he means is, after Nour messaged, asking us to look into things, I messaged Marks because you're all like family. Both of us working on this makes it move faster. Tonight is the only time we've passed this information, and, well, it seems like a clusterfuck, and it is, but everyone is safe. You are safe."

Locke chuckles, "Not sure Nour or Marks are gonna be safe when Rome and Hudson—"

Gwen elbows him again.

Jillian wipes away a tear. "Does he love her?"

I lean back and pull her against my chest, wanting to stop her worry, her pain, her fear, but right now, she not only wants but needs answers.

"I'm not sure if he even knows it yet, but I've known him all my life, Jillian, and I am sure he loves her. I'm sure he loved her that first night he saw her."

"She gave him her taco, and it was all over." Leland chuckles.

"You are not helping matters."

"No." Jillian sniffs. "I remember that night. I saw something."

Gwen grins and claps her hands. "No one is as deserving of love as he is, except maybe Linda Hart. Marks and my moms are together. They're going to freak out when they find out that Marks finally met *the one*."

"So this is his thing, then. He falls in love—"

"No." Gwen smiles. "He's never been in love, not once. No girlfriend, nothing."

"She's asking but not asking for you to give him a chance." Locke explains.

"If she's happy—"

"That's questionable right now," Gwen cuts her off. "She found out about all this much like you did. She's pissed."

"Maybe more than pissed," Locke adds.

Gwen nods in agreement and adds, "Maybe she told him it would never work if he hid things about her children."

"So, you want me to what?" Jillian asks.

"Know that you're safe, know that there are people on you and Rome, and we apparently have a guy in Blue Valley now who looks after them when Marks isn't around."

Locke leans in. "Which Gwen just found out about, and she's not pissed."

"And your mother just found out about it, too." Gwen frowns.

"So, she thinks he's possessive?"

Gwen replies, "I can't answer as to how your mom feels."

"I'm not asking you to. I'm telling you, she feels like he's a creeper."

"That's understandable, but sometimes we do things to ensure the people we love are safe," Gwen explains.

And, of course, Locke goes deeper. "Like when you have their phone and you turn on 'share my location' so you know where they are if you can't find them."

"Yeah, that's overstepping a boundary in a big way too." Jillian sniffs.

"So, you would take issue if, say, Nour wanted you to share locations with—"

"What the fuck, Locke?"

Jillian turns and looks at me. "I think he's trying to support his friend out, chill."

She looks back at the screen. "But in their situation, a new relationship ... hell no."

"I did it. Okay? You two happy now?" I ask, ready for her to flip shit, knowing I deserve it.

She turns around, brow arched. "You're stalking me?"

"When I heard your old man's call that night, I got freaked out that you wouldn't tell Rome. So ... yeah."

She narrows her eyes at me. "But then I did tell Rome."

"In my defense, it is also how I found you tonight."

"Oh, that makes it better." She rolls her eyes and then looks back at the screen. "Is there anything else I need to know?"

"Um, hold on just ... Yep. Bingo." Gwen nods. "We have tags from a street cam and"—she flips the screen—"is this your father?"

"No," I answer, feeling like I may puke. "That's my brother."

"Amira," Jillian and I both say.

"Address?"

I rattle it off as I head toward the door. "Call Amira?"

"Of course," Jillian says.

"Hold on, Nour," Gwen says.

"Fuck that, Gwen. I need—"

"Is this Jillian's father?"

"I don't know, but right now—"

"Show Jillian the phone."

"Fuck, Gwen, my sister—"

"Black BMW is pulling away from your location and heading to her. Stay put. Is this Jillian's father?"

I walk back to Jillian and hold out the phone.

"Yeah."

"Hello?" Amira's voice comes through Jillian's line.

"Hey, Amira, this is—"

"Hey, Dr. Shaw. I can't talk right now. I, um, pregnant cat."

I mouth, "*Name?*"

Jillian shakes her head and mouths back, "*What?*"

I mouth, "*Ask the cat's name.*"

"What's the cat's name?"

"Purple nerple."

I mouth, "*Fuck! Keep her talking.*"

Jillian does exactly that as I sneak into the other room.

"Gwen—"

"Yep, checking Wags surveillance, and no, she's not there. What's purple nerple?"

"Our code for Alton is seconds from going batshit crazy."

"Okay, we have Maze a block from Amira's. Quickest way in?"

"Door code, 6753."

"Perfect. He will bring her to you."

"He's fucking nuts when he's pissed."

"And Maze is an ex-Ranger. That trumps crazy any day," Gwen replies calmly. "Jillian still have Amira on the line?"

"She does."

"Good. He's going in and—"

"Oh no!"

Jillian begins to panic, and I run back to her.

"Amira, are you—"

"Amira Uyar, I'm a friend of your brother's."

"Wait for it," Gwen says.

"The hot one?" a deep voice asks.

"Fuck you!"

"All right, Alton Uyar is secure and—"

"Amira, are you okay?"

"I think so, yes. GI *Someone* just let himself into my home and is taking Alton somewhere?"

"Put me on speaker, Nour," Gwen says.

"On. Amira, are you hurt?"

"Shaken up. He's insane."

"Did he put his hands on you?"

"Oh yes, but I'm fine."

Hands shaking I growl, "I'm gonna kill him."

Gwen chimes in, "No, you're not. You have two women who need you to dote after them and playoffs, and then a World Series to win." She continues without missing a damn beat, "Hey, Amira, this is Gwen York ... well, Locke."

"Oh yes, I know you."

"You do, and it's okay to be freaked out, but I assure you that you are safe. You're going to pack a bag, and GI Maze is going to deposit the not-hot brother in a cop car that should be there in less than a minute. They'll take a statement, and then Maze will bring you to Jillian's place for the night until we figure out what we need to do next. Did he mention the wife? Kids? Parents? Anything we need to know?"

"He said so many things. Oh God, I don't remember, and—"

"That's okay. You're going to put that out of your head and pack an overnight bag if you can. If not, I'm sure Jillian has everything you need, and I am"—she pauses—"sending pizza and wings your way."

"Just relax as best you can, okay, Amira?" Jillian sniffs.

"Now we're going to switch lanes a second. Jillian, your old man was spotted around the neighborhood, and the cops are looking for him. Everyone needs to stay inside tonight, okay?"

"Yeah, of course."

"I don't wanna stay inside. I wanna break his fucking

head like he did hers, and I wanna bust Alton's, too, in case it was him." I clench my fists. "What the fuck!"

"Greed is a fucking bitch," Leland grumbles.

"And you're not going to like this, but Rome and CeCe need a heads-up, and so do the boys on Slugger Row, and Cora, for good measure. I don't want any surprises or missteps this time around."

"Okay." Jillian nods.

"As a woman and a friend, call your mom and discuss with her how you two want to handle this. Maybe keep it under wraps if you think it will mess up Rome's head. Just a thought. You both know him better. Amira, you still there?"

"Yes, of course."

"All this has to stay between us. Not just for your brother and Jillian, but all I's need to be dotted and T's crossed, so whatever charges we can get will stick. Did Alton knock on your door or—"

"He was in my house. He broke a window. My cat is … Oh God, my Noelle is missing."

"Can I tell you a secret?"

"Yes."

"Maze is a cat lover. He has three. You let him know, and I can assure you he'll do what he can to help."

"Okay."

I squat down and fist the sides of my hair.

"When Noelle is found, she is welcome to stay here."

"Oh, thank you, Jillian. Thank you so much." Amira sniffs.

"Did he say why he was there, Amira?"

"Grandmother's jewels."

"Does he have them?"

"Hell no, he doesn't. They were a gift to me."

"Pack them up. If that bitch knows they're there, she'll try to get them, too."

"I know none of you want to hear this, but you need to sleep. Your bodies need rest. So eat, and then sleep. Marks and Linda will be there in a few hours. If you need me, I can—"

"No freaking way," Jillian cuts her off. "*Your* body needs rest. You're growing a life."

22

JILLIAN

Mom

Jillian

HEARING HER VOICE BROKE ME.

"Hey, Mom."

The sound of her voice tells me she's broken right beside me.

"Jillian."

"I'm sorry."

"You have nothing to be sorry for. This is not your fault."

"All I can think about is what if I got hurt so bad I could never answer another one of your calls. What if—"

"Oh, Jillian, sweetheart, that's never going to happen." Mom's voice quivers.

"I'm sorry. I'm sorry I didn't talk to you about, well …" I peer up at Nour, whose eyes are moving between me and his phone screen, but his hand stays gently on my leg. "You know."

"I do know, and I assume you do, too."

"Maybe? I also remember the first taco night and how, um, maybe, *he* looked at you?"

"Well, *he's* on the shit list, and *he* may never come off it," she snaps.

I can't help but laugh, and then I can't stop.

"What exactly is it that you find so funny, child?"

"I'm just so happy you feel like you *can* put him on the shit list."

"Oh, I didn't put him on it; he put himself on the damn thing," she huffs.

"Yeah, well, the fact you trust him in a way that you can tell him you're angry, especially when it's at him, speaks volumes."

"Right now, I'm not interested in reading a single word, let alone a volume." She's pissed, and he's … not even trying to defend his actions.

I start laughing again when I remember the first time they met.

"How hard did he crack you on the head?" Mom asks, sounding less pissed, even a little amused.

"Oh my God, we were on the porch"—I laugh—"and you were all like, '*Have a taco, Zane.*'"

"I did not use that tone."

"Oh yeah, you did." I snort, and the corner of Nour's lips tip up.

"You should get some sleep. *You're delusional.*"

I continue, "And he was all, '*I would love one of your tacos. Thank you, Linda.*'"

She giggles. "Jillian, that's enough."

"Rome looked at Hudson, who was clueless of course, then he looked at me, and I grinned, then to CeCe, who wagged her brows."

"All of that is a lie."

"Oh no. And Rome got all … Rome and hissed, '*Not happening, Red*,' to CeCe."

"I don't remember any bit of this. You're completely delusional," she tries to scold me.

"That's what happens when you get your taco eaten—you lose your—"

"This conversation is not happening. Go to sleep."

I look at Nour, who's looking down, shaking his head.

"There's nothing better than getting your taco—"

He quirks a brow and mouths, "*Nothing?*" and Mom's gasp draws me back to her.

"Young lady!"

"Grown-ass woman, doing grown-ass things." I smile softly at him as I pull his hand up and kiss the back of it.

"Like getting your head cracked."

"Yeah, right after picking up tacos, of all things."

Mom sighs. "I will be at your door shortly. I love you, Jillian."

"Love you. Drive safe."

I end the call and lean into my comfy chair, facing Nour.

"You get pissed, and you don't try to hide it. You dance and sing when you're doing work others would hire out, done. You joke when you were mugged and could have been gravely injured," he states.

"May not be the best coping skills, and yes, a shrink would have a field day with it, but"—I curl into myself a bit—"I don't see it changing."

"I wouldn't want it to." He reaches over and tucks a strand of hair behind my ear. "It's part of your charm, part of what makes you as beautiful inside as you are in the flesh."

"If we're doling out compliments, it's my turn. You're focused, driven, love the people who deserve your love, and don't let those who don't see how amazing you are—you hold back. You love your friends, and loyalty means something to you, which isn't an easy find these days. Your sense of humor is hidden at times, but damn, when you let your guard down, it's incredible. And you're a thinker, which is sexy." I close my eyes and lean back. "You have the hottest ass in baseball, a body that makes me want to be a dirty shirt so I can rub myself all over those washboard abs, and a face that a girl could look at all day. You're the total package, Nour Uyar, and I may be one of the only women in the world who does not regret my first."

"You're tired." He takes my hand and kisses it. "Sleep."

"I'm tired and resting my eyes. I'll sleep after I hug Amira and see for myself that she's okay."

"I know there's a lot going on, and we have no plans for the future, but I need to thank you for showing me that I could love again. And, in the next breath, you taught me I have never known its true meaning. I have been turning myself inside out to make sure nothing I do stops you from being you or causing you any pain. Seeing you like that in an alley, I'm not sure I can stop."

His words, his admittance, just simply him…all of it has my heart throwing punches in an attempt to fight its way to him.

"I'm not supposed to know that New York and L.A. are interested in opening trade agreements. If you don't feel the same, I'm going to accept. If you want to give this a fair shot, I'll lean to New York because it's close and—"

I shake my head and open my eyes. "Any chance Montana is looking for the best ass in baseball?"

"The Mavericks?" he says with zero enthusiasm.

"I told Roman if he doesn't see that all the love he has is crushing me, he can't be part of my life. Montana University sent an email today. I can start there in January."

When his head cocks to the side, I realize my own voice has even less enthusiasm than his.

"It's not fair, you know."

"Oh, see"—his lips twitch up at the corner—"I do understand. But facts being what they are, I want to shake his damn hand because, otherwise, I'd have never fucked a unicorn and fallen in love."

"I love—"

"You don't have to say it because I did. In fact, I'd love the opportunity to earn your love." His eyes light up. "We can turn it into a new project."

"I'm done doing projects for now. But I'd love to do one proving you can't earn someone's love if they don't already love you. Fuck them if they make you earn that. You earn trust, respect, and loyalty, not love. Not the real kind, anyway. I love you and am not afraid to admit it."

"So, your theory bombed?"

"Hell no. I'm right. It was totally sex and not love."

"When did it change for you?" he asks, leaning in slowly, wetting his seriously gorgeous mouth.

"You first." I wet mine.

He brushes his lips across mine. "On three?"

"One …" I press a small kiss to his lips.

"Two …" He presses one to mine.

"Three." I smile against his.

I say, "Barn," and he says, "In the rain."

He gently pulls me into his lap and kisses me. "I cannot wait until you're un-concussed. I'm dying to taste your pussy again."

"Last I checked, my pussy isn't concussed." I smile.

And that's when his phone rings …

AMIRA ARRIVES at the same time the pizza and wings that Gwen Locke sent.

Nour cups her face. "He bruised your face. Where else did he hurt you?"

Rapidly blinking to hold back tears, she holds up her wrists. There are visible fingermarks on them. "He had rope. He tried to tie me up. I pulled his mask off, and he struck me. He threatened to kill me if I told anyone and then threatened to hurt you, as well."

A voice clears from behind as a large, tatted-up man with thick, long, dark gorgeous hair, twisted in a knot, steps into the space. "Excuse me."

"Maze found Noelle." Amira hugs herself.

"Where do you want her set up?" he asks.

"I'll show you Amira's room, but first …" I move between her and Nour and hug her. "You're going to be okay."

"And you will be, too." She takes my hand and Nour's and puts them together. "But you're both better like this."

"Working on it, Amira." Nour wraps an arm around her and pulls her under his arm. "I want to kill him."

Walking away to show Maze where Amira will be staying, I offer to take the massive white ball of fur from him.

"Nah, she and I are doing a thing."

WHILE AMIRA WAS in the bath, her phone was blowing up, and the caller ID showed it was her father.

"Should you maybe just answer it and—"

"Fuck him." Nour shook his head.

I pick up her phone and hold it out to him. "Tell him that. Tell him, *fuck you*."

"Oh, Jillian …" He shakes his head. "I've told him that, and when he laid his hands on me, I didn't cower."

"Good. He probably should have laid hands on the evil twin. Maybe then he wouldn't—"

"Evil is right and has been since we were kids."

"Purple nerple?"

"After enough nannies quit, Amira was left to tend to us when they were away, socializing, spending generations of money. He would go into rages at the word *no*. And man, did he get a look that told you he was looking for a reason to rage. As he got older, his rages became less and less physical and more mental. Amira couldn't have friends over without him making them cry, and he would blame it all on me. Since he was a better show pony, they favored him."

Amira walks out into the room, hair in a towel, holding Noelle. "We had a cat named Snowball. She was just like Noelle—a blue-eyed Turkish Angora. He slammed her tail in a door and broke it. He said it was an accident, but I don't believe him. He tied things to her crooked tail, shut her in closets … awful, just awful. I couldn't wait to go away to school." She frowns at Nour. "And I left you to deal with it all."

"I didn't deal with much. I ignored him and played sports."

"Which they tried to make you quit when Alton tried out for the baseball team and didn't make it."

"Tried and failed, which made him try even harder to cause me to fail."

"That's horrible," I say.

"Thought so, too." Nour chuckles silently.

"Nour always tried to include him."

"Oh, the regrets we have in life," he jokes as Amira's phone rings again.

She picks it up, reads the screen, and huffs as she answers it, putting it on speaker and holding a finger over her mouth.

"Amira, are you there?" a deep, angry voice rumbles through the room.

"I am. How are you, Father?"

"I'm not well. I just received a call from my son in jail. Amira, why would you have your only brother arrested?"

"I have two brothers; one has always been vile, yet he's the one you—"

"I've already had enough of this. Drop the charges, and we'll reopen talks about your trust fund."

I can feel Nour physically tense up beside me.

"I am long past sad that this is what our family has become. Long past trying to rationalize your choices to act as if Nour isn't our family."

Nour shakes his head at her and makes a who-cares gesture.

"I have never said these words to you before but have thought them every day for the past three years. Nene would be ashamed of what you have done to the Uyar family."

A woman gasps, "Amira, how could you?"

"If she were here and saw how you have treated Nour, she would walk past you and never look back."

"Amira." Nour shakes his head.

"He broke into my home through a window, dressed as the common thief he is. When I returned, he tried to tie me up. When I was able to pull the mask free, he struck me, not just once. He told me he'd kill me if I didn't give him the jewelry Nene had given me. He told me he'd kill my brother if I went to the police. He has been a disgrace to this family from the time he was born, and you are a disgrace to Nene for allowing it. So no, Father, I will not be dropping charges. He will get what he deserves for once in his life.

And shame on you both because you made him the way he is."

"That is enough!" Nour's father demands.

"No, not nearly. Nour's friend was also attacked tonight. She was beaten, robbed, and hospitalized. This on the heels of your son and his disgusting wife showing up at one of Nour's press functions and refusing to leave when she asked them to. That is not a coincidence. He'll pay for that, as well."

The man's roar comes through the speaker. "And how will he pay, Amira! Everything is gone! Our fortune is gone!"

Nour leans forward, lip curling as Amira sits back, hands over her mouth, in shock.

"When I find out that you knew he was going to come after my sister because you lost millions, old man, you're going to pay dearly for what you have done." Nour then hits *end*.

A voice clears, and I look up to see Mom and Zane Marks.

Zane Marks lifts his chin. "We'll look into the financials and phone records. If the two connect, they're looking at conspiracy to commit murder."

Nour kisses the side of my head and stands. "Thank you, Marks." He smiles at Mom. "Hello, Linda."

"Hello, Nour."

"I just want you to know that I am in love with your daughter, and your son is going to be very upset with me."

She smiles. "Roman will come around."

"Hudson?" he asks.

"Him, too."

"You?"

She looks around him at me. "You love him?"

"Yeah, totally."

She looks at him. "Me, too, then."

23

NOUR

Workout

Nour

THE PLAN IS to wait until after the playoffs and when we win, which we will now that I have full access to the lucky nips and the magical pussy that, once I dip my cock into, I hit a grand slam. So, yeah, we'll wait until after the World Series.

Linda and Marks? Who knows when they'll come forward? For now, it stays between the Hart women and the men lucky enough to love them.

For now, we stick to Jillian and me.

Walking into the locker room, pretending I'm here to work out and knowing Rome already has, I approach him with fake caution.

"Yesterday—"

"I was out of line," he cuts me off. "That issue is Jillian's and mine, not yours."

"That's not what I'm talking about."

"Okay." He shuts his locker, hitches his bag over his shoulder, and turns toward me. "What's up?"

"Jillian and Amira are resting at Jillian's. Your mother is there, and so is Marks." I inhale, then continue, "To make a long story short, they were both attacked. My brother is the suspect in both attacks, but there's a possibility your father was involved in Jillian's."

He shakes his head, rightfully confused.

"I called Gwen, and she has all the balls rolling in the right direction. Everyone who may need looking out for has a person doing just that. My brother is in custody, possibly facing attempted murder charges for Amira's attack, and they're gathering information to see if he was involved in Jillian's, as well."

"She's pissed at me." He scowls and looks down. "CeCe says she has every right to be."

I clamp a hand on his shoulder. "You're family, a strong family. Go to her. Give Hudson a call. She made your mom promise she wouldn't say anything for—"

"Two and a half more days."

"She has a concussion. She's going to be fine."

"And Amira?"

"Amira, too. Go, make that call, grab CeCe, head over, and lay eyes on her."

"On them. Amira's family, too."

"On them."

"You heading over?" he asks.

"Just left there, but yeah, when I'm done here, I'll be over. Probably have a couple more Jags with me."

AFTER PASSING ALONG the information to the Steel brothers, making sure my family and Jillian's father don't have access to the stadium, I texted AJ and Bennett.

Finding parking was a bit of a problem.

Walking up the two stories to her place and hearing all the voices, my assumption that it was a packed house was right.

"Jesus, took you long enough to get here." Bennett scowls at me as I walk in.

"Had some things to do."

"Another unicorn to fuck? You didn't come home last night."

"I was here, dealing with some things, like my sister"—*and Jillian*—"being attacked by my brother. Probably going to be dealing with some things for a while."

"It's on the news!" someone yells, and everyone hurries in and gathers around the TV.

"*Two women were attacked in Trenton, New Jersey, last night, and we have information for you. Both attacks took place in the downtown area, where violence is seldom seen. One victim was brutally attacked and found unconscious in an alley by a local hero and taken to the hospital where she received treatment and has been released to continue healing at home.*"

What the fuck?

"*Approximately two hours later, another woman arrived home to find a masked man inside her upper-class home on a street that has been always thought safe. The woman was attacked and managed to unmask her attacker, who demanded valuables and threatened her life if he didn't get them.*"

A picture of my brother flashes across the screen. "*Alton Uyar is the twin brother of*"—my photo is splashed across the screen—"*Jersey Jags' rookie catcher, who happens to be the hero who found the first victim and also the brother of the second victim. You'll get more details from Trenton News, channel 12, as our reporters and the authorities begin to unravel this twisted web of crime.*"

"*You* found Jillian?" Rome asks.

"Yeah, I was going to grab some authentic Mexican instead of Taco Bell to celebrate and …" I wave a hand toward Jillian, who looks like she is far too amused to be the same person who decided we'd wait until the Jags' season ended.

"You call an ambulance?" AJ asks.

I shake my head. "Probably should have, but it was messed up seeing her there like that. I knew I could get her to the hospital faster than an ambulance."

"You didn't call Rome?" Bennett asks.

I have no idea how to answer this.

"He knew Jillian had put me on a seventy-two-hour time-out," Roman answers.

I look at Jillian, who lifts her nose in the air.

"You really sticking to that after everything that's gone on, little Hart?" I ask.

"I can add to that list, hotter twin."

I roll my eyes, realizing she's taken a pain med and bracing for the inevitable.

"No joke." CeCe laughs. "He got robbed."

"What's the deal with ugly Uyar?" AJ asks.

Amira is all too happy to answer, in embarrassing detail that includes the shit that went down at O'Donnell's and the phone call with our father last night. Am I pissed? No. It's her story, too, and my hope is that talking about it, she doesn't wake up screaming in terror again tonight.

EVERYONE EXCEPT ROME, CeCe, Marks, and Linda Hart have gone home.

"You wanna head back? We can cover tonight," Rome offers.

"I'm staying," I say, not looking away from where Jillian and Amira are snuggled up in her big fuzzy chair.

"It's really no big deal. I'm sure you didn't get—"

"I appreciate it, but—"

"You looked out for Jillian; we'll look out for Amira."

I turn and look at him, trying to get some insight on if he's trying to bait me or if he's being genuine. But the reality is, it doesn't matter.

"My sister woke up twice last night, screaming in terror. She won't leave Jillian. She probably feels responsible for what happened to her and feel's safer here than at home. I am staying with my sister."

"I mean, why not? You stay with yours; I stay with mine. Totally get it, brother."

"Why not, indeed."

I catch Jillian moving and glance over. She's wide awake, sliding out of the chair, trying not to disrupt Amira's sleep.

Once she's slid all the way down and is on her ass in front of the chair, she crawls over toward us. "Yeah, so, if you're both staying, there's a whole apartment downstairs that's ready to be painted." She stands up and rubs the back of her head. "Three days off, and I'd have had it done until your brother," she says, then looks at Rome, "or your father, played whack-a-mole on my head. I have a tenant lined up."

"You're using this to get free labor." Rome nods.

"Damn right, I am." She smiles and looks toward CeCe and Linda, who are cooking. She then looks back at me. "Amira's not going back. She called a realtor when you were gone. She also took a call in the bathroom and acted off when she came back out."

"What can I do to help?" Rome asks.

"Both of you could try not to feed off all this and focus on kicking ass in the playoffs. We're all on the same team, and everyone could use a win."

"Not easy to let this slide off our backs, Jillian," Rome states.

"Wasn't easy to slide out of that chair without waking Amira, and let go of my three-day break from you, but I did. And I did it with a damn goose egg on my head." She smacks him in the chest. "Suck it up, Hart."

And then Jillian Hart, the woman who has stolen mine, struts away with a big-ass goose egg on the back of her head.

"Mine's falling apart, and yours is acting like a bossy little brat." I look back at Rome. "I want him to rot."

"Same page, Uyar." He agrees

"And if Alton didn't do this, I want your father rotting in a cage beside his." I nod.

"Preaching to the choir."

CECE, Rome, Linda, Marks, and I painted the apartment, and Dromida O'Donnell dropped by to check on the girls. Lena joined us for dinner, and that woman is a treat. After she left early so that she didn't miss her shows, Jillian shared the whole story of how she was bullied by a five-foot, eighty-year-old woman into buying Etta's and how it was one of the best decisions of her life.

Amira was falling asleep at the table over a plate full of food she ate little of and excused herself before anyone was done eating. Is this acceptable? Of course it is, but it wasn't in our home growing up.

I waited a bit for her to get settled in and then excused myself.

I knock lightly before entering and find her sitting in the middle of the queen-sized bed, surrounded by our grandmother's jewelry, silently crying.

"Talk to me, Amira." I walk over and sit beside her.

"Mom's not well. They haven't paid attention to the finances because she's sick. They need money."

"I would really like you to look at me."

She turns and looks up at me, and I use my sleeve to wipe her tears away.

"Four years ago, I was in a very similar position. I was either going to go back and grovel, or I was going to look ahead and never look back."

"She's sick, Nour."

"I am asking you to please wait for us to get the information back from the investigators. Nene gave this to you. It's yours, not theirs. She also gave all of us trust funds to be handed over at the age of thirty. That is yours, too, and they've already taken it."

She clenches her fists. "Why do I feel like I should help them when they may have been in on what Alton did last night? What is wrong with me?"

"You're a kind and caring woman." I chuckle. "And I believe we should thank God daily that we had some amazing nannies and Nene."

"Our mother is awful." She laughs.

I nod and laugh with her. "She totally is."

She places over forty pieces of jewelry into a little fireproof box then gets comfortable in the bed. "Go, be with your found family."

I climb in right beside her. "I'm with you, my family, my sister. You, Amira Uyar, you came here for me, for our family, and you're part of this, too."

She nods, then rolls to her side, I hear the smile in her voice when she says. "Please don't fuck this up for us."

Laughing, I tell her, "I'll try my best, but something tells me you're in regardless."

WALKING out of Amira's room, for now, I find Jillian curled up in the chair, watching …

"You watch *Real Housewives*?"

"Don't judge me," she says, not looking away from the screen.

"*Judge you*? That's part of my game-day rituals." I laugh.

She glances over at me, eyeing me skeptically.

"Swear it."

She moves over a bit and pats the spot beside her. "Tell me more."

I glance around.

"They're gone."

"Linda and Marks?"

"Mom wanted to get groceries. But it wouldn't matter if she was here." She hands me her phone. "She tried to tell me about him and I missed it. The text. Getting her house was her 6th favorite days, she skipped number five on purpose I think. I bet it's because it was the day she met him and she couldnt tell me, but wanted to."

I hand her back the phone. "So how will you proceed?"

"I'm going to be their biggest cheerleader."

I move to her, shove my arms under her ass, and lift her up.

Smirking, she asks, "What are you doing?"

"Deciding if I wanna watch *Housewives* or eat you out." I lean down and grab her nipple with my teeth. "Lady's choice."

"You are a dirty, dirty boy, and I love it."

Heading to her room, I tell her, "That's good because I'm not sure I could be anything but me with you." I kick the door shut behind me and set her on her feet. "No sex."

She pouts out her lip.

"Doctor's orders. I heard her say it. One more day."

"Fine," she grumbles as that sexy little smirk plays on her lips.

I kiss the top of her head and whisper, "Good girl."

To stop a smile, she bites her lower lip as I grip the bottom of her Jags sweatshirt and lift it up and over her head.

"I knew you were braless." I lean in and take a taste.

"Um, a little help here," she says, face still covered, arms in the air.

Chuckling, I pull it the rest of the way off and toss it to the ground.

I'm met with narrowed eyes. "Do you love me or my tits?"

Thumbs hooked in her sweats, I slowly pull them down. "Your tits are part of the whole sexy, beautiful package."

Squatted down, I look over her body, completely bare before me, and I'm going to take my time with her tonight. "No bra, no panties, self-service."

I take her hips, guiding them toward me as I lean in and kiss the soft skin of her waistline, down her left side, from her hip to her knee, and then move to the right, kissing from her knee to hip.

Looking up, I grip her calf, placing her leg on my shoulder, and am at eye level with pretty pink flesh. I inhale her sweetness as I look up and watch her breasts rise and fall quickly with anticipation. Turning, I lick her inner thigh, then press kisses all the way to her pussy lips, watching her face, watching her, the entire time.

"You smell delicious, Jillian."

Her body quivers, and her lashes flutter like wings as I draw a perimeter with my tongue around her sweet little slit.

"I'm about to make you dizzy, little Hart. I want you to sit down so I can properly worship your pussy." I tighten my grip on her hip, stalling her so I can run my nose up her slit. "You smell so fucking good. Too fucking good. I may just do this all night."

"Or at least until they return."

"I can hide out in here"—I open-mouth kiss her cunt—"all night. They'll never know."

I release her hip. "Lay down and spread your legs for me."

She moves up the bed and lays back.

"Good girl."

My mouth starts at her ankle, and I barely touch her as I kiss up her body, mouth never once leaving her flesh until I have nowhere else to go but heaven.

I spread her legs wide, settling between her legs, and slice my tongue through her folds, watching her body arch, tits sticking out. I was so wrong about them; they're one hundred percent real, just like every inch of her.

"Fucking so good." I lick around and around her opening, not ready to go in yet, wanting to just enjoy the moment.

Her breaths become harder, and she grips the bedding as I lick around her clit. Her hips thrust upward as she moans my name. It's never sounded so sweet.

I kiss down her lips and dip the tip of my tongue inside her. She cries out softly, and I do it again and again, continuing to savor her taste. I want it in my mouth until the day I die. Even taking my time, it doesn't take but a minute to get her to the point she's teetering on the edge of orgasm, which is a pleasant surprise.

When she starts to whimper, I know she wants it.

I flick my tongue over her clit, and she stiffens.

I kiss her sweet lips again and groan. "Taste so good. So, so good."

I flick my tongue over her clit again, and she cries out.

"Good, Jillian?" I ask before doing it again.

"Oh God … yes," she pants.

I do it again. "Still good?"

"Nour …" she whimpers.

Rock-hard and aching, I shove my hand down my sweats and give my cock a squeeze while I flick and suck, flick and suck, flick and—

"Oh God. Oh, oh, oh …"

Pumping my cock in my hand, I suck harder as she grabs two handfuls of my hair and comes.

Then, I do it again.

Hungry for more of her, I kiss up her body, grabbing her tit in my hand, and nearly fucking come from the feel of her here, too.

"Perfect. Fucking perfect," I tell her before taking her nipple in my mouth, flicking my tongue over her piercing and sucking hard.

"Oh," she pants. "My," she pants harder. "God."

I move to the other, give it the same attention, and back again. And then I tell her, "I need more of your pussy."

24

JILLIAN

Playoff-Eve

We all hope for swift justice, but the day the Jags flew out for the first playoff game was sooner than we expected.

Street camera footage further confirmed my father was in the area and that Alton Uyar was not. And phone records confirmed Alton was in touch with his mother, father, and wife several times throughout the day he attacked Amira.

Hours after Alton was arrested, his wife and children left the US and are moving around Eastern Europe, making it hard to get an opportunity for the authorities to question her.

The Uyar family is not broke, in real-world numbers, anyway. And yes, Nour and Amira's mother is ill. She has irritable bowel syndrome. Both of them deny prior knowledge of his crime.

Mom, CeCe, Amira, and Cora all decided to act as though we'd be cheering them on from home with the others, but we arranged to surprise them and stay for both games, hosted in Montana. It's best out of five; two games to be played away and then back to Jersey, where, fingers crossed, they'd win the first game, which would clinch the league.

Helena has the business end of Etta's under control and, once again, I asked Lena to come and see what it was all about, to which she shook a bundle of sage at me. "Work. No time for game."

Unbeknownst to anyone else, games were exactly why I pushed for this surprise trip.

We booked a four-room suite at a resort right across the road from the Jags' hotel, my treat as I was rolling in white sage dough and haven't spent any fun money.

Thankfully, everyone crashes fairly early, so I'm able to get ready for a night that we will never forget.

When I walk into the hotel bar, wearing a Uyar jersey as a dress, red-bottom stilettos, a blonde wig, and a brand-new unicorn mask with more coverage than the OG one, for obvious reasons, I'm not easily missed. In fact, Nour nearly chokes on his drink when he sees me.

The boys are in stitches, which makes it almost impossible to keep a straight face. Clearly, luck is on my side because Rome isn't with them, but Locke is.

I hold up both hands, wiggle all ten digits, and nod toward the door. Nour scrubs a hand over his face but lifts his chin.

STANDING AT THE ELEVATOR BANKS, I step in, turn, and watch as he has to jog to stop the door.

"You're something else, you know?"

"Neigh."

He goes to grab my hand, and I shake my head. "Not in here."

He laughs. "Do you know how much shit I'm going to get for this?"

"Tell me it's not worth it," I smirk.

"You're trouble."

"So you've mentioned, with a capital T, if I remember correctly."

"Yeah, you are definitely that."

"I think you like trouble, SMS."

He laughs darkly, hand pressing down on the front of his pants. "How hot are you right now?"

"Hotter than I should be when we're not even alone. As soon as we get in that room, you're gonna have to help me get out of these clothes."

The elevator stops at floor thirteen, and the doors slide open. "After you, GTO."

I step out and glance back at him. "There are two reasons I should be following you; the first, you have the best ass in baseball, and second, I haven't a clue which room is yours."

"This is true." He steps ahead of me, and I follow the hottest ass in baseball all the way to his room.

He opens the door, and I walk in. He follows and kicks the door shut behind him.

"What's the deal with this wig?" He tugs on it as I remove the mask and inhale a deep breath.

"If anyone gets suspicious, they won't question if it's me." I turn and look up at him as I pull the jersey over my head and toss it to the side. "Why do you still have clothes on?"

"That's a really great question."

Together, we remedy the situation within seconds.

He leans in and kisses me. Then he pulls back and brushes his lips across mine while gently pushing me backward until I feel the bed against the back of my legs.

"Jillian, beautiful fucking Jillian. How did you make an impossible situation even more impossible?"

I wrap my hand around his swollen cock and stroke while saying, "There's nothing impossible when it comes to us."

"That's not true." He cups my chin. "It's going to be impossible to stop loving you, so don't you fucking dare ever make me do it."

"That's never going to happen. Not ever."

Beginning to stroke him as I move so that I am facing him on all fours, I grab his cock again, and then wrap my mouth around the head of his beautiful dick.

"Fuck," he growls as I take him in further, deeper, sucking harder and hoping I'm doing it the right way.

"Son of a bitch," he groans as I sink my nails into his ass and pull him closer, taking him further, loving the feel of his head against the back of my throat.

"Damn," he growls again. "Fuck, you do not have to do this, but I'm sure glad you are." He reaches down, both hands on my tits, cupping them, lifting them, pinching and rolling my nipples between his fingers, tugging the tiny little bats that have his number on them. I move up and down his shaft, loving the taste of him, the feel of him in my mouth.

He then maneuvers me so I'm on my knees, one hand wrapped around the back of my neck, gripping tight enough to guide me. "This okay? Fuck, tell me to stop. Tell me to go. Suck faster. You feel so good, so fucking good. Such a good girl, Jillian Hart. My good girl."

And here we are again, with that praise kink, that *good girl* and the way he says it, causing my insides to clench, but there's nothing in there to hold onto.

I am so turned on and wonder: has anyone ever come giving head?

I pull back to get a breath, inhaling deeply, panting as I stroke him faster, more furiously, harder, feeling powerful and powerless at the same time.

Mouth filling with the need to taste him again, I do just that. I pump, I suck, and I deep-throat him until I know I'm drooling, but I don't fucking care if I look like a rabid dog or a unicorn in stilettos. All I care about is I love him, he loves me, and his cock tastes delicious.

He grips the side of my head to stop me, and I try to pull his hands away. I don't wanna stop. I wanna keep going. I wanna suck faster.

"I'm gonna come," he warns, which is confusing. Why would he warn me? I don't warn him. Now is not the time to be polite or a gentleman, nor is it time to stop and tell him that. So, I don't. I show him.

I moan at the first shot of his hot cum, sucking harder, wanting more, telling him with my eyes and my actions, and being rewarded with the way he looks at me with reverence.

I am a fucking goddess. I am his *goddess.*

When he is done, he leans down and kisses me a million times on my forehead, cheeks, and lips. Between kisses are *good girls*, and *I love you*, and *how did I get so lucky* tossed in more than once. Yep, I have a hardcore praise kink.

He turns around and lies down on the bed, maneuvering me so I'm in his arms. His chest rises and falls as he rubs my back, holding me tight.

"That was a World Series winning moment."

"Good?" I ask.

"*Good*?" His brows showed up.

"Yeah, stupid question. Apparently, after I swallowed the confirmation, I forgot."

"Nothing you say or ask is stupid, Jillian. I'm the fucking idiot that keeps forgetting you're not experienced in everything, yeah? You will be. I can't get enough of you. I'm going to ask you this once. Kinda how pissed would you be if you woke up with my face between your legs every morning for the rest of your life?"

"Probably about as pissed as you would be if you woke up every morning for the rest of your life with me sucking your seriously beautiful cock."

He curls up slightly and looks down. "Yep, officially magical. What was that? A twenty second recovery time?"

"See, I could get used to that." I move to straddle him. "You think you could give me that lesson you promised?"

"You want to ride my pole? It's all yours."

One Month Later…

ASIDE FROM GETTING FUCKED in every position known to man, and probably some unknown, so much has happened in the past month.

In no specific order, the Jaguars won their division, they went on to win the league, and Gwen York gave birth on day two of the World Series to the cutest little baby in the world. Blaze Bennett Junior walked off the field in game three, and the manager of the team had a mini-stroke in game four, but the Jersey Jags won the World Series for the first time in their history.

I believe in hard work and although hard work had a lot to do with their success, so did Nour's consistency with his list and ensuring he did everything the same the night before every game and the next day leading up to it. And I also believe that my lucky nips and the mysterious unicorn that showed up the night before the first game of the championship game and the World Series brought the boys a little luck.

Today is going to prove to be challenging. They have a team meeting where it is speculated that Bennett could be traded, a new team manager may be named, and a whole lot of other shit's about to change too. But before that, my *boyfriend* is going to meet up with Roman and tell him that he and I are in love. And just to keep us all on our toes, tomorrow, we're all going to watch the New York Knights play the New York Giants, and together, we're going to tell Hudson.

STANDING IN THE SHOWER, I look up at ... "My boyfriend?"

Smiling, he kisses me.

"My lover?"

Another kiss.

"The man with the hottest ass in baseball?"

Kiss.

"The piano-playing, major league, World-Series-winning, number one catcher in the league, hot as fuck hottie?"

Kiss.

"The giver of many orgasms?"

Kiss.

"Actually, the giver of all my orgasms, aside from the ones I use to give myself."

He bends and takes my nipple in his mouth, and my back arches, pushing further into him. I run my hand down his abs and feel him hardening again. I stroke him, and he moans against my breast. When I pull back, he tilts his head, and his eyes fill with questions. I lick my lips and look down at his beautiful, wide cock. Then I kneel before him, and his body sags against the shower wall as I take him in both hands and stroke him up and down as I watch and feel him harden even more.

"You don't have to do this."

"Try to stop me." I wink as he pushes the hair that has fallen in my face back so that he can watch me.

I flick my tongue across this tip, eliciting a low rumble. I do it again, and he clenches his teeth. I then wrap my lips around just the head and flatten my tongue against it. His eyes roll back into his head.

"You're so good with your mouth, so good."

My pussy clenches, knowing what's coming next.

"So hot. So wet. Fuck, you look even more beautiful with my cock in your mouth. Suck it, little Hart. Suck my cock."

Nour is all of those things I said about him before I went down on my knees, but he is also a dirty talker extraordinaire. *I fucking love it.*

I take him as far as I can and swallow.

"That's it. Take as much as you can."

I tighten my lips around him and move back up and down, slower this time. Lips around his broad head, I suck harder, flattening my tongue as I watch his facial muscles tighten and pop. He's restraining himself when I want him to lose control.

I grip his cock tighter and stroke up and down, up and down, my mouth following my steady movements. His grip on my hair tightens, a sign I know so well.

I stroke him faster now, watching his eyes grow heavier and heavier with each lick. I suck up and down his cock and let my tongue caress the vein on the underside of his erection, and he hisses. Then I cup his balls in one hand as I continue pumping him with the other, sucking on the tip, swiping my tongue across it, and moving up and down his length again, and again, and again.

The taste of his pre-cum makes me even hungrier. Electricity moves inside of me, anticipating what's to … cum.

And, oh God, does he deliver.

"Holy fuck, you're fucking amazing."

25

NOUR

Day of Reckoning

THE AMOUNT OF MONEY I'VE SPENT ON UBER IN THE PAST month is absolutely ridiculous. More ridiculous is that I am a grown-ass man, doing grown-ass man shit, and I'm fucking terrified that this is going to change everything for Jillian and me in a way I'm not ready for it to change, but it has to.

I rap on the door, and Rome answers it.

"Hey, man, what's up? It's early."

"Yeah, I thought I could try to catch you before we all headed down to see what we're facing."

"Not for nothing, but there's no good way to say your manager should have known Junior's dad was fucking with his head. That's on him, not Blaze." He walks over and pours a cup of steaming hot coffee. "You want a cup?"

"I would love one. The season's over. It's time to get addicted to caffeine again."

"Worst things you could be addicted to, I suppose."

For a split second, I thought this was a good segue into the conversation, but comparing Jillian to a worse addiction is a bad idea.

"Season's over, but it's now time to plan wedding festivities. I can't wait to make her mine officially."

And there it is, the opening, and here I am, already preparing to get my fucking nose broken and possibly make some big changes in my career.

"There is no good way to say this, and I hope it doesn't change anything with us, but—"

"Does it have anything to do with the rumor I heard about you possibly going to New York?"

"In a way, yeah, but I don't want to open that conversation until we have this one first." I take a sip of my coffee and lean back in my chair. "I suppose the best way to come out and say this is: I'm in love, and it's not a choice I would have made for myself. In fact, I avoided it for a long-ass time. But as you know, when you love somebody, you can't just turn it off."

He simply stares at me.

"Roman, you are my best friend on this team. Of all of the girls in the world, I would never have chosen my best friend's sister to fall in love with, but I love Jillian with all my heart, and I will treat her better than any other man on the entire planet could. I don't want you to be pissed at me, but I understand that you are going to be, and I don't want that for you, man. I don't want you to hate me and have to see me every fucking day at work, and every time there's a Hart family get-together.

"I was offered that trade, and I don't want it, but I want peace for Jillian more than I want the Jags for me." I wait for him to say something, but he doesn't. "The other option we have is Montana. The Mavericks have made an offer that I am considering, and you know how much I hate the fucking Mavericks. But Jillian has until the end of the month to make a decision about going to grad school there."

We sit there, staring at one another, and I know if I look away, I lose, so I don't. I sit and watch him battle inside of himself, or maybe plan the battle that's gonna be right here, right on the table that we've sat at one hundred times and talked baseball, life.

"Say something, man. Scream, yell, throw a fist, tell me I'm not good enough, and I won't deny it. No man is good enough for her. She's amazing, but you know that, which is why you protected her for years."

"Only fucking thing I have to say to you is: over my dead body."

All right, at least we're talking.

"You have been fucking around with some freak dressed as a unicorn for months now, and you think that I'm gonna let my sister—" When he stops, he shakes his head. "I do not even want to ask this question. I don't want to know the answer."

"All I can say is, then don't, as your friend."

"*My friend*? You've made my sister a fucking laughing-stock, a joke. No. No, you cannot date my sister. You said you weren't gonna hurt her, that you'd never hurt her. You've already done that. You made an ass of her." He forces out a laugh. "No, you've made a unicorn out of her."

"Jillian mentioned her telling you that she went online, put herself in some fucked-up situations in order to date and feel. She said she told you that she lost her virginity to some guy at a hotel. What she didn't tell you was that guy was me, and—"

"Get out. I can't do this with you. I think I'm gonna get fucking sick. I loved you like a brother. I made you family."

"I'm not gonna leave yet, and if you decide you want to drag me out while I'm telling you this story, that's your choice. But the dating app that she and I met on was a hookup app. Neither one of us showed our faces or used real names. And both of us knew what we were getting into. Her reasoning is she wanted to lose her virginity, which, by the way, was not on her fucking period. I didn't know she was a virgin. Not my fucking thing, Roman, and you know it."

"I don't even know what the fuck you are … I don't—"

"She told me she had a girls' weekend in New York City," I talk over him to get through this. "She rented a hotel room. She told me to come meet her. I asked if she wanted to exchange real names and numbers, and she said *no*, that this was a hookup app, and let's not make it anything more."

"So, what? When you showed up and saw who it was, you—"

"I didn't actually see who it was. She was wearing a fucking unicorn mask. She had showered and gotten soap in her eyes, but instead of calling it off, she just wanted to get through it. She had candles lit. She even unscrewed the light bulbs so that I wouldn't switch on the lights and see her eyes because, in her words, she looked like a demonic crackhead or something like that.

"Not the point. The point is, it happened. I didn't know who the hell she was, and when I woke up, there was a message on the app, basically telling me one of her girls got into something and she needed to be with her. She told me to stay in the room if I wanted, but none of that means anything. It has no relevance. I fell asleep. She woke up, went to wash her face, her eyes were no longer burning, and we were gonna go for a round two after a quick …" I stop. "Also information that is completely unhelpful.

"Cliff notes: she knew who I was, saw me after her eyes were cleared up or something, and she left. She had some crazy idea that I did this to hurt you or wanted to ruin your career so that I would get more … I don't know what she was thinking, but she was a little bit of a mess and had no one to talk to about it. Me? I was thinking I was going to get tagged in a unicorn selfie, naked on a hotel bed."

"I really don't want to hear any more of this."

"Okay, I respect that." I stand. "We would really like to be able to be cordial. I never want her to lose you all, and I tried to stay away to ensure I wasn't an issue. But now, I don't think she's gonna accept you all hating the man she loves, either. It's unfair to her. But I'm willing to take the trade and stay here on the East Coast as long as I know that she's happy. Then I'll be happy wherever I am. If this is going to be a problem for you, and you can't take a couple days and put yourself in her shoes—our shoes—and see that this was never done in malice, then Jillian wants to go to Montana. I don't want to, but I will go anywhere to be with her. I love your sister the way I pray a man will love mine one day."

I walk to the door, open it, and then look back. "I need to make a decision soon, so let me know what you can handle, what you can get over, what you can simply see had nothing to do with you. Just … let me know."

My phone rings as soon as I pull out of the driveway. I don't even have to look to see who it is. My girl is obsessed with *Find A Friend.*

"Hey there, beautiful."

"How'd it go?"

"As expected. Give him a couple days."

"Did the unicorn thing come up?"

"Jillian, you know it did."

She clears her throat. "And how did that go?"

"Let's just say you and he may share blood, but he is not nearly as amused about it as you are right this minute."

"Well, all that means is I got my sense of humor from my mom; he got stuck with dad's. Ew."

"I love you, beautiful. I'll see you after the meeting."

Next up, coffee shop. This ought to be good.

WALKING IN, I see AJ and Bennett sitting at a table, waiting.

I walk in and sit down. "How are you doing?"

"I haven't slept since the series," he answers, staring off into space.

"I can understand that."

"I hate him," he says before turning to look at me. "If this is about my father and me, I'm leaving."

"Told you it wasn't, man. Something to share with you guys, and I really want you to be happy for us."

"*Us?*" AJ asks

"Him and Jillian," Bennett answers before I have a chance to.

"How the heck did you figure it out?"

He shakes his head. "Any fool could see the way you two look at each other. It's the way that we all want someone to look at us and the way we one day want to look at someone. And then the unicorn sightings. Jillian has a great rack."

"You tell Roman yet?" AJ chuckles.

"Yeah, I did just a couple of minutes ago. He's not real fucking happy, and I don't blame him."

"Then break up with her," Bennett suggests.

"Not a chance in hell."

And once again, I am graced with a smile from Blaze Bennett, proving he has teeth, good fucking teeth, too. "Then don't you dare."

WHEN I WALK into Etta's, I have a massive headache.

Linda smiles at me from the counter. "You okay?"

"Yeah. How was your day?"

"It was good. Slow for a change."

"Can I ask you a question without offending you?"

"Of course."

"What made you keep the last name Hart?"

She smiles. "They've never shared that story?"

I shake my head.

"Looking back, the name was probably the only charming thing about my children's father. What is more beautiful than a heart? It's where love is said to grow. I didn't have a lot of that growing up. I found it in Etta and my children. When we divorced, I still wanted to share the name with my children, so I tweaked it, softened it a bit. H-A-R-D-T went to H-A-R-T.

"I like that a lot."

"Are you questioning yours?"

"I'm not sure." I point to the clock. "Should I lock up? I'd like to take you H-A-R-T ladies, Lena, and Amira out to dinner."

She nods. "Roman is here. Maybe we should wait a few minutes."

I send Amira a text to let her know it may be a bit longer.

Being down here while she's up there, defending something she shouldn't have to, pisses me off. But there's not a fucking thing I can do without pissing off one Hart or another.

"Oh dear," Linda says, looking at the computer screen.

"Something I can help you with?"

She turns the screen. "The sage is no longer the hot seller."

"The unicorn bouquet." I nod, then shake my head.

"Actually, they're calling it the mystical alicorn bouquet."

"Alicorn is the proper term for the horn." I nod. "Right."

"Two hundred orders." She giggles. "Oh my."

"I don't even want to know."

"There are add-ons." She turns the screen again.

"Vibrators." I nod. "Makes sense."

The door to the back room opens, and Roman and Jillian walk out.

He looks right at Linda. "She needs help."

Jillian slugs him.

Linda scowls at her as he walks by me and opens the door.

"Well, come on."

I give Jillian the look.

"Amira and CeCe are meeting us for dinner. Lena doesn't want to go. She's afraid she'll—"

"Miss her shows." I nod. "Hey." I grab her elbow and ask, "Everything—"

"It's fine. All good." She pushes up on her toes. "Love you."

As I hold the door open for Linda, I whisper, "I'd like to ask you another question."

She smiles, and her eyes get misty. "The answer is yes."

One Month Later…

STANDING ON THE ROOFTOP, looking over the city, bursting in reds and oranges, matching the dozens of arrangements scattered around the rooftop, our friends and family are sipping drinks and waiting patiently for the girls to walk out.

To my left, my brothers, my real and true brothers—Roman, Bennett, AJ, and Hudson—stand with me as I wait.

"You nervous?" Roman asks.

I shake my head. "Not even a little bit."

"Perfect."

"You nervous about yours?"

"No." He looks around. "Just hope I didn't push for extravagant when this is perfect."

"Yours will be, too."

The song begins, and Jillian peeks out around the corner, wearing a headband with a unicorn horn on it.

Everyone laughs.

There isn't a person on the team—hell, maybe not a soul in Trenton—who doesn't know at least part or a version of our story.

She steps out in a stunning cream dress and walks toward me while "Raindrops Keep Falling on My Head" continues playing as her mother and the girls follow behind her.

Halfway to me, she takes off the headband and tosses it behind her. I can't see where it lands, but I assume someone caught it.

When she gets close enough, the guys step away and join the crowd.

I take her hand and give her a spin before pulling her tight against me, reminding myself I can't kiss her until we're pronounced man and wife, which is the only thing traditional about our wedding day, aside from the ring on her finger—a stunning five-carat, champagne diamond that Nene gave Amira to hold onto for me until the day I found the one. A ring Jillian refuses to wear unless it's a special occasion because she's afraid she may lose it.

The minister walks over, stands beneath the arbor that Jillian and I threw together last night, and addresses our family and friends. "It's been a true joy to have been able to meet these two individuals and get to know more about them and their beliefs about love. I'm sure everyone standing here would agree that there is no doubt they're the real deal and will make it through any storm they encounter."

"We love storms," she says quietly.

"We do." I wink.

"There was something very interesting that was discussed in reference to all of you."

Jillian puts her forehead on my chest, and I kiss the top of her head.

"They told me that not one person they chose to be part of today is someone they would not expect to tell them if they saw something that Jillian or Nour may do that wasn't honoring their promise to one another. That was followed by: how lucky are we to have found each other and our true family? So, now I ask you: how lucky are we to be here to witness their promise, their vows, and to feel the love they have for each other and for all of us, too?"

I hear them respond, but I'm too busy watching this version of Jillian standing before me. She's excited, nervous, and would probably climb up me right now, and not in a sexual way, but to be closer.

"I love you," I whisper.

"I love you," she whispers back.

"Oh my God, I can't with these two." CeCe giggles.

We exchange vows and rings, and I keep my eyes fixed on Jillian when the minister says, "Ladies and gentlemen, it is my pleasure to announce to you for the first time, Mr. and Mrs. Nour and Jillian Hart."

Jillian looks at him and shakes her head, and our minister nods to me.

I lean down and whisper, "Not that a name should matter, but I like yours better."

To that, she jumps up, wraps her arms around me, buries her face in my neck, and says, "Mr. and Mrs. Hart."

"Mr. and Mrs. Hart," I repeat, twirling her around.

The End

This is the end of Jillian and Nour's story, but you'll see them again in
Hudson Hart's story
Hart Breaker
Coming This Fall

Is Next!

**Hudson Hart
is coming soon.**

Preorder now

Hart Breaker

This book will place in the
Blue Valley Legacy
world

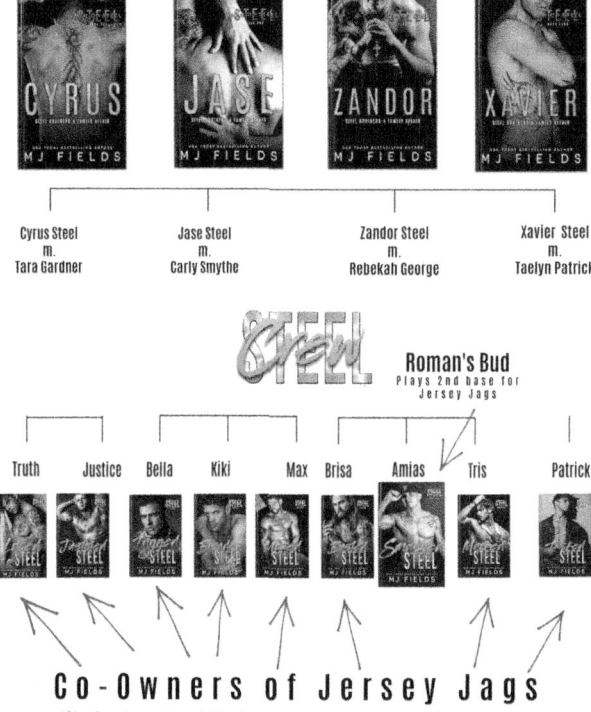

STEEL — MEN OF STEEL

Cyrus Steel m. Tara Gardner
Jase Steel m. Carly Smythe
Zandor Steel m. Rebekah George
Xavier Steel m. Taelyn Patrick

STEEL CREW

Roman's Bud — Plays 2nd base for Jersey Jags

Truth · Justice · Bella · Kiki · Max · Brisa · Amias · Tris · Patrick

Co-Owners of Jersey Jags
'The Crew' purchased the Jags after Amias started playing for them.

Not to be outdone by their kids, the Steel Brothers (our tattooed & pierced bad boys) retired and bought the Revolutionary Field Property

USA TODAY BESTSELLING AUTHOR
MJ FIELDS

Books by MJ Fields
MJ FIELDS

Rounding The Bases
Baseball Romance
Taking First
Steeling Second
Force at Third
Catching Feels

THE STEEL WORLDS
(Recommended reading order)
The Men of Steel Series
Jase
Cyrus
Zandor
Xavier
Forever Family
Raising Steel
Or get the
Men Of Steel complete box set
The Ties of Steel Series
Abe

Dominic
Eroe
Sabato
Or get the
Ties of Steel complete box set

The Rockers of Steel Series
Memphis Black
Finn Beckett
River James
Billy Jeffers
or get the
Rockers of Steel complete box set

The Match Duet
Match This!
ImPerfectly Matched!
or get the
complete duet

The Steel Country Series
Hammered
Destroyed
Wasted
or get the
Steel Country complete box set

Tied in Steel series
Valentina
Paige
Gia
or get the
Tied in Steel complete box set

**Steel Crew
(Generation 2)**
Tagged Steel
Branded Steel
Laced Steel
Justified Steel
Tricked Steel
Busted Steel
Smashed Steel
Marked Steel
Maxed Steel

Mercy West
No Mercy

Taking The Shot
(Recommended reading order)
Hockey Romance
Long Shot
Snap Shot
Hot Shot
Flip Shot
The Holiday Hat Trick

THE LEGACY SERIES FAMILY OF BOOKS
(Recommended reading order)
The Blue Valley series
Football Romance
Blue Love
New Love
Sad Love
True Love

Blue Valley series spin offs

The Way We Fell
The Way The Wildflowers Grow
Coming soon
The Way The Heart Breaks

The Brody Hines series
Rockstar Romance
Wrapped In Silk
Wrapped In Armor
Wrapped In Us

The Burning Souls
Rockstar Romance
Stained
Forged
Merged

Love You Anyway

The Truth About Love Duet
27 Truths
27 Lies

The Firsts series
Football Romance
Her First Kiss
His First Crush
Their First fall
27 Truths About Their First Goodbye
Their First Time

The Norfolk Series
Irons
Shadows
Titan

Timeless Love series
Unraveled
Deserving Me
Hearts So Big
Couture Love

The Caldwell Brothers Series
(co-written w/ Chelsea Camaron)
Hendrix
Morrison
Jagger
Visibly Broken
Use Me

Standalones
Basketball romance
Offensive Rebound

The Holiday Springs series
(co-written w/ Jessica Ruben)
Broody Brit
Irresistible Irishman

About the Author

MJ Fields is a **USA Today bestselling** author of contemporary and new adult romance novels. She lives in New York with her daughter, smoochie faced Newfie, Theo, and diva/terror Ellie
When she's not locked away in the cave, she enjoys spending time with her family, watching sports, listening to live music, taking in a show, singing off key, dancing to her own beat, listening to audio books, and reading— of course.
Forever Steel!
Join MJ's mailing list:
http://bit.ly/MJFNews

Follow MJ on BookBub:
bookbub.com/authors/mj-fields

Check out MJ's website
www.mjfieldsbooks.com

Thank You

Thank you to all of these amazing humans
who have helped bring
Catching Feels
to life
Photographer: Katie, Cadwallader Photography
Cover Designer: Kari March
Editor: Kristin, C&D Editing
Proofreader: Geissa Cecilia
PR: Autumn, Wordsmith Publicity

Printed in Great Britain
by Amazon